the complication with the best man

PIPER RAYNE

about the complication with the best man

One wild night turns into two pink lines.

Sleeping with the best man at my cousin's wedding felt right at the time—he was a hot, available firefighter, and I was the tipsy maid of honor. It's a rite of passage.

No regrets... until two pink lines flipped my world upside down.

Now I'm wildly unprepared and trying to hide my pregnancy in my small Alaskan town where privacy is a myth and gossip spreads faster than frostbite.

But wait, it gets worse.

Baby Daddy just came back to town—with a fiancée in tow.

And guess who she wants to plan their wedding?

Me.

Keeping the secret was hard enough.

Keeping my distance from the father of my baby? Impossible.

Just when I think I have it all figured out, he reveals his own secret that changes everything.

The Complication with the *Best Man*

I force my strained smile to stay in place as the groom goes on and on about how important it is that the wedding reflects his steadfast environmentalism and how he won't be happy with anything less.

I muster all my self-control to resist pointing out that the most effective way to reduce his carbon footprint would be to skip the massive wedding altogether. A wedding with one hundred fifty guests, each invited with paper invitations, seated with paper place cards, and greeted with paper menus on their plates, not to mention the individually wrapped party favors, extravagant floral arrangements, and, of course, the grand finale—an after-dinner fireworks display.

The words *and* my lunch churn around in my stomach, making me nauseous. I think I may have caught a bug or something because I've felt off all day.

Thankfully, the bride returns from the bathroom and sits next to her fiancé.

"Darren was just telling me how important it is to him

to make sure we're thinking of the environment throughout the planning process," I say to her.

She smiles at him and intertwines her hand with his. "We're in agreement there."

Miraculously, I'm still able to hold the smile on my face.

I've been a wedding planner for five years, and I've learned to identify high-maintenance clients at a glance. The couple sitting across from me is now at the top of my list of clients I'm not planning their second wedding for if this one doesn't work out. Usually, it's the brides who make my job harder, while the grooms just go along for the ride—or are dragged along, more likely. But I have a feeling good ol' Darren here will give Katherine a bit of competition in that department.

We continue with the meeting, and I note all their wants and needs, constructing a mental timeline in my head, working backward from their big day.

Once we finish, I walk Darren and Katherine to the door out to Main Street in my small quaint Alaskan town of Lake Starlight.

I took over Aunt Juno's office when she retired from matchmaking a few years ago, which has been a blessing. Working out of my parents' basement didn't scream professional wedding coordinator. As if I needed a sign that said, "Don't worry. You can trust me with the biggest day of your life."

I wave goodbye to my newest clients and go back inside, reaching for my water. I take a small sip, hoping it soothes the nausea that's been plaguing me today, but it only makes it worse.

I haven't thrown up yet, but my stomach has felt unsettled all day, and that damn feeling in the back of my throat won't go away. I vaguely remember one of my cousins texting in the group thread after our big family Sunday dinner about her kid being sick. Maybe I caught something. I better not have. I do not have time to be sick right now.

Summer is winding down, and if I was in the lower forty-eight, that would mean wedding season was too, but in Alaska, a lot of people get married in the fall and winter months. The natural landscapes make for gorgeous backgrounds in wedding pictures. And there's a growing number of people who choose to travel here during the colder months for a destination wedding rather than have one at a tropical resort.

It's actually the season that's grown the most in the past few years and the entire reason I was able to take over Aunt Juno's office in the first place. I've sort of made this time of year my specialty and have put together a social media campaign that brings in a lot of clients.

So while the majority of the wedding industry winds down for a break, I gear up for a busy fall and winter. In fact, I have two new clients who found me online coming into town in the approaching weeks.

I sit at my desk and jot down notes on my computer about my meeting with Darren and Katherine, what their priorities are, and some ideas I want to research so that I can present them at our next meeting. Then, before I forget, I add our next appointment to my phone calendar, along with an alarm to ensure I don't forget.

I tend not to be the most organized person. One glance down at my desk, which is littered with sticky notes that act as my to-do list, gives it away. I have a garbage truck full of day planners I've promised myself I'd use, but I always revert back to scribbling cryptic messages that most times I can't decipher.

Looking over my sticky notes now, I don't see anything

that requires my urgent attention, so I grab my purse and call it a day, heading to Bloom to chat with Maven about Darren and Katherine's wedding while their flower preferences are fresh in my head.

Even though it's a short walk, I get stopped twice for a quick chat.

Taking fifteen minutes or more to get somewhere that should take five comes with being a lifelong resident of a small town. This is especially true for me, as my last name is Bailey. The family name Bailey carries a little more responsibility in this town for several reasons. Not only do a lot of the Bailey family members own businesses here, but also, Bailey Timber was founded by us and employs a substantial number of people in the area. Add on the fact that my dad's parents were tragically killed in a snowmobile accident when he and his eight siblings were young, and the town sort of adopted them as their own and has a vested interest in their lives—at least that's how my dad tells it.

The bell over the door rings when I walk in, and Maven looks up from behind a long worktable scattered with flowers. The shop's walls are painted a rich, deep green, and the floor features a striking black and white checkerboard pattern that adds a touch of classic charm. Lush greenery from a variety of plants cascades from shelves and corners, filling the space. At the back, a large cooler houses an array of fresh flowers.

"Hey, roomie," I say.

Maven recently moved in with me. She's three years younger than me, and when she first approached me about leasing the extra room in the house I rent just outside of the downtown area, I wasn't sure if we'd be a good match. I'm somewhat chaotic and my housekeeping skills lack as much as my day planner keeping. But Maven was desperate to get out of her parents' house, and I related to how that felt, so I agreed.

Good thing I did because it turns out we're a great match. Maven is quiet and shy, neat and orderly, and enjoys spending her nights reading on the couch. If anything, I'm probably a little too loud for her. But she doesn't seem to mind my chaos. In fact, I think she secretly likes it. Maybe since she's the oldest of her sisters, she appears to enjoy picking up after me. She says she finds cleaning relaxing and therapeutic. I don't get it, but more power to her because when I look at a room that needs to be cleaned or organized, I feel paralyzed, never knowing where to start.

She sets down the flowers in her hand. Maven is gorgeous, though I don't think she sees herself that way. Her most striking feature is her dark brown eyes with flecks of gold in the center that are set off by her warm, tawny skin. Today, she has her dark, curly hair pulled back into a ponytail, and she's wearing the same style overalls she tends to work in every day. These are a khaki green with a repeating daisy pattern.

"How's your day going?" she asks.

"Well, I just met with a bride and groom who are going to challenge your ability to not put those scissors through your eye." I shrug. "But they can't all be easy peasy like Palmer and Hudson were, right?"

We both laugh. Our cousin Palmer got married last month, and though I was part of the wedding, I also acted as the wedding planner for it, which was a breeze. Neither of them were really picky about the details of their big day. All they cared about was that they'd be married at the end of it.

For a moment, the best man, Hudson's friend, flashes through my mind. Finn.

I press my thighs together just thinking about him and the night we shared in his hotel room.

Stop it.

I don't do this. I don't get hung up on my one-night stands—especially when they live in Vermont. I push Finn out of my mind and get down to business with Maven.

"These particular clients are very concerned about the environmental impact of their wedding, so I wanted to run some ideas by you to see if they're feasible before I present them at my next meeting with them."

"Oh, I like a challenge. Let's hear what you're thinking." Maven leans over the worktable, chin propped on her hand.

"I thought for the centerpieces, instead of having flowers, we could have potted plants, so people can take them home, and they'll last more than a few days. Or even have herbs? Then guests could plant them when they get back home."

"When is the wedding?" she asks.

"Next spring."

She nods. "That could absolutely work."

A flit of excitement ignites in me from fleshing out my ideas for a wedding. Or maybe it's still my lunch that's not sitting well.

"I also thought we could source the planters we use for the tables from secondhand shops."

"I know a cute little vintage shop in Anchorage that we can check out."

"Perfect." I clap my hands together in front of me.

Maven's eyes light up. "You know, I could also use curly willow to keep everything in place, rather than floral foam."

I point to her. "See? This is why you're the best florist who ever lived."

Maven's expression turns from excitement to cringe, and her hand falls to her tummy. "Give me a second?"

Before I can answer, she rushes through the door to the back of the store.

Shit. Whoever's kid was sick last Sunday must have given it all to us, if Maven isn't feeling well either. Damn it. I had a urinary tract infection a couple of months ago, and that was aggravating enough to deal with. I don't want to be down for the count, hunched over a toilet for three days.

While I wait for her to return, I do a quick sweep of the shop, taking note of what new types of greenery and flowers she's brought in, constantly looking for inspiration that will showcase my services.

A couple minutes later, she walks through the back door, looking pale.

"Did the toddler bug get you too?" I ask.

She laughs. "No, I just got my period." She groans. "Do you have a tampon in your purse? All I have left are pads. One of the weekend girls must've taken the last tampon and not said anything."

"Of course." I set my purse on the scarred wooden worktable and unzip the side pocket of my purse and pull out a tampon for her. "Here you go."

"Thank you. I'll be right back."

She disappears to the back again, and I zip up the pocket of my purse, slinging it over my shoulder.

Then I pause.

Then I think.

Then I calculate.

Then I panic.

I dig my phone out from my purse and pull up my health app to see when my period is due.

Motherfu—

I'm late.

My period was due two weeks ago.

Finn's handsome face flashes in my mind again.

No.

No, no, no, no, no...

I quickly type out a text to Maven that something came up and rush out of the floral shop, walking steadily down the street, only smiling and waving, not allowing anyone to stop me. I climb into my car.

I'm a fast driver normally—just ask the sheriff—but this time when I pull away from the curb, it's as if I'm racing out of the pits with my number one rival right behind me.

HARPER

By the time I drive to Winterberry Falls, pick up a pregnancy test, and get back, it's already dinner time, which means there's a good chance Maven is home. She probably has questions.

The entire drive to the neighboring town, I ran through my options if I am pregnant. The first thing is to keep it out of the gossip that fuels this town. Which means this has to be kept close to the vest.

There's no way I am though. It must be the stress. I'm so careful. Always. I'm on birth control, and I always make the guy wear a condom. No exceptions. This is all just me panicking over nothing.

My fingers wrap around the steering wheel as I make my way down Main Street, gripping so tightly, they're white. There's no sense in freaking out when I don't even know that I'm pregnant. My throat pinches closed with that nauseous feeling again, and I try to put it out of my mind.

If I can't go home and take this test, I'll go to Palmer's house, which is the next best place.

They say you can't choose your family, but I would have chosen Palmer. She's my cousin and my best friend. If I am pregnant, I'm blaming her and Hudson for having such a hot, single, eligible guy for a best man. I mean, how's a girl supposed to resist something like that, especially after a few glasses of wine?

I plow into her driveway faster than I should and slam on the brakes behind both Palmer and Hudson's cars. I would have preferred only Palmer to be home, but that's okay. I'm here all the time, and Hudson won't be suspicious. There's nothing to be suspicious about anyway.

I climb out of my car and rush to their back door that opens into their kitchen, hoping to slip into the bathroom and get this over with so I can see with my own eyes that there are not two pink lines on the stick. Then I can move on with my night.

Of course, they're all in the kitchen. Palmer, Hudson, and their daughter, Adley.

"I gotta go." I wave and beeline to the bathroom, shutting the door behind me. Let them think I have explosive diarrhea.

I strip my pants and underwear down and sit on the toilet before pulling the box from my purse. My family would probably be surprised that this is my first time ever taking a pregnancy test. I carefully read the instructions, which seem easy enough.

I pee on the stick and set it on the counter, starting the timer on my phone. I wipe, pull up my underwear and pants, wash my hands, and sit on the toilet to wait.

And wait.

And wait.

After the longest two minutes of my life, my phone

vibrates in my palm. I inhale one final breath before picking up the stick. My stomach drops out.

Two pink lines.

Two very bright pink lines.

There's no debating this result.

I guess go big or go home.

Holy shit. Maybe I should have bought the two-pack, or two different brands. This could be wrong, right? But those pink lines aren't fading, and the box says it's ninety-nine percent accurate. Huh, that means it's probably right.

I panic, unsure what to do right now. I shove the box back into my purse, unlock the door, and hurry to the kitchen.

"Nice of you to stop by," Palmer says rather than signs.

She must have her cochlear implant on. Her hair is down, so it's hard to tell from this angle.

I glance at Hudson and set my gaze on Palmer again, hoping she'll see my wide eyes and realize I need to talk to her. "I almost peed my pants. I gotta talk to you."

"Okay, want a sandwich first?" she asks, offering me a plate.

So, she doesn't get it.

My hands fidget in front of me. That nausea floats back up my throat. I haven't eaten since lunch. Babies need to eat, and I'd already be failing at this job if I don't give him or her nutritious food. "Yeah, I should probably eat."

"What's wrong with you?" Hudson asks, but I sit at the table and ignore him, taking a bite of my sandwich.

Adley slides down from the table.

"Where are you going?" Palmer asks.

"Bathroom."

I'm so lost in my head that it takes a moment for me to clue into what is happening.

"Oh, wait." I fly out of my chair, realizing that I was in such a panic, I left the pregnancy test on the bathroom counter.

Adley glances over her shoulder, giving me a devilish glare, obviously seeing it as a challenge of who can get to the bathroom first. She runs, and I try to catch her, but she wins and slams the door in my face. I suddenly regret all those games of tag I've played with her over the years.

My palms land on the closed door, sliding down to the doorknob, but the little devil locked the door. "Adley."

"Relax, she'll be out in a second. Is your stomach upset or something? Did you catch whatever Jalon had last night? It's been like one kid after the other today if you follow the cousin chat. I just sanitized everything, and I don't want to do it again," Palmer says.

I keep twisting the doorknob with no luck. "Adley, open up. Adley, come on. Please open the door."

My whine sounds like it used to when Easton would lock me in the basement, thinking it was funny because I thought people were hiding in there when I was eight.

The door opens, and my stomach sinks to the floor. This time, it has nothing to do with the baby in my stomach.

Adley holds the pregnancy stick high, sauntering out of the bathroom. "What's this?"

I snatch it out of her grasp and turn to face the two adults.

Hudson spits his water all over the table, eyes wide, while Palmer stands from the table, her mouth hanging open in shock.

My eyes glue to Hudson. "You!" I point at him. "Your friend did this to me." Tears fill my eyes.

Finn? Palmer signs, obviously hoping Adley doesn't pick up on what's going on.

Palmer had pulled me aside at the wedding and asked what was going on because we were flirting, but we had to stand side by side the entire night. Surely there was going to be flirting. I didn't go into the night thinking I'd land in his hotel room, but it was a nice surprise. His skills were an even nicer surprise.

I grunt. "It's false, it has to be. I'm going to buy every last test they have to prove I'm right." I walk out of the house before either of them has an opportunity to say anything.

They'll have too many questions. Questions even I don't know the answers to yet.

HARPER

P almer called me so many times last night that I ended up turning my ringer off, so I shouldn't be surprised when there's an incessant knock at the front door the next morning.

I'm still in bed, huddled under the covers and trying to avoid the world because nothing has felt real since I saw those two pink lines on the test. It's all way too surreal.

When the knocking doesn't stop, I crawl out of bed with a groan. It's mid-morning, so Maven will already have left for work.

I peek around the curtain, and yep, it's Palmer. After a deep sigh, I swing open the door. Tears immediately spring to my eyes seeing her expression—a mix of concern and pity. She steps forward and draws me into a tight, secure hug that breaks my last piece of restraint.

For the first time since finding out, I cry. The reality of the situation. The weight of the decision that must be made. I've always been careful, practiced safe sex, so I wouldn't be in this predicament.

Palmer squeezes me so tightly I might break, but after a

couple minutes, she pulls away, shutting the door behind her. "How are you?" she whispers, as if Maven could overhear.

"She's at work." My shoulders slump, and I walk into the living room and collapse onto the couch, pulling a blanket over me. "It's starting to set in."

Palmer sits in the chair beside the couch. "The father is Finn? You haven't mentioned anyone else lately."

Her comment stings, although she didn't mean it to. She's curious if I could be pregnant and not know who the father is. Yes, if I'm into a guy, I'll definitely go to bed with him, even though I'm not interested in anything long term. But I don't sleep with every single male with two feet, a heartbeat, and a dick either.

Regardless, I know people will wonder. Will judge me anyway.

"Yes, it's Finn's." I groan and squeeze my eyes shut. "I don't even know how this happened. I'm on birth control, and we used a condom. All three times."

Palmer's eyes bug out. "You did it three times in one night?"

I shrug, pushing the blanket off my shoulders. "The sex was really good. Amazing actually." Probably the best I've ever had, but I'm not going to give her a play-by-play of Finn's bedroom skills when he's her husband's best friend. "What did Hudson say after I left?"

She tilts her head. "He was shocked, but don't worry, he won't say anything. It's not like he and Finn talk every day anyway. Probably once a month unless something's going on."

I nod. I wasn't worried about either of them saying anything when I left last night. I know they would never. Adley, on the other hand...

"What about Adley?"

A mischievous smile creases her lips, and she looks just like Adley when she's done something she's not supposed to. "We told her it was a test you take when your tummy is bothering you to check if you're sick. She bought it. I swear, a huge part of parenting is just lying to them about stuff or figuring out how to tell them a half-truth."

I muster up a small smile, thankful I won't have to worry about that.

"Do you know what you're going to do?"

I wince at her sympathetic tone and shake my head. The idea of having a baby, fathered by someone I had a one-night stand with, is mind-blowing. But the thought of terminating the pregnancy makes me sick. I can't even imagine the idea of adoption.

"I figured. All right, go get dressed." She stands from the chair, hands on her hips as if I'm Adley.

I burrow down further under the blanket, and Palmer whips the blanket off of me.

I curl into the fetal position. "I don't want to go anywhere," I whine. "I'm just going to stay in my little bubble where I don't have to face the world and my new reality."

I'm taking you somewhere. It's a surprise, she signs.

I blow out a breath on a groan. "What kind of surprise? The sugar kind? Because that's about all my vices can be now, but watch, I'll probably have gestational diabetes."

It's not food related.

I groan and kick my feet like the kid she probably just dropped off at school. "I don't wanna."

"Should we set up a playdate?" she asks, glaring at me.

"Playdate? That's how I got in this position."

She bites her lip to not laugh at my joke. "I meant with

Adley. You're acting like I just said you couldn't have a popsicle before dinner." She grabs my wrist. "Come on."

I fight her, but she's right, time to act like an adult, and adults face their problems head on. Right?

"Fine."

Twenty minutes later, I've gotten dressed in a pair of leggings and a T-shirt, and I'm in the passenger seat of Palmer's car with a package of saltines on my lap. I guess it was Palmer's congratulations gift. The pregnancy nausea sucks.

"So when are we going to get there?" I ask for the tenth time, but Palmer doesn't bother answering.

Man, she's really mastered the mom thing. Thank God I have her to help me through this. She just keeps driving out of town until we're on a small road surrounded by trees. I look at everything we pass, unsure where we could be. I thought I knew every nook and cranny of Lake Starlight.

Eventually, she turns onto a short gravel driveway lined with trees in front of a rustic cabin. It too is surrounded by thick woods, and though the cabin looks as if it's seen better days, it has a charming Hansel and Gretel fairy tale feeling to it with the arched door and shaker shingles.

I don't unbuckle and look at her. "What is this place?"

She presses the button, and my seat belt unclicks. "Come on."

"If this is some ambush, I'll never forgive you. Is someone in there?" I open the passenger door but step out cautiously.

"Just come and see," Palmer says.

I follow her up the old brick walkway toward the arched sky-blue door that reminds me of my great-grandma Dori's eyes and the tint of her gray hair. I was in my early twenties when she passed away, and I miss her to this day. She was a force to be reckoned with.

Palmer slides a key out of her pocket and unlocks the door, pushing it open, motioning for me to go in.

The cabin is just as small as it looked from the outside. There's a living room, a small kitchen with a table and chairs, and a short hallway that I assume leads to a bedroom and bathroom.

It takes me a moment before I look at the walls and see photographs of Great-Grandma Dori and Great-Grandpa Philip, a man I only know from pictures and stories since he passed well before I was born. The pictures consist of them here, by the lake, and skating when they were much younger. It's only of them. There are no pictures of my parents, or Palmer's, or any of my aunts and uncles.

"Is this a love den?" I turn to face Palmer.

A laugh bubbles out of her. "It was theirs." Her eyes fall to a picture of Great-Grandma Dori standing in front of Great-Grandpa Phillip on bended knee. It's a tad grainy and age is definitely getting it to, but it was their proposal for sure.

"I didn't think our family could keep secrets. Am I the only family member who doesn't know about this place?"

She shakes her head and explains to me that the cabin was left to our eldest cousin, Calista, by Great-Grandma Dori. She saw it as a place for each of her great-grandchildren to find refuge and peace during a time of need. Calista passed it down to Brinley, who passed it to Lance, who then offered it to Palmer. Each one of them needed a place to escape from their reality, where no one knew to find them.

"And once you feel more settled and have your plan, or if you see one of the cousins struggling, you pass it on to the next person of your choosing." She smiles as she looks around the small, dated space. "It's like a refuge in the storm. When everything beyond these walls is a mess, you can come here to try to make sense of it. You feel her, right?" Palmer wipes a tear on her cheek. "I felt her energy the first time I walked in."

I nod. She's right. It's as if Great-Grandma Dori is here to talk to and give me advice. It's like heaven to have somewhere to disappear to where no one can find me, and I can take the time to figure out what I want for myself.

I draw her into a hug. "Thank you."

When I pull back, there are tears in both of our eyes.

I hope this place will be helpful, she signs.

"It will be." I give her a watery smile, willing the words to be true.

Surely I'll figure this out and come out the other side.

HARPER

For the next two days, I pretend there's nothing going on in my life. Any time I think about the pregnancy or feel nauseated, I push the thought out of my head and continue on with whatever I'm doing.

I'm not exactly conflict avoidant. Well, maybe I am because when a problem presents itself in my life that I don't feel equipped to deal with, I have a bad habit of pretending it doesn't exist until it becomes so overwhelming I have no choice.

And there's definitely a timeline issue this time. First, there will be signs of the pregnancy when my stomach grows. Then I can't just show up to a family dinner with a baby in a carrier and say surprise. Well, I could actually see myself doing that. Oh, who am I kidding, my family would figure it out before my pregnancy ever got that far. They're all like FBI agents when it comes to anyone keeping a secret.

When Saturday comes around, I run a few errands and swing by my parents' house. It was my grandparents' house that my dad inherited and raised my brother and me in. I always feel a mix of nostalgia and comfort when I walk in, something I'm in desperate need of right now. It's as though I woke up this morning and the little boy or girl inside of me said, I'm done with being ignored. Go figure, it's part me after all.

I open the door without knocking. "Hello..." When no one answers, I head through the family room toward the kitchen. "Mom?" I search out the window to see if they're on the deck. "Dad?"

I step just inside the kitchen. "Oh god!"

My dad is furiously tucking his golf shirt into his pants, and my mom is washing her hands at the sink, trying to appear as if they weren't just fooling around during the day. I thought they were in their, like, once-a-year-on-their-anniversary fucking. Not broad-daylight-in-the-kitchen fucking.

My dad shrugs, his cheeks not even pinkening. "A call would have been nice."

"This is my house." I avoid all eye contact, heading over to the fridge to grab a pop. "Tell me I missed your anniversary."

"What? No." Dad kisses Mom on the cheek.

A girl can hope, can't she?

"You should be happy you have parents who still can't keep their hands off one another," Mom says.

A strangled cry erupts out of me as I pop open the can. "Let me live in my bubble please." I still for a moment, the baby pressing on my stomach, asking to be remembered again.

Crap, is pop bad for a baby? I glance up, and my mom is giving me a quizzical look. She probably knows, but I can't ask her, so I set the can on the counter without taking a sip, hoping my parents are so much in their afterglow they don't notice.

I promise, little one, I'll do more research.

"What brings you by, Harp?" my dad asks, sitting at the table with his tablet in front of him. He holds it up toward me. "Did you see Sportsverse did an article on your brother?"

Crossing my arms, I lean against the counter as my mom dries her hands with a towel.

"I guess I missed that one," I say.

I love my brother. I do. But all my life, it's been him and his baseball career and how successful he is. While I'm here toying with the idea of telling them I got knocked up at Palmer's wedding by the best man I'd just met. My brother and I are on different playing fields—literally—when it comes to my parents.

I shrug. "Just thought I'd swing by for a visit. No reason."

My mom studies me, and I see her mommy detective skills go on high alert, like little antennae popping out of her red hair. I attempt to give off an unaffected, casual air.

I must succeed because she just says, "Do you want to stay for dinner?"

Man, I'm really getting better at this whole omission thing.

"No, that's okay. Thanks though."

"Did you watch your brother's game last night?" my dad asks.

I pick up my can of pop and join him at the table. Truth is, I totally forgot about Easton's game last night. He's the short-stop for the Chicago Colts, and I usually try to watch at least part of his games, or at the very least the next day's recap.

"No, I missed it. Did he knock one out of the park?"

He shrugs. "No. Could've been worse. Could've been better too."

My dad missed out on his chance to go to the pros when he had to leave college to return to Alaska in order to raise his siblings with Aunt Savannah after their parents died unexpectedly. He said he's never had any regrets, but I think sometimes he likes that his son got to where he wanted to be too.

"There's always a next game," I say.

My mom sets down a bowl with my favorite trail mix and takes a seat beside me. On any other day, I'd already have my hand in the bowl, but this constant nausea is really putting a thorn in my habit of snacking more than eating a meal. But if I don't have any, those little antennae will slowly come back up.

"Thanks." I take a small amount and eat it. "Is East planning to come home when the season is done?" He usually does, for a while anyway, but I keep forgetting to ask him when we talk.

"I sure hope so. I miss my son," Mom says, covering her heart with her hand.

I refrain from rolling my eyes. My mom dotes on my brother. Not that she doesn't dote on me too, it's just in different ways. My brother's dreams were always bigger than mine. That was clear early on in our lives. He was going to go somewhere while I was... not.

"How's work going?" my dad asks, and I'm thankful he changes the subject away from my brother and baseball.

"Good. Busy. I met with an out-of-town bride yesterday, and another couple is flying in next week."

"Oh, Harp, that's great news. Sounds like business is

going well." My dad peeks over the edge of his tablet and smiles.

"Do you ever think about catering more to the local clientele and not worrying so much about the out-of-state people?" my mom asks.

I grit my teeth and take a deep breath through my nose. My mom was a principal until she retired, and the guidance role that she had with her students trickled down to everything I did, whether I asked or not. She means well, I know she does, but it always makes me feel as if I'm doing something wrong.

"I do cater to the locals, Mom, there just aren't enough of them to keep my business afloat, which is why I cast a wider net. So far, my plan has been working." My tone comes out a little snippier than I intend, and my dad peeks up over his tablet with raised eyebrows.

She raises her hands. "I was just asking."

I know she worries and that she asks out of love and concern for my future, but the fact that years later, she still questions how I'm running my business spurs feelings of unworthiness inside me.

Does she ask Easton if he's really doing everything he needs to in order to win the Golden Glove award this year? Somehow, I doubt it.

"You're doing a great job, kiddo." My dad shares a look with my mom, and she pats my hand.

"Absolutely." She gives me a smile as if she's appeasing me but really thinking that if it was her, she'd do something different.

Deciding that it's best to move on, I change the subject and ask them about the trip they have planned in a couple of months once winter settles in. Ever since they both retired from the high school, they usually spend a month or two in a warmer climate, like Arizona or California.

My parents tell me all about the condo they've rented in Palm Springs and their plans for activities. They're definitely excited, their love for one another shining as they play off each other. My parents' story as to how they met has always been told to me by people in town. How in love they were and still are. The way my dad changed his course because of my mom. On and on, I've heard stories as if they're Lake Starlight's fairytale love story. Which is gross, since it began with them hooking up in the back seat of my dad's Jeep that still sits in the garage. They take it out once in a while during the summer, and after what I just walked in on, I'm thinking I never want to ride in it again.

"You've barely touched your trail mix or your pop. Are you feeling okay?" My mom puts her hand on my forehead.

Leaning to the side, I shift away from her touch. "I'm fine. I just had a big lunch, that's all."

I look between the two of them... I could tell them now. Just blurt out that I'm pregnant even though I'm not completely sure of my decision yet. But when I imagine telling them, all I envision is the look of profound disappointment on their faces. Them thinking that Harper has screwed up yet again.

My parents love me, I know that. But I've always felt as though I can't live up to being Austin and Holly Bailey's daughter. Their names, my family name, is kind of a big deal in this town. My brother never had any trouble living up to being a Bailey. He did well in school, did well in sports, and somehow kept all the shit he did a secret, while every time I did anything, I was caught. And now he's a professional athlete, a hometown hero. He's got a trophy case in the high school, and he's turned everyone into a

Colts fan, and when he comes home, you'd think he was the mayor. And the people always say, "And they have a daughter, Harper. She... well, she looks just like her mother."

I get the difference. I never took school seriously. I was always impulsive and wild and found myself in the usual sort of teenage trouble growing up.

I can't say anything to them yet. Not until I have a plan worked out to present to them. Maybe if that's the case, they won't freak out and give me that look like I just can't do anything right.

One thing is for sure, I have to figure out what I'm going to do and soon.

After I leave my parents' house, I head to the cabin with the hope that solitude will offer some clarity about what I want to do.

As I drive through Lake Starlight's small downtown, I pass the town square and fixate on all the families there. The parents playing with their children, chasing them around and pushing them on the swings and catching them when they come down the slide. Can I really do that? What if I answer a phone call, and my kid flies off the slide and goes airborne?

Once I'm inside the cabin, I open some of the windows to let in some fresh air. Although the weather is growing colder with each passing day, you learn early to take advantage of being able to keep windows open when you live in Alaska. There are way too many months we're holed up inside.

Now, what do I do? I don't really enjoy quiet or solitude. I'm more of a go go go person, socializing with friends and family. My mind travels a mile a minute, so any lack of background noise makes all my thoughts louder.

When I was here with Palmer, I didn't do much more

than take a surface look at everything, so this time I wander around the small space. There are some bottles of water in the fridge and canned food in the cupboards that someone left behind. There's also an unopened box of saltines. I wonder if Palmer left them for me or if one of my cousins has something to share.

This nausea is killing my addiction to food, but I should eat, so I open the box and grab a sleeve of crackers. I take crackers with me as I continue my exploration, taking small nibbles.

The bathroom is small and dated, but clean. In the one bedroom, there's a dresser with a few items of clothing in the drawers. The top of the closet is piled with extra blankets and pillows. As I'm about to shut the closet doors, my gaze snags on something leaning against the wall in the back.

Curious, I pull it—actually them, now that I'm closer— out and set them on the bed.

"Oh my god." I flip through the poster boards.

Great-Grandma Dori was known for meddling in her grandchildren's love lives, but I had no idea she went this far. Each board is designated for one of my aunts and uncles, my dad included. Every single one resembles a crime board on TV when a detective is trying to link a case together. Except these are plans to get them together with their now husbands and wives. Way to go, Great-Grandma!

I giggle reading all her schemes, but then a feeling of melancholy descends over me. I miss my great-grandma so much. She was one of a kind. If she were here, she'd know what to tell me because she had the best advice.

After I put the boards back in the closet, I lie down on the bed. I've been so tired lately. Tired and nauseous. So far, pregnancy isn't much fun.

I let my mind wander, trying to picture the outcome of three options. If I don't continue with this pregnancy, could I pretend it never happened? No way. I'd always wonder what if. Wonder what my baby may have looked like. What his or her personality would have been like. Most of all, whether I made the right choice. I'd most likely always mourn the loss of what could have been.

Which means...

The weight of the decision presses my body into the mattress. I'll be doing this on my own. I'll tell Finn about the pregnancy, but he lives in Vermont. Even if he wanted to be involved, it wouldn't be on a full-time basis. Which means I'd be a single mother. Me. Harper Bailey. The impulsive, promiscuous party girl.

The what-if game plays in my head further. What if my wedding planner business fails? What if I'm a terrible mother? What if I mess him or her up? What will everyone think when they find out?

I breathe through the anxiety tightening my chest and roll onto my side, lightly pressing a hand to my belly. A knowing seeps into my bones. It won't be easy, but I already know my decision—I'm going to be a mother.

HARPER

D ays go by and Palmer doesn't pressure me about what I've decided, but she does check in with me every day to make sure I'm okay.

Last weekend, after making the decision to have the baby, I was terrified. But as the days have gone by, I've settled into my decision and the rightness of it. My plan is to get Finn's contact information from Hudson this weekend and reach out to him. Another dose of anxiety spins around me because I have no idea how he'll react.

My plan is blown to pieces on Thursday night when I'm settled in with Maven to watch TV with a bowl of sour cream and onion popcorn. It's been our thing since she moved in. We try a different flavor of popcorn for every episode we watch. A message from Palmer comes through.

Um... he's here.

Who?

Finn! He just knocked on our door.

> What is he doing here?

> I have no idea, but I thought you'd like to know.

My stomach flips, and before I truly take any time to think about what I should or should not do in this circumstance, I'm off the couch. "I have to run over to Palmer's," I say over my shoulder to Maven.

"Is everything okay?" She sits up, and I hear the concern in her tone.

"Yup." I grab my purse off the hook by the front door and slide into my shoes. "She and Hudson have to run out, so I'm going to watch Adley."

"Is everything okay? Where would they have to go at this hour?" Maven calls after me, but I don't bother answering.

Driving over to Palmer's, I don't give myself an inch to second-guess my decision that Finn being in town is somehow a sign that this is the exact moment for me to tell him he's going to be a dad. I just want to get it over with so I don't have to have another week of dreading reaching out and being like, "Hey, did the condom break, or what exactly happened? Oh yeah, it doesn't matter... congratulations, Daddy!"

My phone buzzes in my purse, but I'm not taking the time to pull over to see who it is. I'm sure it's Palmer. She may not officially know my decision yet, but she knows me well enough to know I'm probably going to show up at her place, and I don't want her to talk me out of it. I need to do this before I chicken out.

I park at the curb since the driveway is full of Palmer and Hudson's cars and what I assume is Finn's rental. I'm not taking any chances of being blocked in by some random family member who decides to pop into Palmer's for a visit for some weird reason. The curb will make for a quick getaway. My head is down, and I head right into their back door that is always unlocked.

"Hello," I call, hoping my tone inflects that this is just an impromptu visit to see Palmer and Hudson.

No one responds, so I walk farther into the house and find the three of them in the living room. Palmer and Hudson are on the couch, and Finn is on an adjacent chair. Adley must either be already in bed or up in her room. I give Palmer and Hudson a cursory glance, and my gaze snags on Finn, seeing him for the first time not as my one-night stand, but as the father of my baby. Wow, weird in a million different ways.

Of course, he looks as good as he did the night of the wedding, minus the tuxedo. He's casually dressed in a pair of worn jeans and a white T-shirt. His tattoos are visible on each arm, and his brown hair with natural golden high-lights is a little longer, reaching his ears. Rather than the clean-shaven face he had at the wedding, he's adorned with stubble. I clench my thighs together to dull the ache of what his face would feel like between my legs now.

I give myself a mental scolding because we are not here for *that*. *That* is exactly what got us in this situation in the first place.

"Hey, guys." My voice cracks, and I clear my throat to sound more unaffected from being in the same room with Finn again.

"Harper." Finn's eyes widen, and he draws back in the chair.

I'm sorry, am I not the one who lives in Alaska? He's the one who flew thousands of miles to get here.

I try not to take personally his clear discomfort that I'm in his presence again. This is new for both of us. One-night stands are meant to never see one another again. But then again, he is Hudson's best friend, so not my smartest decision to pick him.

Finn walks over to me, holding out his hands. I retract a fraction, but he doesn't relent, giving me the most awkward hug I've ever received. "It's good to see you again." His hands pat my back, although our chests don't touch.

Over Finn's shoulder, Palmer gives me a wide-eyed expression, and Hudson's face is the color of the snow still sitting at the tops of the mountains outside. They see the awkwardness too.

I shake off the weirdness because it's now or… well, over the phone. Which sounds nice right about now? I don't have to see his jaw drop.

"Can we talk for a minute?" I ask.

He cocks his head to the side, eyebrows drawing down. He probably thinks I'm a stage-five clinger, and I'm about to tell him that I developed feelings. The only thing I'm feeling is queasy. "Um… yeah. I was hoping we could chat anyway, so that'd be great."

Oh, that's surprising. I guess I read that expression wrong. Maybe I'm misinterpreting this entire exchange, and he's nervous to see me again because he thinks there's something between us? There is. A baby.

It doesn't matter because after I blow his mind with my news, he's no longer going to think of me that way. There's a good chance he'll regret sleeping with me entirely.

Palmer stands, drawing my attention. *Why don't you help me get everyone some drinks in the kitchen?* she signs.

Why is she signing to me rather than speaking since she

has her cochlear implant on? Regardless, I'm so close to getting this news out, and she's not going to derail me.

No, I have to do this before I chicken out.

She widens her eyes at me, clearly trying to communicate something. *I think we should talk first.*

I frown. The whole time Palmer and I go back and forth, Finn is looking between us and Hudson, waiting for him to translate our sign language.

Ignoring my cousin, I turn to face Hudson. "Can you guys give us a minute?"

He gives me a tight nod, stands, and sets his hand on Palmer's lower back, leading her out of the room. She follows, but she keeps glancing over her shoulder at me. I ignore her in favor of maintaining my courage.

I walk farther into the room and sit where Palmer was while Finn sits in the chair he was occupying. His cologne does smell nice. He leans forward, resting his forearms on his thighs, and flashes of our night together play through my head like a movie. Being this close to him reminds me why I fell into bed with him in the first place. The buzz of attraction has only deepened between us. Or at least for me. Maybe I'm imagining it, or maybe it's the pregnancy hormones.

"How are you?" he asks, taking me out of my clustered thoughts.

He has no idea what a loaded question that is.

"I'm good. How have you been?"

He nods. "Good. Good."

An awkward silence cloaks us like a blanket, so I try with an obvious question. "What are you doing in Alaska?"

Finn shifts nervously in his chair. "That's actually what I wanted to talk to you about."

"Oh?" I act indifferent because surely, he's not here on

some mission to win me over. Like I rocked his world so much that night, he can't stop thinking of me.

Not that the attraction between us the night of Palmer and Hudson's wedding wasn't intense, but I'd assumed the drinks helped and the fact that we'd both seen our best friend get married earlier that day. Maybe I've been so hung up on the pregnancy thing, I'd forgotten that.

He swallows hard and looks at his clutched hands together between his knees. Then he straightens out and rubs his hands down his thighs, as if he has to gather courage too.

I decide to put him out of his misery so we can discuss the most important thing right now. "It's okay. I know why you're here."

His shoulders relax. "You do?"

I nod. "It's nothing to be embarrassed about. I felt it too." His forehead wrinkles, but I press on. "The attraction between us was instant. And intense. I've wondered what it might have been like if we were able to explore it more since you left too."

He blinks rapidly, blows out a breath, and pushes his hand through his hair, standing and pacing in front of the couch. "I mean, yeah. It was, but... I... I'm not here to try to hook up again or start something with you."

Heat flames my face, and I inch to the end of the couch, wondering how fast I can escape.

Finn must recognize it because he inches toward me. "Sorry. That came out wrong. If I lived here and things were different, I'd definitely consider dating you."

"Gee thanks." I clench my fists on my lap.

He shakes his head. "I'm fucking this up."

"Just say whatever you were going to say," I snipe, wanting this moment over.

"I'm here because… well… I'm getting married."

The last three words. The most important words come out in a rush, so it takes my brain a beat to string them together to make sense. When they do, I bolt up off the couch.

"You're getting married?" A wave of nausea swells over me, and I swallow back bile rising up my throat. And not from the baby.

There's an underlying sadness or maybe pity in his eyes. "Yes."

Now I'm the one pacing, hand over my stomach because I might throw up in his lap. "You had a fiancée when you slept with me?" My voice is shrill and loud.

Something drops in the kitchen.

"We're okay," Hudson calls.

The only thing worse than getting knocked up by the best man is finding out I'm his other woman.

He frowns. "God, no! Of course not!"

"Then you need to explain how I slept with you a month ago and now you're engaged." My hands fist at my sides.

He blows out a breath. "My long-term girlfriend and I were on a break when I was here for the wedding."

My head rears back. "A break? This isn't an episode of *Friends*. Jesus."

"We got back together when I returned to Vermont," he continues, ignoring my comment.

"You didn't mention her the night we slept together."

Finn scowls. "I'm sorry. I didn't realize I had to give you my entire dating history before I slept with you. Should I have asked you a list of all your exes and hookups before I stripped you out of your dress?"

His words bring an image to my brain of a naked Finn

standing at the end of the bed, gazing down at me while he stroked his length. A tidal wave of heat travels through my body.

I squeeze my eyes shut and give my head a little shake to rid myself of the mental picture. "I would have liked to know you were jumping from her bed into mine."

He groans and runs his fingers through his hair. "I didn't know we'd get back together."

My head cocks to the side. "You didn't know, and yet here you are, a little over a month later, telling me you're engaged?" I roll my eyes.

He crosses his arms. "You can choose to believe me or not, but it's the truth."

I mimic his stance and cross my arms. "I'm going to go with not believe you."

He throws his hands in the air. "Fine. Whatever. But there's more."

My hands drop to my sides. "More? How can there possibly be *more*?"

He cringes and one hand tugs on the back of his neck. "It's the reason we're here."

"We?" I glance around the room. I'm not sure why. Do I assume someone is going to pop out of Adley's playhouse and announce herself?

"Tamra wants to get married in Alaska, so we're here to plan the wedding. And…"

"Oh, for fuck's sake, what?"

He draws out a long breath. "It seems she's hired… you as our wedding planner."

My eyes widen, and my stomach lurches. Again, not the baby, just his or her daddy. "What?"

"Hey." Both of our heads turn toward the archway of the room. A hesitant Hudson's hand is up in the air as if he comes in peace. "Adley's already asleep, so can we keep it down a little?"

He disappears, and I lock my vision back on Finn.

"What are you, some kind of sicko? Why would you allow her to hire me?" I whisper-shout, if that's even a thing.

His chocolate-brown eyes fire with irritation. "Yes, because I want to be uncomfortable the entire time I plan my wedding. And I thought, let me torture myself a little bit." His shoulders lose some of the tension. "I didn't know until we checked into the resort, and she gave me the rundown of what we're doing tomorrow, which apparently involves meeting with you first thing since you're our wedding planner."

Oh my god. The out-of-town clients I'm meeting with tomorrow are Finn and his fiancée? I had her name of course, but I was a second away from throwing up when I was taking her information down. I figured I'd get the groom's information when we met in person.

My eyes widen. "You can't be serious."

He nods, lips pressed together in a thin line. "It was all her doing. Obviously, I had nothing to do with it."

"Of course, you wouldn't want your beautiful fiancée knowing about your dirty little secret, right?" An oily sensation coats my skin at feeling as though I was the other woman.

I've never fooled around with anyone else's man, but I'm familiar with the feeling of other people judging me for my hookups. As if they thought I have to live a pious life until I find my person.

"It's not like that," Finn says, drawing me from my thoughts.

I cross my arms again. "Tell me what it's like then." I don't miss the venom in my voice.

"I just think it would make things... awkward for everyone if Tamra knew. I was hoping we could keep what happened between us."

I guffaw and huff but try to rein myself in. This man is not worth it. "Still making me feel like your dirty little secret."

Part of me wants to blurt out that I'm pregnant, but I need to consider what he's just told me and how it will come into play. There's certainly no perfect time to tell Finn that I'm pregnant, but right now might be the worst possible time.

A piece of me wants no part of this. No part of him and his fiancée and their wedding. I want to email Tamra and tell her I can't take her on as a client anymore. But I can't cut them lose because now more than ever, I need to make money to support my child. And it was clear from the intro conversations that Tamra intends to have a lavish wedding, which correlates to a nice paycheck for me.

"Harper—"

I put my hand in the air. "Fine. I'll keep your little secret."

"You will?" He arches an eyebrow, and his voice raises.

"Yes, but only because it will upset your fiancée. There's no reason to do that if what you say is true, and you weren't together when you were here for the wedding."

"It's true. I swear it." He sounds so earnest that I think he might be telling the truth.

Still, it stings knowing I was a detour on the way to his final destination. Which is a ridiculous thought and must be the hormones talking. I've never once cared what any of my hookups have done after I slept with them. Finn isn't any different. Except he has some kind of magic sperm that weaseled its way into my egg.

I nod. "Then tomorrow when we meet, I'll act like we met in passing at the wedding and nothing more."

"I appreciate that."

I don't bother responding but walk over to grab my purse where I left it on the couch. "I'll see you then." Turning, I begin to the leave the room.

"Wait!" he calls. "You wanted to tell me something?"

I shake my head. "No, it was nothing important."

The lie slips off my tongue, and I walk through the dining room to the kitchen where Palmer and Hudson are. I wave goodbye, and thankfully they don't stop me.

This is going to come to a head eventually, I know that. Just not tonight.

FINN

The door to the hotel room opens, and Tamra waltzes in with two to-go cups. I recognize the logo from Brewed Awakenings, the coffee shop I quickly got addicted to when I was here for Hudson's wedding.

"This little town is so cute! I'm so glad you listened to me and agreed to have the wedding here."

After Tamra saw all my pictures from Hudson's wedding, she insisted that we get married in Alaska. She's always wanted a destination wedding, but I assumed she meant somewhere tropical. But that's overdone, according to her, and no one wants to attend yet another wedding on the beach. She has a point. We've been to three different beach destination weddings together. All of them Tamra's closest friends.

I hate the fact Harper's accusations still run through my mind this morning. No part of me wanted to return to Lake Starlight with my fiancée with the chance of running into my one-night stand, but Tamra wouldn't drop it, and I don't have much of a choice once she gets something in her head. It hurt a little that Harper thought I would cheat on my fiancée, but she doesn't know much about me other than my dick size and the few tidbits we shared when we were forced to hang around one another all night.

At the wedding, Tamra and I were broken up, and I thought it was for good, which I was more than fine with. Tamra and I had been together for three years. The relationship had fizzled, and we figured we were better off as friends. There was no way for me to anticipate everything that went down after I returned home from Alaska.

Now, what would have been an already uncomfortable situation is worse since Tamra hired Harper as our wedding planner. Hence my visit to see Hudson and Palmer—I wanted to ask them what they thought the best way to handle the situation was. I'd only gotten so far before Harper barrelled into the room.

God, she looked as stunning as she did when I first met her at the rehearsal dinner. The fire I love about her was on display last night too. I'm drawn to her take-no-bullshit, I-am-who-I-am persona. But as a firefighter, I know better than anyone how quickly a fire can turn and end up burning you.

Tamra comes over and sits next to me in the small living area of our hotel room, handing me my coffee.

"Thanks." I grab the remote from the coffee table and turn off the sports channel. "Listen, about the meeting this morning. Do you really think it's necessary?"

Tamra turns from where she's digging through her bag, a frown on her face. "Of course it's necessary. How do you expect to plan a wedding when we don't even live in the state?"

"It just seems like a lot of effort to go to when…"

She tosses her bag on the chair next to her and crosses her arms. "When we're not marrying for love?"

"Exactly." I bring my coffee to my lips and take a hesitant sip. The worst is when you burn your tongue and can't taste anything for a few days. My life is going to be in turmoil during our time here, so I might as well enjoy the taste of the food.

She places her hand on my leg. "You knew what this would entail when you agreed to all of this, Finn. If our plan is going to work, it has to be believable, and anyone who knows me knows I wouldn't slap together a half-assed wedding."

She couldn't be more right. Tamra can be a little high maintenance, as anyone who knows her can attest. If we were in love and this were a real wedding, she'd make her parents pull out all the stops.

I sigh. "I guess I see your point."

She squeezes my thigh. "You just need to be present for these things, play the role of the doting groom, and we'll be in the clear."

The same uneasiness I felt when I agreed to marry Tamra in the first place worms its way through my veins. I hate lying to everyone, but I have no choice. I'm doing this for my family.

She stands, taking her coffee. "We need to leave in twenty minutes."

"No problem, I'm ready." I pick up the remote and turn the TV back on. Might as well pass the time watching the sports updates rather than counting down the minutes until I'm in the same room as my fiancée and my one-night stand.

I PARK the rental truck on Main Street and soak in the quaint downtown. It really is postcard perfect, and I can't come up with one reason Tamra wouldn't want her wedding here.

When I don't immediately undo my seat belt to get out of the truck, Tamra pats my leg. "This may not be a real wedding, but planning is so fun." She claps her hands in front of her, excitement radiating off her. "C'mon, let's go."

She wouldn't be as excited if she knew who Harper was to me and the fact that I haven't stopped thinking about her since I left Alaska.

Last night, I considered telling Tamra what went down with Harper. After all, we weren't together, and she'd have no reason to be upset. But I figured it would only make everything more awkward, so I kept the information to myself. Not that I think Tamra would be jealous or anything. She definitely would not. Hell, knowing her, she might tell me I could hook up with Harper as long as I kept it on the down-low.

But Tamra not knowing about Harper, and Harper not knowing the truth about Tamra and me, serves a bigger purpose as well—it keeps me away from the temptation Harper is.

One night with a woman like her is one thing, but extending it to anything beyond that could prove danger- ous. I have my issues from my past and being with a woman who is wild and spontaneous and who clearly likes to live life without much thought for the future isn't the best for me.

And so, as awkward as it is, I'll walk into Harper's office today and play the loving fiancé who bows to his bride's every whim because nothing can jeopardize each of our reasons for doing this. My family is depending on me, even if they don't know it.

I round the front of the truck and meet Tamra on the sidewalk, sliding my hand into hers. It's something we've done a thousand times, so it shouldn't be a big deal, but her hand no longer feels as though it fits with mine. It's like I'm trying on a size too small. It works, but it's not right.

We walk down Main Street toward Harper's office while Tamra comments on every storefront we pass, talking about how adorable and charming each business is, from the bakery to the baby store.

I take a big breath when we stop in front of Harper's office with the Hitched & Happy Co. sign on the front door window.

"She told us to go on in when we arrived." Tamra releases my hand and opens the door. "Harper?"

I follow Tamra inside as Harper comes out of the back area. She looks different than any time before. I've seen her casual with her hair in a messy bun like she was last night. I've seen her dressed up like she was for all the wedding events. Never have I seen her in high-waisted navy dress pants and a short-sleeved cropped cream blouse with her hair slicked back into a ponytail.

This is professional Harper. And it looks fucking fantastic on her.

But that's no surprise because she's probably stunning no matter what she wears.

She's all smiles to Tamra, not sparing me one glance let alone two. After she shakes Tamra's hand, it's Tamra who puts her hand on my back to introduce me. I'm a fucking slimeball who Tamra has no idea knows what Harper looks like underneath that pantsuit, nor the fact that I want to see it again.

"And this is my fiancé, Finn."

Harper's gaze meets mine, but I'm pretty sure she's looking over my shoulder instead of at me. Her fiery temper from last night isn't there, nor the playful spirit when we met at the rehearsal dinner. There's only what I'd classify as cold indifference, though Tamra doesn't notice.

Harper nods. "Good to see you, Finn." She gives all her attention to Tamra.

A dagger right in the heart.

Maybe this is how she is with all the grooms. I can't imagine a lot of grooms really give a shit about what color the flowers are and whether the chair covers match the designated wedding color.

Harper waves and leads us over to her desk. Through my own reprimand, I shamelessly check out her ass in her pants. Fuck, I'm an engaged man. I can't be checking out another woman.

I hold out Tamra's chair for her, and after she's seated, I take the chair beside her, opposite of Harper's desk. Once we're settled, Tamra shocks me by intertwining her fingers with mine.

Harper's eyes fall to our adjoined hands before she raises her gaze to me, then her posture goes rigid, and she concentrates on her computer screen. "All right, let me just open your file so I can see my notes from our conversation. Just to confirm, are you still hoping to have the wedding at the end of October?"

"Absolutely," Tamra says, turning to me with a wide fake smile. "We're anxious to make it official."

She's not lying. It's just not for the reasons that Harper assumes.

I do my best to give a natural smile back to Tamra.

"All right, well, that's a little more than two months

from now, so that is going to limit where the wedding can be held. What kind of ceremony and reception are you dreaming of?" Harper's eyes don't detour to me once, all her attention on Tamra.

I'm surprised how much her ignoring me is bothering me. I shouldn't be worrying about Harper. I should be focused on making sure this wedding goes off without a hitch so that Tamra and I both get what we want.

"I had this idea that we could do something different— maybe get married at night under the Northern Lights. Wouldn't that be beautiful?" Tamra shoots me some fluttering eyelashes, and I want to say she's laying it on a little thick.

Harper clears her throat, and Tamra shifts her vision to her. "Well, there's no way to guarantee the Northern Lights will be on display the night of your wedding, but it is a good time of year for them. Beyond that, you should know that it can dip below freezing at night in October. I'm not sure if you plan on wearing a traditional wedding gown, but if so, you might find it to be on the cold side." She laughs, but it's forced, not the real laugh I heard that night.

Tamra frowns. "Oh, I didn't think about how cold it would be here. Of course, it's Alaska."

"Maybe we have the ceremony inside, but during the reception we can be sure to take a few shots outside? Even if there are no Northern Lights, it will still be beautiful," I say, hoping Tamra will just agree and it gets us out of here faster.

My suggestion perks her up. "That's a great idea. I knew there was a reason I'm marrying you." She leans over and gives me a kiss on the cheek.

My eyes zero in across the desk at Harper, and again, I

feel like an asshole. Our eyes meet briefly before she tugs hers away.

"Indoor ceremony it is. How many guests are you expecting? That will determine what our options are."

"Oh, I hadn't considered that yet." Tamra lists off the names of friends and family, keeping a mental tally of who she thinks would travel for the wedding. "Who do you think will come from your side?"

I shrug. "My parents. And Hudson and Palmer."

Tamra drops my hand and shifts in her seat to better face me. "Aren't you going to invite the guys from the fire station? What about people who work for your parents at the ski resort?"

I'm trying to limit the number of people who get drawn into this farce, and unlike Tamra, I don't come from the type of family where I feel beholden to invite certain people because of their social status. Yes, my parents own a ski resort they inherited from my grandparents, but it's a small one and not as lucrative as it once was. One of the reasons I'm in this chair now.

"I don't want any of my coworkers to feel like they have to spend the money to fly out here, and I'm pretty sure my parents will feel the same about everyone who works for them."

The corners of Tamra's mouth pinch in, and it's clear she doesn't appreciate my answer. She faces Harper, who tries to play it off as if she wasn't watching our exchange.

"All right then." Tamra inhales to regroup. "Best estimate is around one hundred people, I guess."

Harper notes it in her computer. "A hundred people will limit the number of places we can look at, since we can't consider smaller venues or restaurants. And what about the ceremony? Do you want a church wedding, or do you want to have it in the same place as the reception?"

"Definitely not a church," I answer, and Tamra whips her head in my direction.

I'm not religious, but either way, I'm not saying real nuptials to my fake fiancée in a church of all places.

"I like the idea of having it all in one place. Seems simpler." I shrug, as if not wanting a church wedding has anything to do with the fact we're not marrying for love.

"All right then," Harper says.

"Okkaayy, I'm fine with that." Tamra forces a smile and runs her hand down my arm.

Jesus, she's laying this on thick. In the three years we were in a real relationship, she rarely showed me any affection.

"I know you're familiar, Finn, because of Hudson's wedding, but Tamra, are you at all familiar with Glacier Point Resort?" Again, she only concentrates on Tamra, ignoring me.

"That's where we're staying," Tamra says, then cocks her head. "Wait, did you plan Hudson's wedding too?" She turns from Harper to me. I really hope she doesn't see Harper glaring at me.

"Yes," Harper answers.

I blink and look at Tamra. I could leave it at that, but it only stacks another lie to my list. "Actually, Harper's cousin was the bride."

Tamra inhales a breath, but I never see her release it. Her back goes straight, and her hand wraps around the armrest until her knuckles are white. "Oh, so you're telling me you two know each other already."

"We met in passing," Harper says. "Nothing memorable."

My hands clutch the armrests of the chair until I'm white-knuckled. What a perfect pair Tamra and I are. "Yeah, nothing worth mentioning."

Our eyes meet across the desk. Though we're lobbing grenades at each other, I still fucking want Harper with her anger pointed in my direction.

"The reason I ask is because my uncle owns the resort, so I have a bit of an in. I'll make a call and see if they can accommodate not only the wedding but also enough rooms for your guests." Harper's fingers move across the keyboard.

"Oh, thank you, that would be wonderful. There's something else I wanted to ask. I would love to develop an itinerary of fun things to do in the area for our family and friends while they're in Lake Starlight. Would you be able to help with that?" Tamra asks.

"Great idea. I can brainstorm a list of activities, and depending how adventurous your guests are, my uncle and twin cousins run an adventure tour company. I'll check what they might have available during that time of year."

"Oh my god, this is so awesome, Harper. Is your dad the mayor? You have an in with everyone in this town. Isn't this great, Finn?" Tamra's smile only grows wider. She's obviously ecstatic that she's going to get everything she wants. The only thing missing is a groom she loves.

"Wonderful." I plaster on a fake smile.

Tamra's phone rings in her purse. "Sorry, I thought I turned the ringer off." She fishes it out of her purse and looks at the screen. "Shoot, sorry." She stands and puts her finger in the air. "I've been expecting this, but I'll be super fast. Sorry."

"Go. No problem." Harper waves at her to take the call and not to feel guilty for wasting her time.

Tamra takes her purse and phone outside with her. I'm

not surprised Tamra interrupted wedding planning to take a business call. That's why she's marrying me after all. But it means I've been left alone with Harper, who is now glaring daggers at me.

I understand why she's upset, but I don't know why she's acting as if I'm the enemy. Does she actually think I was lying when I said I was single the night of Hudson's wedding?

"Something on your mind, Harper?" I arch an eyebrow and lean back in my chair, bringing my leg up to rest my ankle on my opposite knee.

She leans back in her chair as well, crossing her arms. "You don't find this entire situation untenable? Sitting here with the woman you slept with while you were on a break from the woman you're about to spend the rest of your life with?"

I lean forward and rest my arms on my thighs. "Yes, it's uncomfortable, but I wasn't lying when I said that we were over at the wedding."

She cocks her head. "Explain to me how you go from things being over to planning a wedding in a month."

Damn it, I should have been more affectionate. She suspects something is up with this quick marriage. The only reason I wasn't touching Tamra and pretending that I love her was because I didn't want to shove it in Harper's face.

I play off her remark with a shrug. "There's nothing to explain. We love each other. We'd been together three years and hit a rough patch. Realized how empty our lives were without each other, and when we got back together, we decided we didn't want to waste time before taking the next step." The lie tastes bitter.

"So, that makes me what? Your rebound?"

I have to get her off the scent that there's anything questionable about my engagement. "Yeah."

Something changes in her demeanor the moment the word leaves my lips. Some of the fiery light leaves her eyes, and I hate myself for being the one to extinguish it.

Harper nods. "All right then."

I almost take it back, tell her the truth—that I haven't been able to stop thinking of her since she left my bed that morning. But even if I were single, pursuing a future with her wouldn't be wise. She's everything I want, but nothing I can handle.

Harper's office door opens, and a fresh breeze blows in. "Sorry about that." Tamra walks back in and joins us.

This time when she sits beside me, I'm the one to show affection. I pick up her hand and kiss her knuckles as though I couldn't bear to be parted from her for that short amount of time, all while I avoid diverting my gaze to Harper's. That's not to say I don't feel her staring at the side of my face. Pulling off this fake wedding just got a shit-ton harder.

seven

HARPER

After my meeting with Finn and Tamra, my head is a mess, so I decide to take the rest of the day to relax at the cabin so no one can bother me. On my way, I make a pit stop.

I hope this isn't a bad idea, though I'm pretty sure it's not.

After my showdown with Finn last night, I talked to Palmer on the phone, letting her know I had decided to have the baby and that I didn't tell Finn after he sprang the news he's getting married. She understood why I'd kept the news to myself but encouraged me to tell him soon. I asked her and Hudson not to tell Finn I'm pregnant. I'll do it soon, but on my time.

But there's another person's perspective I'd like to get on this whole situation first.

I've always been close to my aunt Sedona. Maybe it's because she was my parents' surrogate and carried me for nine months, or maybe it's because I've never felt that she judged me. Sure, she always gives me her opinion on something, but it's never in a way where I feel like she's looking down on me or that I'm disappointing her as I do with my mom.

No doubt her own past will give her a unique perspective on the situation.

I pull into her driveway, gather my courage, and go knock on the door. Maybe I should have called first to make sure she was home.

Relief fills me when I hear the pad of footsteps behind the door. Then it swings open, and my aunt looks surprised.

Palmer looks so much like her. They share the same dark hair, though I suspect my aunt's color might come from a dye box now. The same pale skin and arresting eyes adorn both their faces.

"Hi, Aunt Sedona." I muster up a smile.

"Harper, how are you? Come on in." She opens the door wider.

I step into the house, looking around to see if anyone else is here. "Where's Uncle Jamison?"

"He's at the sports complex finalizing the schedule for fall. Did you need him?" She tilts her head, looking at me with concern.

"No, I was hoping to talk to you."

Her body relaxes, but she has no idea what she's in for. "Of course, sweetheart. Is everything okay?"

"Yeah." I nod and give her a wan smile.

She picks up on the fact that this isn't an ordinary visit to catch up and leads me into the living room. The big stone fireplace is void of fire since it's not cold enough outside right now, but I remember many times when Palmer and I cooked marshmallows over the fire and got in trouble for dripping the gooey goodness on the hearth when we pulled them out because we'd let them cook too long.

It's a fond memory for me. I can't help but picture the

child I'm carrying in my belly doing the same someday, and my nose tingles with emotion that just won't stay back anymore.

We sit on the couch, her on one end, me on the other. Tears build in my eyes now that I'm here.

She shimmies closer to me and takes my hand. "Sweetheart, what's going on?"

"I'm pregnant," I blurt because I have no idea how I'm supposed to ease into something like this. It seems better to put it out there before I lose my nerve.

Her eyes widen, and she sucks in a breath but recovers fast from her surprise by squeezing my hand. "Okay."

I give her pleading eyes.

"Can I ask who the father is?"

God, I hate that she even has to ask. But that is the number one question everyone will be asking when the news comes out.

"Finn. The best man at Palmer's wedding." Tears leak down my face, and I wipe them away with my free hand.

She nods, face full of empathy. "You're scared?"

I nod.

"I remember how I felt when I found out I was pregnant with Palmer."

She was much younger than I am when she found out she was pregnant, but she knows what it feels like to have an unplanned pregnancy. Although hers was with a long-time boyfriend and not from a one-night fling.

"I'm scared and confused and embarrassed. I don't know. I have a million things going through my head."

She releases my hand and cups my cheek. "And that's all perfectly normal. It would be weird if you didn't have all those big feelings. Have you decided what you want to do?"

I set my eyes on hers, wanting her to see I've taken the

time to think and I'm certain about my decision. "I'm going to have the baby."

My aunt pats my cheek, and her hand drops. "Great. We're going to have a new baby to love. That's exciting." She smiles a genuine one that says she really does think this is good news.

Even with her understanding and excitement, tears topple down my cheeks from the relief. I didn't realize how much I needed to hear that from someone, anyone. She draws me into an embrace and rubs my back until my sobs calm down.

"Aunt Sedona?"

"Yeah, sweetie?"

"Do you think I can do this?"

She draws back, and her lips tip into a smile. "Of course you can."

"But... I'm not really responsible."

Her lips dip into a frown. "None of that matters. Aunt Phoenix was the least responsible of us all and look at what a wonderful mom she is to Jack and stepmom she's been to Maverick. And don't get me started on Uncle Denver."

We both laugh, but she sobers quicker than me. "And you are responsible. You've started a business on your own, supporting yourself. There isn't one definition of what it means to be a great mother."

"But do you think I can do it? You were a single mom. Can I handle it?"

My aunt left my uncle when she was still pregnant with Palmer, and he didn't come back into their lives until Palmer was eighteen months old.

"I'm not going to lie, it's hard, though you've never shied away from a challenge. But, Harp, did he say he didn't want to be a part of the baby's life?"

I shake my head and divert eye contact before explaining what happened last night at Palmer's house when I was ready to tell him, but he told me he was engaged first. "Everything has just gotten so much more complicated."

She sighs. "Yes, that definitely makes this all the more sensitive, but he deserves to know. You have to tell him."

"I will. I'm just not sure when." I groan and flop back into the couch. "I don't know what's worse—the idea of telling Finn or telling my parents."

Aunt Sedona sighs and presses her hand on my leg. "Harper, your parents love you more than anything in this world. They're going to be here to support you. Don't doubt their love."

I sit up. "I'm always disappointing them. I'm failing them when I just want to make them proud. That's all I've ever wanted."

She grips my hand again, squeezing it between both of hers. "Why do you think you haven't made them proud?"

I roll my eyes and chuckle. "What's to be proud of? I'm almost thirty, with no real accomplishments in my life to speak of. I'm single and knocked up with a stranger's baby, and he's about to be married." I point at myself. "And I'm his wedding planner!" I groan and throw myself back down into the couch.

"Stop putting yourself down. I know you feel as if you're in Easton's shadow, but just because you don't hit homeruns in a baseball stadium doesn't mean that what you're doing with your life is any less of an accomplishment."

"He's a professional baseball player. He's hit a level most never do. It's insane to think that out of all the baseball players everywhere, my brother is one of the select few to really make it big and make a name for himself in the league."

She tilts her head in a calm manner. "Yes, Easton is a great baseball player. And he worked hard to get there. But you work hard too. And your parents do not have favorites. They love and believe in you just as much as they do Easton."

"Hmm... I'm not sure, but I think the tables have definitely turned now," I mumble, looking down at my stomach.

"Yes, your pregnancy will surprise people, there's no stopping that. But once the shock wears off, they'll be happy to have another little one in our family, especially your parents." She pokes my arm. "You're having the first grandchild."

"From a one-night stand."

"Hey, you want me to tell you about the Buzz Wheel post about your mom and dad in the back seat of his Jeep—"

"God no."

She laughs. "You're being too hard on yourself. And you can do this, Harper. You'll be a great mom. Look how good you are with Adley."

I love that kid as if she's my own, but there's a difference between being the fun aunt and being the person responsible for making all the decisions and raising a child to be a good person.

"I guess."

She nods as if I'm in complete agreement about my mothering skills.

"Thank you for talking to me. Obviously, don't say anything to anyone yet."

She moves her fingers over her mouth as if she's zipping her mouth closed. "My lips are sealed."

I lean in for a hug, trying my best to soak in the confidence she has in me. "Thanks for letting me vent."

"Anytime, sweetheart. If you need to talk some more come by any time, all right?"

We pull away, and she opens her mouth but shuts it.

"Be careful, I might be over here every day," I say.

"That's okay."

I have to figure out when and how I'm going to tell Finn about the pregnancy. There're already too many people who know besides him, and I'm afraid that if I don't tell him soon, someone else will. I'm not blind to the town I live in and how there are eyes everywhere.

I ARRIVE AT THE CABIN, and the moment I step through the door, the tension leaves my body.

This is exactly why I'm here. Something about this place is healing. I'm not someone who usually enjoys solitude or quiet. I don't hang out on my own, preferring to be around other people. I'm shocked I haven't brought my portable speaker or my laptop so I can watch TV by now. But something about this place lets me enjoy being with my own thoughts.

I flop down on the couch with a groan, and my mind instantly travels to the day I've had.

It was so awkward today with Finn and Tamra. And not just because watching him be lovey-dovey with someone else while I'm pregnant with his child and neither of them has any idea is messed up. But because I felt almost... jealous. Which is absurd. I barely know the man.

When she reached for his hand or he kissed her knuckles, I wanted to leap over my desk and rip them apart. The pregnancy hormones must be to blame. Something in my subconscious must see Finn as mine because his baby is growing in my belly. That's the only explanation because I never get hung up on a guy. I have my fun with them and move on. End of story.

One thing is for sure, I have to tell him soon. I'm barely pregnant right now, but eventually I'm going to show, and then there will be no hiding our little surprise bundle.

Just the idea of telling him makes me sick to my stomach. How will he react? What will Tamra do? Fire me for sure. Meanwhile, Buzz Wheel will have a field day with me.

"What a mess."

Thirsty, I get up off the couch to get a bottle of water from the fridge, but I stop when I spot an envelope on the table. I walk over and pick it up. My name is written in Great-Grandma Dori's handwriting.

How did it even get in here?

Taking the envelope with me, I walk back to the couch and pull my phone from my purse, texting Palmer.

> Did you leave me a letter at the cabin?

Her response comes in less than a minute.

> Just open it.

> Explain. I don't need any more surprises in my life right now.

> Great-Grandma left a letter for each of us. I got one too when I was staying at the cabin. Open it... please.

Tears prick my eyes at the thought of my beloved great-grandma leaving me a letter.

Abandoning my drink, I bring the letter to the couch and sit down. I set my phone on the worn coffee table and stare at the envelope in my hands. I'm afraid to open it. Afraid of what it might say. Where she might have thought I'd be at this stage of my life. Could I be a disappointment to her too?

It's not that I think she'll have said anything mean. Maybe it will be a harsh truth I'm not ready to face. So rather than opening the letter, I slide it into my purse until I'm ready. Ready to face myself.

FINN

Tamra and I are only in Lake Starlight for another two days, so our schedule has been nonstop. Turns out there're a lot of things to decide for a wedding. More than I ever could have imagined. More than there should be for a fake wedding for sure.

So today, Harper has arranged to take us around the few choices we have for the wedding and reception venue.

Lucky me, we're starting with the Glacier Point Resort, which is the same hotel where Harper and I snuck into an elevator and up to my hotel room a little over a month ago. I was already plagued with flashbacks the minute Tamra and I checked in and took the elevator to our room. It was all I could do to get out of the confined space. This won't be awkward at all.

"C'mon, we have to go meet Harper downstairs," Tamra says, still putting on her makeup in the mirror.

"I'm ready," I say, sitting on the chair set against the wall in our room. I've been aimlessly scrolling through my phone for twenty minutes, waiting for Tamra to be done.

"I'm ready too."

I stand, pocket my phone, and watch her apply gloss to her lips. "I'm not sure you understand the meaning of ready."

She straightens her back, giving herself a once-over in the mirror before leaving the bathroom. "Come on."

Tamra grabs her purse from the nightstand next to her bed since we're sleeping in separate beds and joins me at the door.

It's cooler today, so I'm wearing a long-sleeve Henley and jeans, but the collar of my jacket gets tighter and tighter the closer we get to the lobby of the resort.

Harper and I didn't have any agreement that our tryst would be anything more than one night together, but it's hard to be around her with Tamra and not feel as though I'm doing something wrong. Something very, very wrong.

The elevator doors ding open, and Tamra encases my hand in hers as we step off. Harper is waiting for us at the far end of the vast, lavish lobby. She's wearing another set of dress pants, cream this time, and a dark green silk long-sleeve blouse that perfectly outlines the swell of her breasts —which look a little larger than I remember. The color of her blouse sets off the red of her hair, which draws a memory of her on top of me, when I had my hands through her thick tresses. Her body stiffens slightly before she puts on a fake smile.

"Morning." Tamra drops my hand and hugs Harper. She's always been a hugger.

Harper's gaze meets mine over Tamra's shoulder before pulling back.

When the two women part, I give Harper a nod and murmur, "Good morning."

"Morning." She turns her attention back to Tamra. "As

we discussed, we'll start here before we take a look at the other two places that are available on such short notice."

"This is so exciting. Thank you so much for all your help, Harper." Tamra looks at me as though she's waiting for me to communicate my gratitude.

"Uh… yeah. Thanks." God, I sound like a fucking idiot. Harper's probably wondering why the hell she ever slept with me in the first place.

Tamra cozies up to my side, wrapping her arms around me and leaning into my shoulder. "Excuse my fiancé, he doesn't realize how much work goes into making sure the huge day goes off without a hitch."

Harper smiles at Tamra, but it's forced. "Let's go take a look."

She leads us up one level to where all the event rooms are located and escorts us to a room at the far end of the hall. The large wooden double doors are already wide open, and I can see the view before we even enter through them. The grand windows lining the wall overlook what I know will be ski runs once the snow settles in for the season.

"Wow." Tamra drops my hand when we reach the threshold and steps in, admiring the space. "I mean, the room is great, but that view."

"It's pretty special, isn't it? I thought you could have your ceremony so that your guests are facing the view, and that way all your pictures would have the perfect backdrop too." She walks to a set of French doors at the far end of the space. "You can also use this outdoor space for pictures, if the weather cooperates." She raises her crossed fingers. "Northern Lights."

Tamra swivels around and raises her eyebrows. "What do you think, honey?"

I almost wince at the pet name.

"It's great." It's hard to be enthused. I couldn't care less if this wedding happens down at city hall as long as it happens, and I get what we've agreed on.

Harper continues explaining our options. "The space is being set up for an event this weekend, so you can get some idea of how it could look. Of course, this bride and groom have chosen circular tables, but you could also set up several long tables that run the length of the room. Those are gaining popularity. That setup would leave more room for a dance floor, if that's a priority of yours as well."

"And it's available in October?" Tamra asks.

"By some miracle, it is," Harper says, then meets my gaze. "Did you enjoy Palmer and Hudson's wedding?" She looks at Tamra. "It was in another room at Glacier Point." Harper's gaze flicks back to mine in challenge.

I clear my throat. "It was very memorable."

Harper rolls her eyes since Tamra isn't looking at her, but when Tamra turns her way, she plasters on a big smile. "Well, let's move on to our next stop?"

"Sounds good." Tamra turns toward me and gives me a look as though she wants to know what's going on with me. Can she tell I'm acting weird? "We might as well all ride together. Do you mind driving the rental?"

Great. Now I'm trapped in even smaller quarters with the two of them. This day keeps getting better and better.

"Of course not. Let's get going." The sooner we leave, the sooner this is over.

Tamra strikes the next venue off the list right away because, as she says, "It reminds her of her country club back in Vermont, and if that's what she wanted, we'd have our wedding there." It's a ways out of town as well, and Tamra insists she wants to stay in Lake Starlight so our guests can enjoy the quaintness of the town while they're here.

I've punched the address for our final destination into the truck's GPS, and we're about two minutes out when Harper speaks up from the back seat.

"I should warn you before we go to this next place..."

"That sounds ominous," Tamra says, shifting in her seat to look at Harper behind us.

"It's a little unconventional. We're heading to a retirement home."

I glance at Harper through the rearview mirror and see there's no joking smile on her lips. "We're not that much older than you."

Harper laughs, and I'm sure it's despite herself. "They started renting out their event space last year. And though we're going to go through the main doors, the day of your event, your guests would drive around the building and go directly into the event space."

"Oh okay, that doesn't sound so bad." Tamra squeezes my forearm on the armrest between us.

"Fair warning, some of the residents in this place can be... well, I'm not sure I even have a word for it, but you'll see what I mean when we get there."

"I'm sure it's fine. Just a bunch of old people." Tamra says.

When we reach the end of the winding road surrounded by trees, I pull into the parking lot and see that Harper wasn't joking. It's a retirement residence.

"They are," Harper says. "But they've got a lot of life left in them, believe me."

She chuckles to herself, obviously reliving some memory, and I risk a look in the rearview mirror, wanting to see her eyes sparkle. Since I've arrived back in town, I haven't seen the woman who stole my attention that night. Harper catches me looking, and I dart my gaze, finding a spot and parking the truck.

We get out of the vehicle and make our way to the entrance, the automatic doors sliding open for us when we get close.

Harper walks in as though she's been here a million times and heads straight to the reception desk. "Hi, Leann. How are you?"

The older woman behind the counter smiles at us. "Great, Harper. How have you been?"

"Pretty good. You're expecting us. I have a happy couple who's here to see the event space." Harper motions to Tamra and me behind her.

"Of course, Dougie knows you're coming. Let me just call him so he can unlock the space for you." She picks up the phone and presses a few buttons, holding the receiver to her ear. She smiles nervously at me when no one picks up before hanging up the phone. "He must've gotten called to one of the residents' rooms. Why don't you head to the space? I'll track him down, and he can meet you there."

"Sounds good. Thanks, Leann." Harper circles around to us. "Well, brace yourself in case we run into anyone on our way."

Before I can ask how off-center a bunch of senior citizens could possibly be, she turns to lead us down the hallway. I do my best not to check out her ass as she walks ahead, but it's an impossible feat.

We've only made it twenty paces into the building before every head in the leisure room to our right swivels in our direction. There are probably ten or so people in what seems to be a TV room of some kind. Most of them keep watching, but three of them get up and slowly make their way over to us.

"Harper," an elderly lady with red hair calls.

Harper's shoulders sag from behind, but when she stops and turns to face the woman, she's smiling. "Hi, Alice."

"Good to see you," one of the old guys with Alice says.

"You too, Melvin. You're looking good."

I swear Melvin's cheeks get a little pink under Harper's praise.

"Are you guys a throuple?" he asks.

I choke on my own saliva as Tamra's eyes narrow.

"What's a throuple?" the third man, who uses a cane, asks.

Melvin shrugs. "Some new arrangement thing my grandson told me about."

Harper holds up her hands. "We are not a throuple." Her gaze darts to mine for a beat. "I'm here to show my clients the event space. They're considering renting it for their wedding." She gestures to Tamra and me.

Tamra looks confused, but I nod in hello at the three of them.

"Speaking of which, we have to be going. We need to meet Dougie." Harper walks away without waiting for them to respond, giving them a wave. Once we're out of earshot, she looks at us over her shoulder. "Sorry about that. They can be a lot."

Tamra laughs. "They're adorable. I can't believe they thought we were a throuple."

I stare at my feet walking along the carpet, I'm so uncomfortable, I just look ahead and pray that we wrap up this wedding planning sooner than later.

nine

HARPER

God, I'm so tired. The nausea has subsided this week, but I've been dragging ass everywhere I go. In the middle of the day, I'll wake up with my head on my keyboard, and my bedtime has been hours earlier than it once was. I can't even get through one reality TV show that Maven and I usually watch together. If she has noticed that I'm dosing off during every episode, she hasn't said anything. Not to mention, we haven't tried a new popcorn flavor either.

It's my twin uncles Rome and Denver's birthday tonight, so a bunch of us Baileys are getting together at Uncle Denver and Aunt Cleo's place. Since our family is so big, and growing by the day, it's sure to be a packed house. Even when only a handful of us can make it, it would make even a kindergarten teacher run.

The laughter and music are already so loud when I arrive, I don't bother ringing the doorbell. Sure enough, it's standing room only. I set the Greek salad I brought on the buffet table. Our gatherings are always potluck and buffet-style.

I spot Brinley and Calista on the couch with their new Bailey additions. Calista's little boy, Jaxon, is a few months old now, but Brinley's daughter, Ivy, is a newborn. At least I think she's still considered a newborn. When are they not newborns? One? Then they're toddlers? But what if they aren't walking? Aren't all toddlers able to walk? I exhaust myself and realize I need to learn this stuff before he or she arrives.

God, just the thought of childbirth spurs too much anxiety. A big part of me wants to avoid Calista and Brinley because they represent everything I'm facing in the next year, and they probably handled it so much better than I ever will. Just as I think I've dodged them, they catch my eye, leaving me no choice but to at least say hello.

"Hey, guys, how are the little ones?"

Jaxon's wide eyes track me as he sits on Calista's lap, so I make a funny face and earn a smile out of him. Ivy is swaddled and asleep in Brinley's arms.

"I'm so glad you came over. Can you hold Ivy for me for a minute? I have to pee so bad." Without waiting, Brinley hands Ivy off to me, leaving me no choice but to accept her.

Thanks to Adley, I know how to hold an infant, but when I look down at Ivy's perfect little face, I wonder what my baby will look like.

Ivy might not be my baby, but this is how it will be when I have my own. As if my brain fast forwards, suddenly I'm holding him or her and the enormous weight of what that means. All the changes my life will incur. How hard it'll be doing it on my own.

"Are you okay?" Calista asks me, forehead wrinkled. "You look a little pale."

I muster a smile I hope masks the anxiety ratchetting inside me the longer I have Ivy in my arms. "Yeah, just tired.

Didn't sleep well last night. So how is Jaden taking to being a big brother?"

The two of us chat about Jaden not being the best big brother since he's suffering from not being the baby anymore until Brinley returns. I stand and pass Ivy to her under the guise of being starving.

After making a small plate for myself, I sit at one of the long folding tables next to my cousins Callum and Jason, who seem to be deep in conversation. They'll never ask me any questions like my girl cousins, so it's like my own little safe zone.

They stop discussing whatever was so enthralling, and both turn to look at me.

"Swapping stories, boys?" I pull my chair closer to the table.

"Just coming up with a plan." Callum leans back in his chair until it's on the back two legs. He and Palmer couldn't look more opposite for being siblings. Callum looks so much like my uncle Jamison, it's a tad creepy.

"And what exactly are you two conquering?" I ask, picking at a roll on my plate.

"The Anderson twins," Jason says, and he and Callum fist-bump over the table.

I roll my eyes and shake my head. "Why do you need a plan? You don't think your personalities and good looks can seal the deal?"

Jason pushes my shoulder, and I laugh. "We do just fine," he says.

I start to give my younger cousins—by only a year— shit about how to be good guys, but then their phones must go off because they pull them out of their pockets and stand. Apparently, they've secured their double date with the Anderson twins.

The rotation keeps coming when my cousin Rohan sits across from me. I usually love seeing him, but I keep worrying someone is going to figure out my secret, and soon I'll have a big spotlight on me in the middle of our family function.

"What's good, Harp?" He digs his fork into his meal.

"Nothing much. Can you believe your dad and Uncle Rome are getting so old?"

If you look up young at heart, you'll see a picture of Uncle Rome and Uncle Denver. I can just see them racing their wheelchairs at Northern Lights at eighty.

Rohan chuckles. "Uncle Rome, yeah. My dad…" He shakes his head. "Not sure he'll ever really grow up."

The sound of a high-pitched giggle draws our attention, and Adley pushes her way through everyone, clearly on a mission toward us.

"C'mere, squirt." Rohan scoops Adley up, setting her on his lap. She picks up the fork and piles food on it.

"You my baby," she says to him, and he opens his mouth, allowing her to slide the fork between his lips.

"Actually, I've been meaning to talk to you," I say to him.

"What's up?" Adley holds a roll in front of his mouth, and he opens, nibbling the bun.

"Good, baby," Adley says. "Now you have to eat your veggies."

While Adley tries to fork the salad, I say, "I have some clients from Vermont, and they want to arrange activities for their guests while they're here for the wedding. Alaska stuff. Like, go home and brag you did what you can only do in Alaska stuff."

"I'm your man. What time of year?" He opens his

mouth and Adley pushes in one tiny piece of lettuce that's dripping with dressing.

"End of October."

He nods slowly, pretending to chew, I think, just so Adley doesn't try to feed him anymore. After he swallows, he continues, "I'll put together some options and send them your way."

Adley squirms on his lap, clearly done with Rohan being her baby.

"What do you think, squirt? What should we do with the city folk?" He tickles her sides, and she laughs and wiggles in his hands. Rohan groans and sets his hand on his stomach, leaning back in the chair.

"Baby full?" Adley asks, looking at his hand with concern.

"Yeah, this is baby's second plate." He gives her a smile.

Adley puts the fork back on the plate. "You need to take one of those tests."

Rohan cocks his head. "What tests?"

The hair on the nape of my neck stands on end. My biggest fear is about to come true. Adley is going to rat me out without even knowing it.

"We had one at home. Mommy said you take it when your tummy is upset to see if you're sick."

"What kind of tests are these?" Rohan smirks, looking over her at me, probably thinking I'll share the same amusement as him. Meanwhile I'm internally screaming no, no, no, over and over again.

"Two pink lines is sick."

Rohan laughs, again his eyes catching mine, and I let out a fake laugh to appease him.

I close my eyes because it's out. Here it comes. My entire family is about to find out at my uncles' birthday party that

I got knocked up by my one-night stand. Open up, floor, and swallow me whole.

Palmer is clearing some plates at the other end of the table, and her head whips in my direction. We stare at each other wide-eyed. Damn Adley for being too smart for her age.

Rohan looks at Palmer, but she's already on her way to us. "Something you want to tell us, cuz?"

I close my eyes and inhale a few deep breaths to combat the tightness in my chest. I open my eyes, and I'm about to spill the news and save Palmer the trouble of having to think of some lame-ass lie, but she speaks before I can.

"Well, this wasn't exactly how I was going to announce it, but yes, Hudson and I are pregnant." She stares at me the entire time she delivers the news.

My mouth drops open. She's pregnant?

Emotions war inside me. I'm excited for my cousin and best friend, but I'm hurt that she didn't tell me. There's also another part of me that is thrilled we'll be pregnant together.

"Mommy, you're having a baby?" Adley jumps off of Rohan's lap and rounds the table, rushing over to hug her mom.

Hudson must hear the commotion of everyone cheering and offering congratulations because he makes his way over. "What's going on?" He kisses Palmer's temple and wraps his arm around her back.

Palmer runs her fingers through Adley's hair. "Our daughter was just talking about the sick tummy test she found at home." Hudson's gaze flickers to me briefly. "So I came clean with it and announced my pregnancy."

"Congrats, man." Rohan stands and reaches across the table, holding out his hand.

Rumblings of Palmer's big news spreads, and family members turn in our direction. Within seconds, our family makes their way over to the happy couple to offer their congratulations, being sure to congratulate Adley, too, on being a big sister, which makes her swell with pride.

I walk the few steps to join my family, but Adley stops me.

"Are you excited to be a big sister?" I ask her.

She jumps up and down. "I'm gonna be the best big sister ever. I'm going to teach her how to talk to Mommy with sign language, and I'm gonna pick out her outfits. I'll even let her borrow my favorite doll but only if she gives it back before bedtime because I can't sleep without her."

"And now you'll have a baby of your own to feed anytime you want," Rohan says, and Palmer gives him a "thanks a lot" look.

I ruffle the hair on top of Adley's head. "You're going to be a great big sister, I know it."

She hugs my legs, and my eyes meet Palmer's.

"I'm going to get some fresh air. You guys are making me claustrophobic." Palmer laughs and nods toward the back of the house.

Once she's a minute or two in front of me, I follow, heading onto the back deck.

"Congratulations." I pull her into a hug, and she squeezes me tightly. "Thanks for saving me out there." I pull away. "Why didn't you tell me?"

I hate the sad smile she gives me. "You have enough going on. I didn't want to further complicate things. I'm ecstatic about my pregnancy, but you weren't planning yours, and I know exactly what that feels like from when I was pregnant with Adley. It didn't feel right to tell you, but you know that under any other circumstance, you'd be the first one I'd tell." She draws me in for another hug.

I squeeze her tightly, hating that she didn't feel like she could share her good news with me because of my own situation.

"I'm sorry you had to tell everyone like that. I feel awful." I cringe.

My parents already knew, and we planned to announce it soon anyway, she signs.

I nod, though I still feel horrible that my circumstances affected when and how she told the family she was having another baby.

"How are you hanging in there?"

I shrug.

"It must be weird hanging out with Finn and his fiancée." Palmer cringes.

"It's not ideal, no. All I can think about the whole time I'm with them is how I have this giant secret that's going to blow up both their lives when I tell them." My shoulders sag.

You need to tell him soon, she signs.

I nod. "I know, it's just figuring out how to do it. They're supposed to be back next weekend for a few days to make some more decisions on the wedding. I'll see if there's some way for me to get Finn on his own and tell him."

She squeezes my upper arms. "It will all work out."

"I wish I had your confidence."

Palmer hugs me again and draws back to sign. *At least we get to be pregnant together. Our kids will be the same age.*

"Not gonna lie, when you shared your news, I was excited about that too. I know nothing about pregnancy or having babies or anything. Can you just make two appointments for everything? We'll do it together?" I laugh, although I would love to have her by my side through all this.

"Have you made an appointment with the doctor yet so you can figure out a due date?"

I stare at her blank-faced.

"Started taking prenatal vitamins?"

I blink at her.

"Cut back on your caffeine?"

I groan, and my head rocks back. "See? I'm already a terrible mother."

"No, you're just new to it. You'll figure it out."

I've been keeping my head in the sand as though that would make this situation a little less real, but it's time for me to dig in and educate myself on what's to come. Because no matter what, this time next year, it won't be Ivy in my arms, it will be a baby of my own.

FINN

I'm back in Lake Starlight, but this time, I'm alone. Tamra was supposed come, but she had a last-minute business emergency she had to stay behind to deal with. I'm not sure if this is a good thing or a bad thing, given my history with Harper.

Though it was awkward as fuck between Harper and me, having Tamra around was a buffer. Especially when it came to my attraction to Harper. Tamra's presence was a constant reminder of why I shouldn't be checking out Harper and replaying the way she rode me that night over and over in my head.

Now that it's just the two of us this weekend, I suspect it will prove more difficult to keep my mind from wandering. Because of course, we're meeting at a romantic restaurant in town to try the menu for our rehearsal dinner. According to Harper, Terra & Mare is the fanciest restaurant in Lake Starlight, and it's the vibe that Tamra wants. The irony that Tamra wants to get married in the quaint little town of Lake Starlight because of its ambience, and yet she wants everything about the wedding to be formal and high end, is not lost on me.

I step into the restaurant and brace myself. Harper is already seated at a table near the window. She gives me a tight smile then looks behind me, probably expecting to see Tamra. When she realizes I'm alone, she frowns.

She's wearing another green top that sets off the deep red of her hair, making her a beacon guiding me across the restaurant.

"Hey." I sit in the chair opposite her.

"Is Tamra running behind?" Maybe I'm imagining the hope I see in her eyes mixed with terror that we'll be having dinner just the two of us, but I don't think so.

"Tamra had to stay back in Vermont unexpectedly. Something came up with work."

Tamra is in IT and is trying to get an app off the ground, so she's constantly working. Her work was the reason we drifted apart originally. She's never around and rarely put any importance on us. Eventually, we broke up until we came up with our plan.

"So, it's just the two of us this weekend?"

"Yep."

"Awesome." Her tone suggests it's anything but.

My shoulders sag. "I'm sorry this is so awkward. I'm going to tell you again. I really did think things were over between Tamra and me." I wish I could tell her the lie I'm living—the words are on the tip of my tongue—but if I tell Harper the truth, and she tells anyone else, it ruins my family.

"Do you regret it?" The vulnerability in her voice is like a quick knife to the chest.

With that, at least, I can be honest. "Only that it hurt you."

She mumbles something under her breath.

I lean forward. "What?"

Harper stares at me for a beat, and there's a glimmer of tears in her eyes. She opens her mouth to say something, but before she can, the waitress steps up to the table, welcoming us and asking if we'd like something to drink.

I motion across the table for Harper to order first. "Oh, um... I'll just stick with my water." She holds up the glass in front of her and gives the waitress an awkward smile.

"No wine?" I'm surprised. I'm not sure I saw her without a wine glass at the rehearsal or wedding.

"Trying to cut back." Her lips press together.

I give my attention to the waitress. "Sparkling water if you have it."

"Coming right up. Colin said to let you know he'll be bringing out the samplers for the first courses shortly."

"Thank you." Harper nods, then turns her attention to me. "Nothing to drink for you either?"

I shift uncomfortably in my seat. It's not that I'm embarrassed, but me not drinking isn't a topic I love talking about. I could chalk it up to a long travel day, or not being in the mood, but for some reason, I want Harper to know. "I'm an alcoholic."

She blinks a few times, eyes wide. "Oh. Wow, sorry I wouldn't have asked if I'd known."

I shrug. "Don't apologize. Been sober for four years."

"That must have been difficult." She reaches for her water again.

"It was. But no more difficult than waking up each morning wondering what the hell had gone on the night before, or if I did happen to remember, being embarrassed about something I said or did."

The corner of her lips tips. "Huh, so tipsy wasn't the reason you took me to your room that night?"

God, is that what she thought? "No."

She doesn't say anything but takes another sip from her water.

The waitress interrupts with a bottle of sparkling water and an empty glass. She sets the glass on the table and pours the water from the bottle, setting it to the side when she's done. "Food will be out in a minute."

"Great, thanks." Harper looks at me. "Now that we've gotten all the awkward stuff out of the way, let me tell you how it's going to work tonight. Each course will be served with a variety of options, and you just have to decide which ones you prefer."

I lean back in my seat. "Sounds easy."

"Should be, but trust me, the food here is delicious, and it's going to make your job hard."

I chuckle. "Well, I look forward to the difficult task."

We share a smile over the table, and for the first time since I returned to Lake Starlight, the easy, relaxed feel between the two of us from that night has returned.

Again, I swear Harper looks as if she wants to say something, but an older gentleman approaches the table with two plates in hand and sets one down in front of each of us.

"Hey, Colin, how are you?" Harper asks.

"Living the dream, you know how it is."

Harper smiles a genuine smile, one I miss being on the receiving end of. "Finn, this is Colin. He's been the sous chef for my uncle Rome for decades. Colin, Finn. He's a client of mine. His lovely bride couldn't make the trip."

I nod and reach out to shake his hand. "Good to meet you, Colin." My head whips in Harper's direction. "Wait.

Your uncle owns this place? Does one of your family members own every business in town?"

"Pretty much." Colin laughs.

"I mean, statistically speaking, with the number of people in my family, it's not that surprising." She shrugs playfully.

"So..." Colin interrupts. "I saw on Buzz Wheel that Palmer is pregnant."

"She is. Isn't it so exciting?" Harper claps her hands in front of her.

"She is?" I ask. I had no idea. Hudson hadn't told me.

"I'm sure you're pumped. I know how close you are to Adley," Colin says.

"She's going to be the cutest big sister."

I allow them to go back and forth, Harper very relaxed with Colin, and Colin seeming to know more about her life than me.

"What's Buzz Wheel?" I ask.

Colin shakes his head with a grin. "Harper can explain that one to you, but first, let me tell you what you have in front of you."

He goes on to explain each of the appetizers on our plate and tells us to let him know if we have any questions. We thank him, and he ventures back into the kitchen.

"So, what's this Buzz Wheel thing he's talking about, and why is it talking about Palmer being pregnant?"

"Just one of the perks of small-town life." She rolls her eyes. "It started a long time ago and was basically a gossip blog. Nowadays it's an app that churns the Lake Starlight rumor mill. People can send gossip in and include pictures if they like, and it refreshes every day. You never know who's watching."

My mouth drops open. "Are you serious? That sounds horrific."

She shrugs. "It sounds invasive, but honestly, it's a small town. If you're the topic at hand, then yeah, it sucks. But if you're the one reading, it tends to be entertaining. Depends which side of the fence you're on."

I can't imagine having all my shit out there for anyone to read. Then I realize...

"They didn't report anything... about us, right?"

Harper laughs, and I watch the easygoing façade slip off her like the bridesmaid dress she wore the night we slept together.

"Don't worry, Finn. Your dirty little secret is safe with me."

eleven

HARPER

I somehow make it through dinner without either strangling Finn or blurting out he's going to be a daddy.

A big part of me did want to lay it out there, but my uncle's restaurant is not the place. There're too many people around, too many prying eyes and listening ears. Finn's face was fear-stricken when he thought our little tryst was on Buzz Wheel, so no way he could handle the news we're pregnant after one night together. But we need to have the conversation this weekend. Tamra not coming is actually a blessing in disguise, even if it means I have to be alone with him for the next two days.

The worst part is, I'm still attracted to the damn guy. When he walked in the door wearing a deep blue button-up and charcoal dress pants, his hair slicked back, I instantly felt my libido roar to life. But he's not mine to gawk at. I'm only carrying his baby, he's marrying someone else.

This situation is already messy enough. It doesn't need to be further complicated by my attraction to a man who isn't available.

We finish dinner, and I've made notes in my phone about all of Finn's selections. After thanking Colin for all his help this evening, we make our way out of the restaurant and onto Main Street.

The sun is just setting and has painted the sky in hues of burnt orange and golden yellow. It's beautiful, and if we were on a date right now, it'd be the perfect romantic backdrop.

"I'll meet you at the flower shop tomorrow morning then?"

Finn is looking at me in a contemplative way. I'm not sure what's going through his head. "Harper, I just want to say how sorry I am that you've been caught up in this. I know it's not an ideal situation, but I appreciate you being so professional and helping us out with everything for the wedding."

"Well, you're paying me." I give him a wan smile.

The way he's looking at me reminds me of how he looked at me the night of Palmer's wedding before he invited me back to his room. His gaze travels from my face, down, and back up again.

I clear my throat and pull my gaze. "Okay, well, I texted you the address for the flower shop, but it's right down the street there." I motion in the direction of Bloom.

He's still looking at me as if he wants to take me back to his hotel room again, not saying anything.

"I'm going to go." I turn to head to where I'm parked down the street.

What the hell was that about? He's an engaged man. There's no way he was looking at me as though he wanted me to be his dessert. I have to be imagining things.

I'M SETTLED into bed with the TV on, thinking of all the things I have to do next week—book an appointment with my doctor, get prenatal vitamins, head to Sunrise Bay to The Story Shop and see if they have any books on pregnancy to educate myself, and find the app Palmer told me to sign up for that will send me a weekly update as to whether my baby is as big as a pea, a walnut, or a melon.

My phone buzzes on my nightstand, and I pick it up to see my cousin Jack's name on the screen. I'm surprised he's calling since we usually communicate through memes. He lives out in Los Angeles with his wife, Shelly.

"Hey, Jack, how's it going?" I answer.

"That's what I'm calling to ask you."

I still, putting him on speaker and scrolling to the Buzz Wheel app. Oh shit, did someone find out? Who? I've been so careful.

"What do you mean? I'm fine." Buzz Wheel is taking forever to pull up, and I try to even out my voice so I don't sound as if I'm hiding something.

"Are you sure?" He sounds skeptical.

"Yeah... why?" Come on, fucking Buzz Wheel.

"You haven't sent me any memes in weeks, which is not like you. Thought I might have to send out a search party." He chuckles, but the concern remains in his voice.

My shoulders deflate as Buzz Wheel finally loads on my phone, and I read about my cousins and the Anderson twins at Lucky's.

"I've just been busy with work. I have some out-of-town clients taking up all my time." I try to keep my voice light.

"Bullshit."

I cringe.

"Be real with me, Harp. If you don't want to talk about whatever it is, that's fine. But don't bullshit a bullshitter."

I sigh. It's not that I don't want to tell Jack. Hell, everyone will know soon enough. But I know that he and his wife have been struggling to conceive a child for a couple of years. It feels insensitive to complain to him about an unplanned pregnancy.

Then again, if I don't tell him, when he finds out in a few weeks, he's going to be upset with me. Especially since he asked me directly.

"Fine. But you can't say anything, okay?" I say.

"You know I can keep my mouth shut."

"I'm pregnant."

He's quiet for a few heartbeats, and I worry that maybe I made the wrong decision in telling him. Then he laughs. "Don't ease into it, Harp. Leave it to you to just blurt it out like that."

I shrug, though he can't see me. "I am who I am."

"I'm guessing from your tone of voice this is not something you planned?"

"Well, let me see... I slept with the best man at Palmer's wedding, and now I'm the wedding planner for him and his fiancée's October wedding, so no. Not planned."

Another beat of silence. I swear I have some uncanny ability to silence people.

"What the fuck? Are you serious?"

I explain the whole situation to him, including Adley almost outing me with her pink lines sick test and how I plan to tell Finn tomorrow.

"Jeez. Harp, that's a lot. I'm sorry."

"It's my own fault. Everyone always told me this would happen." I laugh, but I can hear the shrill note to my voice.

"Hey, stop that. I never liked those jokes, but even so, you're entitled to live your life however you want. You're not hurting anyone."

"Are you sure? Because I'm about to throw a grenade into a happy couple's wedding plans tomorrow morning." I cringe.

"I'm pretty sure he was there too. You didn't end up in this situation alone."

I love Jack and didn't realize until right now how much I needed his advice on this matter.

"I know." I drag my finger over a line in the print on my comforter, following its path. "But I hate this so much."

He sighs, and even over a phone line, I feel his empathy for my situation. "If you need anything, let me know, all right?"

"Will do. Enough about me though. How's Shelly?"

Usually when I ask this question, he starts in on some story about something funny or amazing his wife has done, but he doesn't do that this time. I can't help but wonder if it's because of the news I just told him, and he's wondering how he gets off the phone and tells his wife that I got pregnant in one night.

"She's good. Listen, I need to take the dog out, but let me know how things go tomorrow, all right?"

Yeah, I'm pretty sure that's what he's thinking about. Maybe it bothers him too because he wants to be a dad so badly. "Thanks for checking in on me, Jack."

"Send me a meme, and I won't harass you with phone calls." He laughs, but it's not his usual one. "Bye, Harp."

I hang up with him and connect my phone to the charger.

I'm nervous for tomorrow, but a part of me is looking

forward to finally getting it over with. No more tiptoeing around Finn and Tamra, knowing I'm holding back something huge.

I look at my purse where it hangs on the hook on the back of my closed bedroom door. Great-Grandma Dori's letter has been burning a hole through the leather since I put it in there. I've pulled it out a few times, thinking I was ready to read it, but every time, I just haven't felt ready. It's so unlike me. I'm usually the one who jumps headfirst into everything. But this feels different. My hand falls to my stomach.

Pregnancy.

I'm going to be a mother.

This feels monumental, whereas all the other impulsive things I've done in my life I just figured they'd work out one way or another. Head down the black diamond run on the mountain before I was ready? What's the worst that can happen? I break a leg? It will heal. Go on a date with a guy I know there's no future with but sleep with him anyway? So what if it's a bad lay, life moves on, and if it's a good one, all the better. Go out partying the night before a big test rather than study? I'll do better on the next one, and if I don't, it's not the end of the world.

But having a baby is not something I can take lightly, and not something I can afford to mess up. There're no do-overs.

Pulling the comforters back, I slide out of bed and retrieve the letter from my purse. I crawl back in bed and position my back against the headboard, staring at the envelope for a minute, my mind casting back to all the great memories I have with my great-grandma.

I run my finger along the seam, open the envelope, and unfold the letter.

Seeing her handwriting and reading the first line, I pause and take a deep breath before I start reading.

My Dearest Harper,

I never told you this because I would never want the other great-grandchildren to be jealous, but I always saw a lot of myself in you. You have that passionate spirit and chase after what you want, never afraid to tell it like it is. Believe me, I know better than anyone how much trouble that can get you into, but it's a characteristic to be valued. People never have to wonder where they stand with you, and let's face it, you're always the life of any party.

But the downside of being bold and feisty is that people will judge. Hell, people are always judging whether they admit it or not, but when it comes to women like us, they tend to do so a little more vocally. Please don't let that stop you from being the brave, headstrong, and free-spirited woman you are. There's a good chance they're just jealous because let's be honest, it's kind of fun being us, isn't it?

I laugh and wipe a tear from my cheek. Yeah, it is...

Until it isn't.

I have to assume if you're reading this letter now it's because you're going through something hard. Something difficult. If I were still there, I'd give you some epic words of advice to be sure, but since I'm not, all I can tell you is—you can handle this. Whatever it is, I know you have the strength to get through it. Just continue being yourself, and you'll figure it out, this much I know. Face the path ahead with the same wild abandon you bring to every-thing. Charge forward with confidence and let your heart and gut lead you in the right direction.

It's a miracle you were brought into this world, and it was for a reason. Never let life snuff out your flame. You burn so bright, my darling, and the world deserves to bask in your light. Let that same light guide you through the dark times and come out the other side even stronger than you were before. It's what you were born for.

Love always,
Great-Grandma Dori

I set the letter on the mattress and weep into my hands, purging all the self-doubt and uncertainty I've been feeling, releasing all the shame and fear. And when the final tear falls, I refold the letter and slip it back into the envelope, knowing Great-Grandma Dori is right.

I *can* do this. I may not have it all figured out yet, but this will not break me. No, in fact, this just might be the best thing that ever happened to me. I'm going to be a mother, and I'm going to be a damn good one.

FINN

I slept like shit last night despite the time change. For some reason, I couldn't get Harper out of my mind. Finally, I admitted defeat and got up early to take a drive around. I knew there was a neighboring town called Sunrise Bay, so I decided to check it out. I grabbed a coffee from a place named The Grind, and now I'm walking around their cobblestone streets. Almost all the stores are closed, but no matter, I'm just killing time anyway.

I swallow the last of my coffee, my sore throat from this morning not having gone away like I hoped. I better nip this cold quick, so I stop by the drugstore to grab some cold and sinus medicine before I head back to Lake Starlight to meet Harper. The medicine I need is behind the counter, so I follow the big pharmacy sign on the back wall.

There's a long line, so I check my watch and see I have some time.

A woman is asking the pharmacist a million questions. I can't hear what it's about since I'm too far back in line, but it's clear from the pharmacist's expression that his patience is wearing thin. I wonder how long she's been here. The guy in front of me turns around and raises his eyebrows, clearly annoyed to have to be waiting for this woman.

There are several different bottles on the counter in front of her, and she keeps picking up one then another. It appears she's asking a bunch of questions about each of them.

The guy in front of me grumbles, and I can't say I blame him. I just want to get my medicine and get out of here.

Finally, the woman settles on one of the bottles, pushing the others toward the pharmacist, who looks like at her with more annoyance than the guy in front of me.

She turns to leave, and she's wearing sunglasses. The hood of her sweatshirt is over her head. She keeps her chin down against her chest so she's practically staring at the floor as she walks away from the counter.

Since I'm standing where the line curves, and she has no choice but to cut through, I take a step to the side to let her pass, but she moves in the same direction I do because she's looking at the floor. She bumps into me, and the bottle she's holding falls, making enough noise that everyone else in line turns in our direction, giving us a look like "what now?"

"Sorry." I get down on my haunches to pick up the bottle for her, seeing that it's prenatal vitamins. I'm not as annoyed that she took so long—she's pregnant and wants the best for her baby. Who could blame her? "Here you go."

As I straighten, holding out my hand to pass the woman the bottle, she gasps, and I quickly look from where her hand is held out to her face.

"Harper?" My head rears back.

How did I not realize it was her? Then again, I've never

seen her in baggy jogging pants and a hoodie with over-sized sunglasses. But I'd know the shape of her face and the strand of deep red hair that's peeking out from under her hoodie anywhere.

She whips her head around to see if anyone is paying us any attention, but the people in line have turned back around, eager to be waited on.

Like an idiot, it takes me a minute to put together why she's so panicked, the bottle I just handed back to her, and why she's in disguise like some movie star.

"Holy shit." I blanche.

The bottle of prenatal vitamins slips from my hand, and I'm sure if I could look anywhere but at Harper, I'd see the people in line are staring at us. Harper bends over to pick up the bottle, grabs me by the forearm, and tugs me farther away from the line. I mindlessly follow her, trying to put all the puzzle pieces into place.

"Are you pregnant?" The question comes out sounding more like an accusation than I'd like, but I'm so in shock, and my mind is flipping through the consequences double-time, that I can't stop myself.

"Keep your voice down." She scans both ends of the aisle and sighs. "We need to talk."

My stomach turns over, and I feel as if I might be sick. "You think?"

"Somewhere someone won't see or overhear us. Let me pay for these, and you can follow my car." She doesn't wait for me, heading up to the front of the store to pay.

Needing some fresh air, I decide to wait for her outside on the sidewalk.

I'm jumping to conclusions. No way the baby is mine. She would have told me by now. I'm not loving the jealousy

I feel thinking about another man's hands on her. But she's a single, hot-as-fuck woman who has every right to sleep with as many people as she wants. And I'm fucking engaged.

But that's all bullshit because if I wasn't the father, she wouldn't have been all jittery and panicked when she saw me.

The sweat along my forehead increases the longer I'm waiting and thinking about what this all means, so I take my ballcap off my head, smooth my hair back, and put it on backward. It's still a little chilly out this early in the morning, but I feel as if I'm baking in the hoodie I'm wearing though I know it has nothing to do with the temperature and everything to do with the woman who is leaving the drugstore and walking toward me.

"Where are you parked?" she asks.

"In the parking lot behind the stores." I gesture in the general direction.

She nods. "Me too. Follow me, and then we can talk."

Talk?

That one little word confirms I'm going to be a dad.

FORTY MINUTES LATER, we pull into the driveway of a cute little cabin set in the middle of the woods.

Is this where Harper lives?

She doesn't address me after she parks. Simply climbs out of her car and makes her way to the front door, unlocks it, motions for me to go in first. She's removed her sunglasses and her hood is down, but she doesn't meet my gaze.

The moment I step inside, I know it's not Harper's home. The place is too dated, too sparse. I can't picture a woman like Harper living here. It feels too tame.

I walk into the living area, though I don't sit. I have too much anxiety coursing through my body and need to pace. "What's going on, Harper?"

She draws in a big breath and stands at the opposite side of the small room. "I'm pregnant."

"I gathered. Is there something else you need to tell me?" I hold my breath, waiting for her to admit it. How long has she known? Why hasn't she tried to tell me? I attempt to calm the questions in my head before my anger gets the best of me.

"You're the father."

A buzzing sound rings in my ears, and I hear nothing after that except those three words on repeat.

You're the father.

You're the father.

You're the father.

With numb legs, I sit on the couch, afraid they won't be able to support me, and I'll collapse.

"We used condoms, and you said you were on the pill." I look up at her through my eyelashes.

She shrugs. "I don't know. I was on antibiotics a week before the wedding, which may have lessened the effectiveness of the pill, but we used condoms too, so...I guess the universe just really wants us to have this baby." When I glare at her, she holds up both hands. "Sorry, too soon for jokes."

"How long have you known?" If she's joking about it, I suspect she's known for a while.

She frowns. "A little bit before you showed back up to town."

"You've known the whole time you've been helping Tamra and me with the wedding?" I take my baseball cap off and set it on the cushion beside me then push my hands through my hair.

Shit. Tamra. What does this mean for the wedding? For everything that hinges on a successful marriage with her?

"I'm sorry, I didn't exactly know what to say. I was still in shock myself. I was going to tell you the night I went to Palmer's, but you announced your engagement first, and I got scared. I couldn't do it. And I was still figuring out what I wanted to do."

There's fear in her eyes, even as we have this conversation.

She's right. Did I expect her to blurt it out while she was showing us potential venues for our wedding? "Oh, by the way, Tamra, your fiancé knocked me up, sorry about that."

"I assume based on the fact that you bought prenatal vitamins that you've decided to keep the baby?"

She nods, and I blow out a breath.

I can't even fathom telling Tamra this news, but more importantly, I live in Vermont, and I'm pretty sure Harper isn't leaving Lake Starlight. I've never pictured myself living apart from my kid.

I bolt up off the couch. "I need to clear my head. I'm sorry, but I can't do any of the wedding shit we had planned today."

"I understand," she says, and I hate how small her voice sounds.

I don't want to hurt her, but she's had the time to process this news, and I haven't. I just need to straighten my head around the news, then we can talk more.

"Can we meet for breakfast tomorrow before I fly out in the afternoon?"

"Sure, of course. Meet me at Lard Have Mercy at eight, or is that too early?"

"That's fine. I'll see you then." I rush from that cabin so fast I'm surprised I don't leave burn marks.

But there's no denying I can't outrun the fact that I'm going to be a dad.

thirteen

HARPER

I sit in Lard Have Mercy with my foot bouncing under the table, anxious for Finn to arrive. I'm not sure why. It's not as though anything he says is going to change my decision to have this baby. But if he comes in here guns ablazing and blaming me, I'm going to fire right back. Jack was right, it took both of us to make this happen.

The bell over the door dings, and Finn walks in. He's wearing another hoodie this morning. It's hunter green, and he has on a pair of worn jeans. I raise my hand in greeting, and he spots me, giving me a tight smile as he winds his way through the morning crowd.

"Hey." He slides into the booth.

Maci arrives at our table immediately to offer him coffee. She's a second-generation Lard Have Mercy waitress as her mom used to work here back when my dad was growing up, or so I'm told. She fills his coffee and looks at me. "You sure you don't want some, Harper? Usually, you'd be on your second refill by now."

I play off her comment with a laugh. "I'm sure. Read a

study about how too much caffeine isn't good for you, so I'm trying to cut back."

She shrugs and asks if we know what we want. I order some maple blueberry waffles with whipped cream, and Finn asks for bacon, eggs, and toast without looking at the menu.

"Coming right up," Maci says and heads back to hand in our order.

"So..." I say, leaning back in the booth, needing a little more space between us.

"So." Stress lines his face. A part of me feels bad for having been the one to inflict it, which is ridiculous. That should be the least of my worries right now.

"Listen, Finn, I just want to make something perfectly clear that I probably should have gotten out yesterday. I didn't tell you because I don't expect anything from you. I'm ready to do this on my own, I just... You deserved to know, that's all. I'm not looking to blow up your life."

He pulls the paper ring off his silverware and folds it over, making it smaller and smaller until he can't fold it anymore. "I'm glad you told me. I mean... Jesus, my brain is still spinning, but thank you for telling me."

I sit quietly, waiting for him to say more. It seems as if he's still working out his thoughts.

Finally, he meets my gaze. "I know you don't know me well, but I'm not someone who shirks my responsibilities. You didn't find yourself in this situation on your own. I was a more than willing participant." He chuckles. "I don't expect you to deal with any of this on your own."

My cheeks heat at his reference to the night we spent together.

A part of me is relieved that he wants to be involved, though I'm not sure in what capacity. It would be nice to not feel as alone as I am now. But he's getting married in less than two months...

"I can't imagine Tamra is going to take the news well. I'm sorry."

Maci arrives at our table and sets our meals in front of us. "Need anything else, you guys?"

"I think we're good. Thanks." I give her a smile, then look over at Finn when I feel him wrap his large hand around my wrist before I can pick up my silverware.

He waits to speak until Maci is out of earshot. "You need to stop apologizing. No, Tamra is not going to be happy about this. But it's no one's fault. What's done is done, and now we need to figure out the best way to move forward."

I press my lips together and nod. "I'll understand if she doesn't want me to handle your wedding anymore."

He sighs and picks up his fork. "I have to go home and talk to Tamra about what this all means, but then I'll be back. I have a bunch of vacation days banked, so I'll spend some time here in Lake Starlight while we figure everything out."

"You don't have to—"

"I do, Harper." He holds my stare for a beat. "I want to."

I push back the small amount of excitement in my belly. This man is engaged to another woman, and while it's great that he wants some kind of involvement in our child's life, it doesn't mean anything for us. There is no us.

"Okay." I unwrap my silverware and pick up my knife and fork.

He nods. "In the meantime, do you need anything before I head to the airport this afternoon?"

I shake my head. "No. The next step for me is telling

everyone that I'm pregnant. Not something I'm looking forward to."

"How do you think your parents will react?" He brings a forkful of eggs to his mouth.

"Honestly? Not well. They'll probably see my unplanned pregnancy as another sign that I'm their screwup child." I cut into my waffles. My stomach has been pretty good the last couple of days, so I plan to take full advantage while I can.

He frowns. "They think you're a screwup?"

I shrug, concentrating on my blueberries oozing out of the waffles. "They've never come out and said that, but they don't have to. I am, especially compared to my brother."

He finishes chewing a bite of toast. "What's the deal with your brother?"

"Do you follow professional baseball? He plays for the Chicago Colts."

He stills with his fork halfway to his mouth. "Wait. Your brother is Easton Bailey?"

I'm not surprised that he knows him. Easton's team might have played like shit this year, but my brother is the best shortstop in the league. "The one and only."

He nods, trying to act as if he's not impressed.

"Anyway, I've always felt like I didn't fit into the box my parents hoped for me and..." What the heck am I doing confiding in Finn as though we're on a date or something? "It doesn't matter. The point is that I'm dreading the disappointment I'm sure will be on their faces when they find out."

Finn reaches out over the table and squeezes my wrist. "Maybe it will go better than you expect."

He's trying to be supportive, but I really wish he'd stop

touching me. It makes it too easy for my mind to blur the lines.

"Thanks." I pull my arm away, and he retracts his hand.

"If you want to wait until I come back, I can go with you when you tell them."

"You'd do that?"

His forehead wrinkles. "Of course. I'm not gonna lie. I'm scared as shit, but for you, I'll be there."

I give him a small smile. That's really nice of him. "I appreciate it, but I think it's better if I do it alone."

He nods and digs back into his breakfast.

"Do you plan on telling your parents?" I bring a bite of my waffle to my mouth.

"Hadn't really thought of it yet to be honest. I'm more worried what I'm going to say to Tamra." He cringes.

Suddenly, my hunger disappears.

We're both quiet for a while, in our own heads while we eat.

I'm glad Finn knows, and he's taken it better than I expected—or at least he's putting up a great front—but I feel terrible for how upset this will make Tamra. Broken up or not, no woman wants to hear about her new fiancé sleeping with another woman while they were on a break.

We make idle chitchat for the remainder of breakfast, and when we're finished, we slide out of the booth.

"Oh wait. You left this at the cabin, so I brought it for you." I hand him the baseball hat he was wearing yesterday.

"Thanks." He takes it and slides it onto his head backward.

I don't know what it is about the look that he has going on right now with his hoodie and the backward baseball cap, but he looks so hot that the space between my thighs buzzes.

I clear my throat. I cannot be attracted to this man. Not only is he engaged, but he's the father of my unborn baby. Things between us need to be simple, not an even bigger tangled mess.

"All right, well this is kind of awkward…" I swear his cheeks pinken as we make our way out of the diner onto the sidewalk.

"More awkward than your pregnant one-night stand planning your wedding to another woman?" I chuckle.

He grins, but it doesn't reach his eyes. "Can we exchange numbers?"

"You're right, that is more awkward." I pull my phone out of my purse and hand it to him.

He inputs his number, then texts himself so that he has my number.

"I'll text you when I know when I'll be back in town, but if you need anything before then, just let me know." He passes me back my phone.

"Sounds good." I slide my phone into my purse and stand awkwardly for a moment. "Finn, I just want to reiterate that I don't expect anything from you. I—"

He raises his hand. "Enough with that, okay? I don't know what this is going to look like going forward, but I do know that I'm not going to just pretend this isn't happening." Finn looks at me expectantly, and I nod. "All right, I have to go pack my things then head to the airport. I'll be in touch."

We look at each other for a beat, further awkwardness spreading over us like a blanket. If he's like me, he's wondering how we say goodbye—do we shake hands, hug, do none of that? I'm the mother of his child, but at the same time, I'm nothing at all to him. This whole situation is weird.

In the end, I thumb over my shoulder. "I'm parked that way, so I'll see you when I see you, I guess."

He nods, lips pressed together, and I turn and walk down Main Street toward my car.

So far, this has gone better than I expected. So why do I feel as though I'm waiting for the other shoe to drop?

FINN

I arrive back in Vermont with dread pooling in my stomach. My life has been a series of one-hundred-eighty degree turns in the past couple of months.

Even the long flight back didn't settle the fact that I'm going to be a father. I know it's the reality of my situation, but it still feels like an idea, a vague concept. Me? A dad? I blow out a breath.

I'm completely on edge. When the flight attendant stopped by my seat on the plane, for the first time since I got sober, I had the urge to order a drink. I'm going to have to be careful how I navigate my path forward and make sure that I continue my recovery. I won't be any good to anyone if I start drinking again.

So, the first thing I do the next morning when I wake up is attend an Alcoholics Anonymous meeting. When I get back in my car afterward, I feel as though I have my head on straight, and I'm ready to talk to Tamra. We already have plans for me to meet her at her place this evening.

She's expecting me to give her the updates on what Harper and I accomplished for the wedding this past weekend. I feel like a total asshole knowing I'm going to pull the rug out from under her instead.

I spend the day going to the gym and putting in a longer-than-normal workout, then I head to the fire station to arrange for some time off. All the while, I consider my options.

If I don't marry Tamra, the people I love will be affected. Hell, I don't even know if Tamra will want to marry me after she hears what I have to say. Though I think that she will, given what she's getting from our deal.

But marrying Tamra will mean living in Vermont for at least a few years, until our obligations are over, which means being away from my son or daughter.

Is that the kind of father I want to be in my child's life? The one who flies in for birthdays and holidays and sees my kid more through a screen than in person? No, it isn't.

Growing up, both my parents were active in my life. I had a wonderful upbringing in a solid family unit, and I want the same for my child. Harper and I aren't a couple, but that doesn't mean we can't be great coparents. Just look at Hudson and Palmer and how well they coparented Adley before they got together.

The idea of giving anything less to my child feels abhorrent.

I know what I have to do, but in doing so, I'm going to end up hurting some of the people I care most about.

When it's time to head to Tamra's, I take a deep breath before climbing in my truck. I don't take the hurt I'll be inflicting lightly. The only thing guiding me is that I need to be a presence in my child's life. I'll have to figure out another way to help my parents.

I knock twice when I reach Tamra's house, then walk in as I always do.

"I'm in the kitchen," she calls from the back of the house.

Her place is about four times the size of the place I rent since she comes from wealth. It's where we planned to live after the wedding. The wedding that will no longer happen.

I walk into the kitchen to find her dishing out food from Chinese takeout containers onto a plate.

"Hey." She looks up from what she's doing then back down at the plate. "Figured we could talk over takeout. I'm starving."

I couldn't eat right now if there was a gun to my head. Not with what I have to tell her. "I'm not really hungry, but you go ahead."

"Oh." Tamra frowns at the plate she prepared for me. "I'll just wrap it up and save it for tomorrow then." She takes her plate over to the kitchen table, so I sit across from her.

As she scoops fried rice onto her fork, I watch for a minute, wondering how to go about bringing this up. It's something I've pondered all day but haven't come any closer to figuring out. Now that I'm here, it seems even more difficult.

She looks up from her plate, forehead wrinkled. "You're quiet. What's going on?"

I blow out a breath and push a hand through my hair. She clues in that something is going on with me because she straightens up and slides her plate to the side.

"I need to tell you something."

"Why do I feel like I don't want to hear whatever you have to say?" She holds my stare.

"Because you're not going to like it."

"Did something happen this weekend in Alaska? Did the event space at the resort fall through?"

I swallow hard. "No, everything with the wedding plans is fine."

Her shoulders relax, and she slides her plate back in front of her. "Oh, thank God. You had me worried for a moment. If it's something—"

"It's not about the wedding."

She closes her mouth and blinks a couple times, finally seeming to get the gravity of what I have to tell her. "Go on..."

"You know when were broken up, and I went to Alaska for Hudson's wedding?"

"Yeah."

"I slept with Harper." I let my words sink in for a moment before I continue. "She was the maid of honor, and as you know, I was the best man, and we spent a lot of time together and well... we ended up sleeping together."

The disbelief on her face morphs into anger. "You slept with our wedding planner, and you didn't tell me?"

"I didn't know she was who you hired until you mentioned her name when we got to Alaska. And yes, I should have told you. But let's not pretend I betrayed you in any way for sleeping with her in the first place. We were broken up and had no plans whatsoever to get back together. I was a single man." I hate that I have to keep reminding people I didn't cheat on anyone when I slept with Harper. I wasn't committed.

She ignores my comment. "Did something happen between you two this weekend?" She leans back into her chair and crosses her arms in an accusing way, which only pisses me off. "And more importantly, if so, does anyone know? You could royally fuck our arrangement, Finn."

I shake my head. "Nothing happened. We might not be

romantically involved, but to the world, we're engaged, Tamra. I wouldn't do that to you."

"So, the two of you have just been keeping this little secret from me the whole time." She throws her hands in the air. "I look like an idiot."

Tamra's not mad because she's jealous. She's pissed because she wasn't in the know, and I don't blame her. I should have just been honest with her from the start. Had I known then what I know now, I would have been.

"It's not like that. I just didn't see the point in upsetting you and making you uncomfortable when there was nothing between Harper and me. I never thought I'd see her again."

"So why are you telling me this now?" She tilts her head, and it reminds me of a dog sussing out its prey.

"Because Harper is pregnant."

She bolts up out of her seat, presses her hands to the table, and leans toward me. "Pregnant?" Her face is filled with horror, no doubt already knowing what this means for us. "Are you serious, Finn? You got her pregnant? Jesus, didn't you use a fucking condom? How stupid are you?"

"We did use protection, but no protection is fail-safe," I snipe back at her, sounding like my freshman health class teacher, Mrs. Barnes.

"I can't believe this." She walks away from the table, hands threading through her hair. "I can't believe this." Tamra keeps saying the sentence over and over as she paces beside the table. After a minute or so, she whips around to stare me down. "How long have you known?"

"I just found out this weekend when Harper told me." I leave out the part where I found out accidentally. I believe Harper when she said she planned to tell me.

Tamra rolls her eyes. "How nice. The minute I'm not around, you two cuddle up to play happy little family."

I stand from the table. "It's not like that, Tamra."

"Sure, it's not." She crosses her arms.

It's understandable why Tamra is upset. I'm throwing all her plans into a lurch. But if I'm honest, I feel worse for Harper. I cringe when I think of her, secretly pregnant with my baby, watching Tamra and me trying to sell that we're a loving, engaged couple. What the hell must she have thought? How must she have felt watching and knowing she had to somehow tell me her news?

"I'm sorry, Tamra. I had no idea it was even a possibility."

"Newsflash, Finn, it's a possibility when you fuck her!" Her voice is irate, and her face is red.

I step forward. "I didn't do anything wrong in doing so. We weren't together, and we had zero plans on ever being together again. You're upset because I'm fucking up your plans, I get it. But let's not pretend it's because we have any romantic interest in each other. I didn't scorn you, Tamra."

She huffs and tears her gaze away from me. "So, what does this mean?"

"I can't marry you." The words drop like a lead weight between us.

She whips her head back around to look at me, eyes wide before they soften. The scary thing about Tamra is how fast her demeanor can change when something she wants is in jeopardy. "No. We can still make this work, Finn. We'll just tell people it happened while you were on a break. That you didn't cheat."

"I *didn't* cheat." My voice grows louder. I'm so damn sick of sticking up for myself.

She waves off my words as if they're of minor consequence, and my anger grows hotter.

"People will judge us, but that doesn't matter. As long as we still look like a loving, committed couple, we'll both get what we want."

Money. She means we both get our money.

Tamra needs funds for her company to finish building out the app she's been developing for years. She doesn't want to take on any investors because she's convinced it's going to be a success and wants full control and all of the profits.

When her grandfather passed a couple months back, she found out at the reading of the will that she'd been left a trust, but it would only be dispersed once she was happily married. Apparently, he was an eccentric man who was married to his wife for more than fifty years before she passed away a year before him.

When she came to me with the idea of pretending to get back together for the sake of the trust, she sold me on the idea by offering me enough money to give my parents. They own a small ski resort that has fallen on hard times. Climate change means each ski season gets shorter and shorter, and you have to have the resources to be able to make an abundance of snow to keep the runs open when Mother Nature isn't cooperating.

The market became more and more competitive as the decades rolled on and huge conglomerates gobbled up all the small resorts and invested heavily in making them over. The money Tamra was going to give me would have allowed them to upgrade the lifts and purchase more snowmaking equipment as well as overhaul the lobby and add on to the small family restaurant at the resort so it could be a real après-ski destination.

My parents have refused to sell over the years whenever they've been approached, but each year, the margins get tighter. I'm afraid that if they don't do any upgrades, they won't be able to compete, and they'll lose the resort.

"Say something," Tamra demands.

I shake my head. "That's not going to work."

"What do you mean it's not going to work?" She grips my shirt. "You made a promise, Finn. We can still make it work. Think of your parents. Think of all their employees losing their jobs."

She's so fucking good it's scary. I reach for her wrists and pull them away from me so that she lets go of my shirt. The desperation in her eyes makes me feel bad for her, but I refuse to let her ambition keep me from being a great father.

And if my parents had any idea what I had planned and the real reason I was going to marry Tamra, they'd agree.

"I'm sorry, Tamra. I am. But if I marry you, I'll be forced to stay in Vermont. My child is going to grow up in Alaska. So, that's where I need to be."

Her face contorts, and she glares at me. "So, now you're going to up and move to Alaska and play the role of baby daddy?"

I inhale a cleansing breath, grabbing for any ounce of my patience. I understand why she's upset, but I don't like the way she keeps referring to my unborn child or me as a father. Hell, the baby probably isn't the size of a peanut yet, and I already feel protective.

"I'm going to do what's right. And marrying you is no longer it."

My words hang between us for a minute.

She must see the resolve in my face because her anger shifts to cold indifference. "Fine. The only thing I ask is that you let me announce our breakup and that you don't tell anyone about our arrangement. I'd rather people look at me with pity than think I'm desperate."

I inwardly roll my eyes. This is the reason it never worked out with Tamra and me—her consistent need to make sure the narrative was her own. "Fine. Whatever."

I don't really care what people will think or say about me when they find out our engagement is off. But I'm going to have to bring my parents up to speed before I return to Alaska so that they're not blindsided at the one-eighty my life just took.

"I hope someday you find someone to marry for the right reasons."

She huffs and rolls her eyes, so I see myself out.

I can handle disappointing Tamra. And my parents. But I don't think I could live with feeling as though I disappointed my child, which is why I know I'm making the right decision.

HARPER

The other shoe drops a couple days later when Maven and I sit down to watch the latest installment of a Netflix reality show. She's on the couch scrolling through her phone while I put the finishing touches on the flavored popcorn. Tonight, we're trying a brown-butter lemon recipe I found.

I drizzle the mixture over the popcorn then use my clean hands to mix it all up. When it's properly coated, I wash my hands again.

I'm bringing the bowl into the living room when Maven gasps. When I turn the corner, I see that she's looking at her phone, mouth wide open in shock.

"What's going on?" I set the bowl on the coffee table.

She looks at me, her eyes falling to my stomach, and wordlessly holds out her phone. I frown, already knowing just by the shift in her eyes what I'm going to read, but I take it, turning it around so I see what's on her screen.

No surprise when I see the Buzz Wheel app.

DID OUR WILD CHILD BAILEY GET MORE THAN SHE EXPECTED?

Seems our very own Harper Bailey may have gotten a little more than expected, in that she's expecting! Pictured below is Harper with who is believed to be the father. Reports are that the two of them looked pretty cozy at Hudson and Palmer's recent nuptials, and it seems that the magic in the bedroom may have resulted in a little magic bean!

Harper was spotted in neighboring Sunrise Bay buying prenatal vitamins, baby daddy in tow. Maybe it's finally time for our forever bachelorette to settle down.

Congratulations to the expectant parents!

I scroll a little further down, and there's a picture of Finn and myself in the store, and I'm holding the prenatal vitamins. As I hand back the phone, my eyes close, and I breathe in slowly. Fucking Buzz Wheel. I can't believe it outed me before I've even told my parents.

My parents.

"I'll explain later," I call out as I rush to the front door, grab my purse and my keys, and bolt out of the house.

I fire up my car as soon as I get inside it, and my tires squeal as I back out of the driveway, heading toward my parents'. I've been trying to drive more responsibly since I found out I'm pregnant, but I throw all those intentions to the wind as I speed over to my parents' house, praying I get to them before they catch wind of this from someone else. Or from looking at that damn app. It's like a Lake Starlight ritual—finish your dinner, settle in for the night, pull up the app, and get the scuttlebutt of what's going on in town.

I squeeze the steering wheel as I turn onto their street, heart racing.

I'd planned to tell them tomorrow, I really did. And I wasn't looking forward to it. But them finding out like this makes it even worse.

As soon as I stop in their driveway, I throw the car in park and kill the engine. I pull the keys from the car, but leave my purse on the passenger seat, not wanting to waste the extra few seconds it would take for me to grab it.

I run up to the front door and don't bother knocking. I just whip open the door and go inside, slamming it behind me, praying I don't find them in the kitchen again. "Mom? Dad?"

No one answers, so I look through the house. They're not in the dining room, not in the kitchen, but I stop short when I find them both in the living room.

"Is it true?" my mom asks with tears in her eyes.

My stomach sinks, water pooling in the corners of my own eyes. "Yes."

I dissolve into tears and stand on shaky legs that might give way until my dad's arms wrap around me. I hug him back, squeezing him tightly and not wanting to let him go. His scent reminds me of my childhood and the way he would always comfort me whenever I was upset or hurt. He always made me feel safe. He still does.

So I stay in his embrace until I have no more tears to shed. He gives one last rub down my back then pulls away, looking at me with concern. He squeezes my shoulder and leads me over to the couch to sit.

I force myself to look at my mother, bracing myself for the disappointment I'm sure I'll see there. But it's not disappointment, it's sadness.

"Say something," I croak past the lump in my throat.

"Why didn't you tell us?" Her voice is a near whisper.

"I was scared."

She takes my hand and squeezes it. "But we could have been there to support you. Why did you feel like you *couldn't* come to us?"

"Because I didn't want to disappoint you." I crumple into tears again, and this time, it's my mom's arms that wrap around me.

Whereas my dad's hugs have always given me a feeling of safety, my mom has always given me strength. I try to soak in some of that strength now. I gather myself and draw back.

My mom wipes the tears from my cheeks. "Sweetheart, we could never be disappointed in you."

A sarcastic laugh barks out of me. "Yeah, right."

My mom frowns, glances at my dad and back at me, waiting for me to explain more.

"You guys are always disappointed in me whenever I mess up. Whether I brought home a crappy grade from school, or you didn't approve of my taking a year off after high school to figure out what I wanted to do before going to college, or how much I date. Sometimes it feels like all I do is disappoint you."

My mom shares a look with my dad, and it's him who speaks next. "Harp, there's no doubt you kept us on our toes when you were growing up, and yeah, there were times that you made us angry, but it never meant we were disappointed in who you are as a person."

My mom squeezes my hand, so I turn my attention back toward her. "We love the funny, spirited, and caring woman you've grown into."

"Really?" The weight I've been carrying around falls off me and melts into the floor.

"Of course. It's upsetting to think that you didn't already know that." She brings me in for another hug. I glance at my dad while I embrace my mom and realize he looks a little misty-eyed. "I'm just upset that you didn't feel like you could come to us with this." My mom pulls away and palms my cheek. "I would have liked to be there for you."

I give her a watery smile. "Sometimes I just don't feel good enough. Easton is, like, this amazing professional baseball player, and you two have your whole love story that everyone in town obsesses over. It's easy to feel like I'm not living up to everyone's expectations for me."

Mom shakes her head. "Love story?" She fights her smile, looking at Dad. "We had a one-night stand in the back of your dad's Jeep. I could have very well become pregnant that night." She pats my cheek and lets her hand drop. "Your story is your own, Harper."

"The only person whose opinion of your life you should worry about is your own," my dad adds. "From our perspective, if you're happy, we're happy."

I exhale a relieved breath. "Really?"

"Yes," my mom says, wrapping one arm around my shoulders. "And believe me, your brother is just as wild as you. We've probably fawned over his accolades in baseball too much, but he's far from perfect. No one is. No one should be. I'm sorry we've made you think we weren't proud of you."

I nod and rest my head on her shoulder. "He's out there making a big splash."

Dad laughs and comes to sit on the other side of me. "And so are you. You started your own wedding planning business and are making a name for yourself. Just because more people out in the world know your brother's name doesn't make what he does any more successful than what you're doing. Everyone in this world has their own paths and their own dreams. East's dream was to play professionally, and we supported him. He made it, but had he not, that love we have for him wouldn't have waned. He wouldn't have disappointed us."

"And you aren't disappointing us. I love the fact you never take my suggestions. It shows I raised an independent woman who thinks for herself and has self-confidence in her decisions. As much as I've praised my parenting for that, I see now where I might have some work to do in other areas."

"That's the thing you'll find out when it comes to being a parent. You second-guess everything you do, and hindsight really kicks you in the balls when you mess up." Dad places his hand on my knee.

"Your dad is right—well, except for the whole kick you in the balls thing. You're always worried you're making the wrong decision. Sometimes they turn out great, and other times you wish you had a do-over, but good thing kids are resilient." Mom smiles at me as if she's joking. "Now..." My mom's gaze drifts to my stomach. "Can we talk about..."

I cringe. This is so uncomfortable talking about my one-night stand with my parents. "Yeah."

"How are you handling the news?" she asks.

I blink a few times. It's not the reaction I expected. I thought she'd grill me for all the details of how and when and why and dig in on how I plan to do this alone. "Well, better now. At first, I couldn't believe it. It didn't feel real. But I've gotten used to the idea now."

"So, you're keeping the baby?" She holds my gaze.

I nod. "Yeah, I am."

Her stoic face morphs into a huge grin, and she places a hand over her heart. "Oh, that makes me happy."

My head rears back. "Wait. You're excited?" I look between my parents.

"Of course. A baby is always a blessing. You know how hard it was for your dad and me to have you and your brother. We'd never look at a grandchild as anything but a gift. Oh my god, I'm going to be a grandma!"

Tears well in her eyes again as she laughs to herself and looks at my dad. There's so much love between them when they look at each other like that. It used to gross me out as an adolescent, but now as an adult, I realize how lucky they are to have found each other.

"I can't wait," my dad says. "Do you think they could call me Pops instead of Grandpa?"

I can't help but laugh myself. "If that's what you want."

"Don't look so surprised, sweetie. Jeez, are we really that bad?" My mom shakes her head.

"No, I just... I thought you'd be upset with me. Angry maybe."

She takes my hand again. "Honey, if you mean would we prefer that you were happily married when you had your first child, then of course we would. Only because it would mean you'd have the full support of the father, that's all."

I guess that makes sense. It hadn't dawned on me.

"Does the father know?" my dad asks.

I nod. "I told him last week."

"It's the guy from Buzz Wheel?" my mom asks.

"Finn, yeah."

"How did he react to the news?" My dad's voice is gruffer now, like if Finn acted poorly, he'd be hunting him down and making sure to set him straight.

"Surprisingly well. I mean, it's not like he was excited or anything, but he didn't lash out at me."

"And he'd better not in the future either," my dad says.

I roll my eyes "I know, Dad."

"He's quite handsome," my mom says with a grin.

"Eww, Mom. Gross." I cringe.

She shrugs. "I'm just saying."

"Well, stop saying." A full body shiver works its way through me. "I don't know what is going to happen with Finn at this point. He lives in Vermont, so..." I shrug. "I'd like him to be involved, but we'll see what he says. He plans to return to Alaska this week. It might take some time to figure out."

"Well, you know your dad and I are here for whatever you need. *Anything* at all." My mom drills me with her eyes.

I smile at them both. "Thanks."

Now that my parents know, this pregnancy feels more real than ever. I stay for a while longer, and when I get back into my car, I check my phone. It's blowing up with phone calls and texts—no doubt I have Buzz Wheel to thank for that.

But I don't want to deal with anyone else tonight, so I turn my phone onto silent, then back out of the driveway. There will be plenty of time to deal with all of that tomorrow.

sixteen

HARPER

The next morning when I turn on my phone, there're even more calls and texts. It all feels overwhelming.

Scrolling through my phone, I ignore all the other messages in favor of one from Finn.

> I'll be back in town this evening. Think we can meet up?

I don't know why I get nervous reading his message, but I do. I wonder how Tamra took the news.

> Want to come to my place?

I know that Maven will be working late tonight, so we'll have the place to ourselves.

> That works. Text me the address. See you then.

I send him my address then scroll through the rest of the messages, determining if there's anybody else I want to answer. When I see my brother's name in the list, I click on his message.

> What the fuck, Harp? I have to hear that I'm gonna be an uncle through fucking Buzz Wheel? Jesus Christ. Call me back.

I go to my missed calls and see that he did indeed call me three times last night.

I'm close with my brother, but I hate when he treats me as if he's my father. I roll my eyes and reluctantly hit his name on the screen, wanting to get this over with.

"What the hell, Harp?" he answers.

"Hello to you too, East." I roll over on my side and put the phone on speaker.

"You're pregnant?"

"Save the lecture, *Dad*."

"I'm not gonna lecture you. But I am gonna ask why the hell I had to find out from Buzz Wheel."

I groan. "I don't know. Because that stupid blog outs everyone's crap?"

"True, but..."

"I was going to tell you after I told Mom and Dad today. Buzz Wheel did that for me though. I talked to them last night."

His laugh rings out through my room. "How'd they take the news?"

"Shockingly well."

"I'm not surprised."

"You're not?"

"Are you kidding? Mom and Dad are dying to be grand-parents. Maybe now they'll stop bugging me about finding a nice girl to settle down with."

I laugh. "I can't wait until you find your girl. I'm going

to constantly remind you how often you said you're never settling down."

"Yeah, yeah. So, I'm gonna be an uncle, huh?" The pride in his voice makes me smile.

"You will."

"You could have planned this better, ya know?"

"It wasn't planned at all."

He laughs again, and it makes my heart ache, missing him. "You're going to have my niece or nephew when I'm in season. Not cool, Harp."

"Maybe when you have your own little one, you can plan to have the baby in the offseason." Although I'm giving him shit, it makes me happy he wants to be such an integral part of my baby's life. Sometimes Easton feels so far away, always on the road and living halfway across the country.

"Nice try. Tell me about the guy. Do I need to take a short trip home?"

He's just as overprotective as my dad.

"No, I think he's a good one. But we're just coparents."

He laughs again. "So were Uncle Rome and Aunt Harley. If you follow in their footsteps, you'll have enough kids that Mom and Dad will lay off me entirely."

"Funny, East. Let me get through this one and make sure I don't screw them up." I run my hand over my stomach. Although flat, it still shocks me that my baby is growing inside me.

"You won't."

I don't say anything.

"You know that, right, Harp? Sure, you might have to pick him or her up from preschool because they threw a pencil at someone or some shit. And I'm pretty sure the sheriff might be your best friend when they're a teenager, but you're not going to screw him or her up. You're going to be a great mom."

Tears well in my eyes. "Jeez, thanks for reminding me I can no longer control my emotions." I wipe my face with the back of my hand.

"What's a big brother for? Sorry to cut this short, but I gotta get to the airport to lose another fucking game."

"Good luck tonight."

He laughs. "Congratulations. Next time, I'm at least your third call, okay?"

"Sure... and East?"

"Yeah?"

"Thank you." I hope he hears the weight of my words. I'm not just thanking him for calling me, but more for his affirmation that I've got this.

"Anytime. Also, we might suck, but that kid is a Colts fan. Remember that."

"He or she will only wear your jersey. I promise."

"Good. Love you."

"I love you too."

We say goodbye, and I feel a lot better, though the number of calls and texts to return is still daunting.

Maven will have already left to open up Bloom, so I plan to swing by before I go into the office and let her know what's going on. She's welcome to stay here as long as she doesn't mind the spare bedroom turning into a nursery and an infant for a roommate.

The other thing I have to do is talk to Maven's mom, my aunt Stella. She's a family doctor, and I'm hoping she'll agree to see me for my first appointment at least. All of this is so new, and I'd be much more comfortable if I saw my aunt.

I lie in bed longer than I should, trying to picture what

the next year is going to look like for me. Certainly not how I thought it would. But for the first time since I found out, that doesn't feel like a bad thing.

I'm determined to do right by this baby, and today is the first step.

***

I PACE MY LIVING ROOM, waiting for Finn to arrive. He texted me a half hour ago to let me know he'd be here soon.

I'm not sure why, but this conversation feels more monumental than the one when I told him I was pregnant. Maybe because I'm assuming he's going to tell me how he really feels about all this now that he's had time to think on it. That, and I'm expecting to hear that Tamra was very displeased by the news, and I feel badly for that too.

When I hear his car pull up outside, I rush to the front window and pull the drapes back to see a truck I don't recognize. That must be Finn in his rental car. I blow out a breath and walk over to open the door.

I put more effort into my appearance today since the last time he saw me, I looked like I was auditioning for the role of a woman who'd given up on life.

The truck door opens, and Finn steps out, giving me a tight smile. He's dressed in a pair of jeans and a deep green Henley, and damn he looks good. What else is new though? I really wish he wasn't this good-looking.

I'm beginning to wonder if my attraction to him will ever fade. Are we going to be celebrating our son or daughter's thirteenth birthday, and I'll still be gazing across the table at him in awe? It's then I remember that even if that is the case, he won't be alone. Tamra will be there on his arm. That's the splash of cold water I need right now.

"Hey, how was your flight?" I ask as I step aside to let him in.

"It was good. I managed to sleep for a bit, so hopefully that will help with the time change."

I close the door behind him and turn around. Suddenly, it feels awkward with just the two of us in an empty house. My house. I watch him glance around.

Finn pushes his hands in his pockets. "Do you live here alone?"

"Used to." I walk past him into the living room. "My cousin Maven moved in with me a bit ago, but she's at work right now, so it's just us."

He holds my gaze.

Oh god, did that sound like a proposition or something?

"I just mean that we can talk in private, that's all. Do you want something to drink?" I ask, changing the subject.

"Water would be great. I'm dehydrated from the flight."

I nod and head into the kitchen to grab him a bottle of water from the fridge. Our fingers brush against each other's as I pass it to him, and I snap my hand back.

"Have a seat." I gesture to the couch.

He sits on one side, and I sit on the other.

"How are you feeling?"

For some reason, his question takes me back, but I guess it's normal for a man to wonder how the woman carrying his baby is health-wise, even if they're not a couple.

"I'm doing good. The nausea I was feeling before is mostly gone now. Sometimes I still get it, but at least I don't feel like skipping every meal anymore. But I do miss coffee.

God, do I miss coffee." I groan, but it comes out sounding more like a moan for some reason.

Finn snaps his gaze away from me. "Sorry, that must suck."

I shrug.

Neither of us speaks for a minute.

When I can't stand it any longer, I finally ask the question that's on my mind. "How did it go with Tamra?"

He blows out a breath and pushes a hand through his hair, something I'm starting to realize he does when he's uncomfortable or stressed.

That well? Awesome.

"You first. Did you talk to your parents?" he asks, looking concerned.

I smile. "I did, and it went way better than I thought. I mean, they'd definitely prefer if I were married and in a loving relationship when I'm having a baby, but overall, they were really great. They're excited actually."

"Really?" He arches an eyebrow. "That's awesome, Harper."

Hearing my name on his lips does something to me, and I have to work to appear unaffected. "Yeah, I feel way better now that they know, but to be honest, they didn't find out from me originally."

He cocks his head in question.

"You need to know that we were in Buzz Wheel. Someone took a picture of us in the pharmacy that day."

"Hudson told me when he called to tell me about him and Palmer expecting. How bad is it?"

I cringe, then nod. "Yeah, so I've been dealing with everyone I know calling or texting me. Good times."

He shakes his head. "That's bullshit." When I don't say anything back, he continues. "You shouldn't have to deal with that kind of thing in your condition. You should be able to tell people if and when you want."

My chest warms at his need to protect me. I know it's not about me. It's about the baby or maybe himself, but still... it feels good to have someone in my corner willing to fight for me.

"I guess I'm just used to it since I was raised here. It's always been a part of my life."

"Is our child going to have to deal with this growing up?"

Panic makes me still, and I glower at him. "I'm not moving, so it's irrelevant, Finn. I know you're the father, but my entire family lives here, and I'm going to need their support since you live thousands of miles away. But to answer your question, Buzz Wheel doesn't report the goings-on of minors."

He raises both hands in front of him. "I wasn't asking because I was going to demand you move."

"Good." I nod.

"And about that other thing..."

I frown. "What other thing?"

"The part where you said I live thousands of miles away." He clears his throat. "I won't be that far. In fact, I won't be far at all. I'm moving to Alaska."

It takes a moment for the words to form in my head, and when they do, my mouth drops open. "You and Tamra are moving here?"

He palms the back of his neck and cringes. "Yeah, about Tamra and me. There's something you should know."

Why do I get the distinct feeling I'm not going to like whatever he's about to say?

"Okay..." I shift in my seat.

"Our engagement was fake."

His words land between us like a grenade with the pin pulled. I blink at him several times.

"I wasn't lying when I said I had no intentions of getting back together with her. But when I got back from Hudson's wedding, she approached me about getting married, pretending we'd gotten back together so that she could have access to her trust from her grandfather. It was a stipulation in his will that she be happily married before she received the funds."

"So, you were marrying her for money? Was she paying you or something?"

"Yes, but not how you think. I mean yes, I was doing it for money. But I was doing it to save my parents' ski hill. They could've used the influx of cash to make repairs and upgrades to the place that would bring in the skiers and snowboarders. There's a chance they could lose the business, so when Tamra suggested what she did, I was receptive. Believe me when I say I didn't think we'd ever see each other again, and I was as shocked as you were when I found out that Tamra had hired you."

I look at my hands in my lap and take in everything he's saying, remembering being around them when I was helping them with their wedding. How I used to think that Finn looked at me with need every so often, then figuring I was crazy because he was happily engaged.

"Say something. Please."

I look up at him, and guilt coats his features. "It sounds like something I would do."

He bursts out laughing.

"You think I'm kidding." I grin.

"You don't think I'm the biggest piece of shit you've ever met?"

I shake my head. "Not at all. You were doing something

to try to help the people you love, and you weren't hurting anyone."

Finn holds my gaze. "I was hurting you. God, Harper, if I'd known you were pregnant, I never would have been holding Tamra's hand and acting that way with her. Not that I'm saying you cared, but I wouldn't have made it even more awkward than it was."

He's clearly telling the truth. I'm not sure that Finn has a dishonest bone in his body.

"I believe you. But you had no way of knowing." I give him a small smile. "So Tamra agreed to move here so that you can be near the baby, and she can still get her money?"

He shakes his head. "No. I called the wedding off. You're my priority now." My eyes widen, and he hurries to correct himself. "I mean the baby. The baby is my priority."

"Yeah. Of course, I didn't think otherwise." Neither of us says anything, and I don't love silence, so I ask another question, "But your parents? The business?"

Finn's gaze dips to my flat stomach. "I know. I'll have to try to figure something else out, but one thing I know is that I'd never forgive myself if I wasn't a part of my child's life."

The warm feeling flowing throughout my entire body should probably sound the alarm bells for me, but instead, I lean into the feeling. I'm not going to have to be a single mom. My eyes get watery. "Thank you, Finn. That makes me really happy."

He doesn't say anything, just swallows hard and nods.

"Where are you staying in the meantime until you find a place?"

He sighs. "Honestly, I'm not sure yet. I was going to look for something more budget-friendly than Glacier Point

Resort, seeing as I have a child on the way, and I'm about to be unemployed."

My brain spins with possibilities of how I can help fix either one or both of those situations. It's the least I can do when this man is leaving behind everything and hasn't even asked me for a paternity test. Then it comes to me. "I might be able to help."

He rolls his eyes playfully. "Let me guess, you have a relative who can pull some strings for me to either get a job or lodging."

"Well... kind of. My uncle Kingston has worked at the Anchorage Fire Department forever, and he could definitely put in a good word for you. There and at the local station."

Finn chuckles. "Is there no end to the Bailey clan?"

"Not really." I pat my stomach. "And it's about to get bigger between Palmer and myself."

He shakes his head. "So which family member owns a cheap motel for me to stay in?"

"I can do better than that." I smile broadly. "You can live with me."

seventeen

FINN

Her words are like a record scratch, bringing all my thoughts to a standstill.

She can't be serious. Live with her?

"Just until you find a place of your own," Harper continues. "It's a small town, and there aren't a ton of options, but we can figure it out. In the meantime, you can stay here for free."

"Why would you do that?"

She gives me a "come on" look. "You're upending your entire life, Finn. It's the least I can do."

"What about your roommate?"

She looks as if maybe she hadn't considered that. "Good point. Let me talk to her first."

While her offer is well meaning, it's an example of how impulsive this woman can be. What if she wakes up tomorrow and doesn't want me here?

"Unless you don't want to." She holds up both hands. "No pressure."

I try to picture it, being in close proximity with her every day knowing how attracted I am to her. But I'm not an animal. Surely, I can control myself, and it wouldn't be forever. Just until I can find a place.

"If your cousin is okay with it, I would appreciate it. But I promise I'll find a place as soon as I can."

"I'm sure she'll be okay with it." She smiles. "Plus, money you save goes to the baby." She laughs, her hands falling to her stomach.

I follow her movement, wishing she was mine so I could cradle where my baby is growing. I wonder what it's like to go through life like Harper does, always assuming that everything will work out for the best. At least that's how it seems she is. I guess I don't actually know her that well, which is something I need to rectify since she's going to be the mother of my child.

"I'll admit that I don't know a lot about pregnancy. Is there anything you need from me?"

She twists her mouth to the side as if she's considering, and I wait for some smartass comment. "I have an appointment with my aunt later this week to make sure everything is okay with the baby and to figure out a due date. You can come along if you'd like."

My adrenaline spikes. "Could there be something wrong with the baby?"

She holds up a hand. "Relax. It's just a part of the process, nothing to be concerned about."

My heart rate begins to return to normal, and I nod. "Okay, yeah, I'll be there. Just send me the info."

"Okay." We stare at each other for a beat. "So, we're really doing this."

"We're really doing this."

I hold her gaze, feeling drawn in. This woman is like a magnet, and I'm helpless to resist. If she were any closer to me on the couch, I'd probably be leaning in to kiss her.

"Thank you for being here, for doing this," she says.

My forehead wrinkles. "You don't have to thank me, Harper. You didn't get pregnant on your own. This isn't just on you to deal with."

She nods slowly, holding my gaze. "Maybe, but not every guy would see it that way."

I shrug. "Well then, they're assholes."

We both chuckle, and I stand. If I stay here any longer, I'm afraid I'll say something I'll regret. "I'll go check in at the resort for the night. You let me know about the spare room, and if it's a problem, no worries, I'll figure something out."

She stands and sees me to the front door, swinging it open for me. "I'll text you later after I talk with Maven."

"Sounds good." As I stare at her, the tension feels more like I'm leaving after a date than a conversation. Maybe it's just because the only way I've ever really spent any time with this woman was in a hotel room when she was riding me. "Talk to you tomorrow."

I force myself to leave and make my way to my rental truck. Another issue I have to take care of—transportation. Do I sell my truck in Vermont and buy a new one or drive it here?

I get in the driver's seat and give Harper a wave. She's leaning against the doorframe, watching me leave, and I have the sudden vision of what she might look like months from now, belly swollen with our baby. The level of pure male satisfaction that image gives me is a surprise. She waves back, and I reverse out of the driveway and head to the resort. Everything in my life is about to change. As crazy as it is, I'm excited for the future.

My grip on the steering wheel tightens. I hope I'm up for the challenge. One thing is for certain, I'm going to need to find out where AA meetings are held around here to make sure I stay on track.

THE NEXT MORNING, I wake up to a text from Harper.

> Maven is ok with you staying here for a while. Let me know what time you're leaving the hotel, and I'll meet you to let you in the house.

> Please thank her for me.

> And you. Obviously. Thanks.

Jesus, it's like I've never talked to a woman before. I need to kick this attraction to Harper to the curb.

> I'll get a key made this morning so you have one.

> Great. Want to meet there at eleven?

> See you then.

I figure I'll go down to the restaurant here in the resort, then pack up my things. I have to make a few calls about my job and figure all of that out too. Deal with my lease in Vermont. And I need to see where the AA meetings in the area happen.

I blow out a breath. There's a lot to do when you're upending your life apparently.

Around eleven, I pull into the driveway of Harper's

house and see her car already there. The door swings open before I even knock, almost as though she's been waiting for me.

"Welcome home." She smiles and gestures inside.

It's one of the things that first attracted me to her—her positive energy and zest for life, that touch of craziness and wild abandon. It was fine for a night of hot sex, but I have to question whether it's good for me in the long term. I think she'll make an amazing mother, no doubt, but since I've gotten sober, I've valued predictability and the status quo, knowing what to expect next.

Why the hell am I even thinking about this? It's not as though Harper has indicated that she wants me at all, other than that she wants me to be involved in our child's life.

"Thanks." I step inside with my two suitcases. It's all I brought with me.

I knew when I flew out here I'd have to head home to pack up the rest of my belongings once I had somewhere to send them. Finding a place to live and a job are my two main priorities at this point.

"Is that all you have with you?" Harper asks.

She looks beautiful today. Her long red hair is pulled back off her face, highlighting the arch of her neck, and she's wearing a form-fitting dress that looks as though it's made of a thin knit. No sign of her pregnancy showing yet.

"For now. Until I find a place."

She nods. "Follow me. I'll show you your room."

I follow her up the stairs, bags in hand, trying my best not to be a perv and watch her ass the entire way. I fail miserably.

When we reach the top of the stairs, the bathroom is directly in front of me. There's a bedroom with the door open to the right and two doors to the left. Harper goes left and stops at the first door, stepping inside.

"It's not much, but hopefully it's okay for now. Sorry about the girly décor."

I glance around with a chuckle. It's definitely heavy on the female influence in here with a lavender and cream bedding set and a host of inspirational quotes for art on the walls.

"You mean this doesn't scream rough-and-tumble fire-fighter?" I point at the picture that says, "What if I fall? But oh, my darling, what if you fly?" She laughs as I walk farther in and set my bags on the mattress. "Thanks again for letting me stay here."

"All right, that's the last time you can thank me." She walks over to the door. "I have to go meet a client, but I left the key on the kitchen counter. Help yourself to anything you want in the kitchen. I'll be home around dinnertime."

Before I can say much else, she's gone, heading down the stairs, then I hear the front door close.

I glance around the room again. I certainly didn't think that this was where I'd end up months after the night I slept with Harper. Surprise.

eighteen

HARPER

"Mmm... nice view."

I whip around from where I'm looking out the sliding glass door to see Maven with a shit-eating grin.

"I don't know what you're talking about." I turn and walk away from the window.

She laughs. "Sure you don't."

When I arrived home from work, I called for Finn, since his truck was here, but couldn't find him in the house. When I looked outside, I saw him shirtless and in the midst of some kind of workout routine in the backyard.

I walk over to the fridge to figure out something for dinner. There's not much in here. "It doesn't matter anyway. Now that we're going to be coparents, we can't be anything more. No way am I going to risk screwing up that relationship for my kid."

When I come up empty in the fridge, I search through the cupboards.

"Is that what you two have agreed on?" she asks.

I shrug. "Not in so many words, but I'm pretty sure

we're on the same page." I sigh. Grilled cheese and tomato soup it is. I'm going to have to learn how to cook better meals if I'm going to be a mother.

"What if you two could be a real couple? Wouldn't that be even better for the baby?" She slides onto one of the stools at the breakfast bar.

"In a perfect world, sure. But there's no guarantee we wouldn't end up hating each other if we tried."

She rocks her head back and forth. "True, but there are no guarantees for anything in life."

Movement out the window catches my eye. "He's coming back in."

Maven turns on the stool when she hears the sliding glass door open. "You must be Finn. We met briefly at Palmer's wedding, but I didn't get to know you as well as Harper did apparently."

"Maven!" My mouth hangs open.

Finn chuckles good-naturedly and walks over to her, hand extended. At least his shirt is back on now, though it clings to his sweat-dampened skin. "Good to meet you, Maven. Thanks so much for letting me stay here."

"Of course. The pleasure is all mine. Especially if you keep doing shirtless workouts in the backyard." She chuckles.

Finn blushes, and damn, it's sexy. "Sorry, I haven't found a gym here yet. Just trying to stay in shape in case I have to do a fitness test, if I can even get an interview around here."

Maven's head cocks. "What do you do?"

"I was a firefighter back in Vermont. I'm hoping I can keep that going here in Alaska."

"You should talk to my dad."

Finn glances at me where I'm buttering the bread at the

counter. "Is he the one who works in Anchorage? Harper mentioned him."

Maven nods. "The one and only. He'll put in a good word for you."

"We're going to see your mom in a couple days to figure out my due date, so I planned to mention it to her when we're there." I pull the drawer open and reach for the can opener.

"Good plan. The way to get my dad to do anything is through my mom." She smiles, her amber eyes lighting up.

"Do either of you want a grilled cheese and tomato soup?" I ask, holding up the unopened can of soup.

"Not me," Maven says, sliding off the stool. "I actually have a date tonight."

"Oooh, do tell." I set the can of soup on the counter.

"Not much to tell. I met him at the gas station when I was in Greywall. I know that doesn't sound romantic, but beggars can't be choosers."

I laugh. "Well, have a good time. Send me your location, all right?"

"Yes, *Mom*." She emphasizes the last word as she always does when I tell her this kind of thing. But this time her eyes grow wide and get an excited gleam. "I just realized that actually fits now."

I shake my head and roll my eyes. "Have fun. I might be gone by the time you come back down, but make sure you send me your location," I call after her as she leaves the room.

"Where are you headed?" Finn asks.

"I'm going by Palmer's place to catch up."

"I have to pick Hudson up later. We're heading out to do the same. Want to head over together?"

It shouldn't be a big deal to say yes. I mean, it only

makes sense. Why would we take two cars? But it also feels like a couple thing to do.

I'm probably overthinking it, so I say, "Sure. You didn't answer me about dinner though. You hungry?"

"If you don't mind. I was just going to take a quick shower." He nods in the direction of the stairs.

"No worries. You do that while I get this ready. I'll call you."

He smiles and thanks me before heading out of the kitchen.

Seeing him sweaty reminds me of the night we spent together. I give my head a shake.

Don't go there.

I prepare dinner, and when it's ready, I call up the stairs for Finn, but he doesn't answer. I try one more time, and when I hear nothing back, I head up the stairs. Maven is in her bedroom with the door closed, music going, so I figure maybe he didn't hear me.

The bathroom is opposite of the stairs' top landing, and when I'm almost at the top of them, the bathroom door swings open. What I see can only be described as the beginning of a great porno. Or maybe it's just these damn pregnancy hormones.

Steam surrounds Finn where he's stopped in the threshold wearing just a towel around his waist. His tanned skin glistens over his muscled chest and abs. I can't help but let my gaze roam over him and all the tattoos down his arms, his chest, and further. My tongue licks my lips of its own accord, and I have to stifle a moan because I know exactly what that bulge under the towel is, and I know how well he can use it.

Finn clears his throat. "Dinner's ready?"

My eyes snap up to meet his. "Um, yeah. I called, and you didn't answer."

He thumbs over his shoulder. "Sorry, probably didn't hear it with the bathroom fan. I'll be right down."

I nod and turn, holding the railing and hurrying down the stairs to give myself some space from this man I don't seem to be able to remember I should be staying away from —at least romantically.

AN HOUR LATER, Finn pulls his rental truck into Palmer's driveway.

"Do you want me to just send Hudson out?" I ask, but I see the door open, and Hudson is already headed our way. "Never mind."

We both chuckle.

"I'll text you to let you know when we're on our way back," Finn says.

"Okay. Have fun. Don't do anything I wouldn't do."

He laughs. "I'm not sure that really leaves any options out, does it?"

I playfully roll my eyes and get out of the truck, saying a quick hello to Hudson as I pass him, then heading inside. I'm not sure if Palmer has her cochlear implant on, so I don't bother calling for her. I check the living room first and get lucky, finding her and Adley.

"The party can start, I'm here!" I hold my hands up over my head, as well as the bag of chips I brought—salt and vinegar, Adley's favorite.

Adley squeals and jumps up off the couch, rushing over to give me a hug.

"How are you, kiddo?"

She pulls away and takes the chips from me, running back over to the couch.

"Adley, that was rude," Palmer says out loud but also signs to Adley. "Harper asked you a question, and you don't just rip a bag of chips out of someone's hands."

Adley frowns at her mom. "But she brought them for me."

"Guilty as charged," I say and sit on the couch beside Palmer.

She turns to look at me. "Not helping."

I raise my hands in front of me. "My bad."

She nods toward the kitchen. "Let's go hang in there."

We get up and make our way into the kitchen to afford us a little more privacy.

"Your bump is starting to show," I say.

She glances at her stomach where there's now a slight swell. "Yeah. Seems like you start showing earlier the second time around. At least I am. Do you want anything to drink?"

I shake my head. "I'm good."

"Hudson tells me that Finn has moved in with you?" she asks as soon as we're seated at the kitchen table.

"Jeez, men are just as big of gossips as us. He's moved in, but he's not moving in. He's just staying with me until he can find a place to rent."

"Mmm-hmm."

I cock my head. "Why are you saying it like that?"

She shrugs. "No reason. What's his fiancée think of that?"

I shift in my seat. "Actually, he's not engaged anymore."

Palmer nods slowly. "Had a feeling that might happen."

"I can't say anything more than that. It's not my story to tell. I'm sure Finn will probably fill Hudson in tonight, and he'll tell you."

Her forehead wrinkles. "Interesting. So, he's moving

here for good I take it?" I nod. "And how do you feel about the fact that he's single and available?"

My head rocks back. "What do you mean? It makes no difference to me."

"Mmm-hmm."

I cross my arms. "Okay, what's with that tonight?"

She shrugs. "It's just that I saw you guys the morning after the wedding, and you two seemed pretty smitten with each other. I guess I'm just wondering if the two of you plan to see if there could be something between you."

I'm already shaking my head before she finishes talking. "Not happening. The priority is the baby."

"Is that what he says?" She arches a dark eyebrow.

"Well, we haven't talked about it, but..."

"But... you have no idea where he's at then. I understand not wanting to complicate things, I do, but you two need to have a conversation and make sure you're on the same page."

She's right, I realize. As uncomfortable as it might be, we do need to talk about it.

I groan and let my head drop back, not looking forward to having that conversation. But I guess this is what it means to become a parent—choosing to do the hard things.

nineteen

FINN

"Wow. Didn't see that coming." Hudson tips back his beer.

We're at the bar in downtown Lake Starlight called Lucky's. I know a lot of people with a drinking problem won't even step a foot into a bar, and I didn't at first, but now it's easier for me. Back when I was drinking, I wanted to drink whether I was at work or smack dab in the middle of a bar. The location made no difference.

If I walked in and felt the pull any more than I do on a normal day, I'd walk right out. But as it is right now, I'm fine.

I sip the ginger ale in front of me. "Yeah, not my proudest moment, agreeing to a fake marriage, but I just wanted to help my parents out."

"It's that bad?" When I nod, he cringes. "I'm sorry, man. We grew up on those slopes."

Most of our childhood was spent at my parents' ski resort. It was our go-to place as teenagers with all of our friends. "I know, but it's taking a toll on them to keep it up. Might be worth just closing. I don't know."

"I wish I could do something."

I shrug. It's not his fault. "I'll see if I can figure something else out, though I don't know what."

"Let me know. You know I'll do whatever I can."

"Congratulations again on you and Palmer expecting." I change the subject, still feeling like a horrible son for not being able to help my parents when I thought I was going to save their business.

Hudson's grin is one of true happiness. In fact, besides his wedding and Adley's birth, I don't think I've ever seen him this happy. "Thanks. I'm hyped about it. How are you feeling about everything going on with you?"

I blow out a breath. "A little overwhelmed. So much is changing so fast. But I don't know, I'm getting more used to the idea with every day that passes. It's starting to feel more real."

He nods as though he understands. And he probably does, given that he and Palmer were friends who hooked up one night and then found out she was pregnant as a result.

"I'll tell you what I could do without though," I say, and Hudson arches a brow in question. "That damned Buzz Wheel app. I finally downloaded the damn thing and looked up the article Harper told me about. What the fuck, man?" I shake my head.

"I hear you. That thing can be annoying as fuck sometimes." He picks at the label on his beer, not really adding anything else.

"Why the hell would someone think it's okay to put something like that in there? I mean, she hadn't even told her parents."

He claps me on the shoulder. "You knocked up a Bailey, man." He looks at me as though I'm a fucking idiot for not being able to read between the lines.

"Okay... and?"

Hudson shakes his head before taking a pull from his beer. "I didn't get it before I moved here either, I guess. The Bailey family is a big deal in Lake Starlight. They own Bailey Lumber, which is the biggest employer around, but more than that, they come with their own lore."

He goes on to explain to me how Harper's grandparents died when their nine children were still relatively young and how Harper's dad and her aunt Savannah dropped everything in their lives to keep the family legacy going. Her aunt took over running Bailey Lumber, and Harper's dad, Austin, took on the role of raising his siblings.

"Basically, they're like royalty around here," Hudson says. "Everyone in town has a vested interest in their happiness."

"Wonderful." I guzzle back a few good swallows of my pop. "So what you're saying is that every single thing I do around here will be under the watchful eye of Buzz Wheel?"

Hudson shrugs. "Just the interesting stuff. Don't go getting caught in the alley kissing." He laughs.

I sigh. "It just feels like a lot, along with everything else going on."

"I promise you'll get used to it. It might take a bit, but you will. It's actually not done in a harmful way, but I only see that now that I've lived here as long as I have."

"And what about fatherhood? Will I get used to that too?"

He studies me for a beat. "Honestly, yes. It will take some time. What I can tell you is that when you meet your child, you'll know right away that you would do anything for them. Anything. If you let that lead you, you'll be fine."

Thus far, I haven't let myself daydream about what it might be like to have a son or daughter. Taking them for walks in a stroller, pushing them on the swing, the first day of school or the last day of school when they graduate. Now that I am thinking about it, a warm feeling fills me and a weight settles on my shoulders. What if I fuck it up?

I have great parents, and I want to be that for my own child.

"How steep is the learning curve?" I ask.

Hudson chuckles and leans back in the chair, calling out to the bartender, "Hey, Van, how steep is the learning curve with a new baby?"

The bartender looks at us and sets down the glass he's wiping, coming from around the bar and over to our table. He has dark hair and a sleeve of tattoos down his arm. In addition to that, he also has dark bags under his eyes and looks as if he hasn't slept in a week.

"Who's asking? You or my wife?"

Hudson laughs and looks at me. "Finn, this is Van. He's married to Harper's cousin Brinley."

"The baby daddy." He holds out his hand to me. "Good to meet you."

I want to cringe at the moniker, but I suppose it's to be expected given that we aren't in any kind of relationship. "Good to meet you. I take it you have a new baby at home?"

He blows out a breath. "I do. And Ivy is the shit, believe me. I'd die for her, but I would've thought my military background prepared me more thoroughly for the lack of sleep and the constantly evolving situation. No such luck though."

"Awesome." I frown. I make a mental note to do my own research so that I'm better prepared for what's to come.

"But it's worth it. Every damn second of it, believe me. I'd do anything for my little girl," he says.

Hudson gives me a look like, told you so.

It does make me feel a little better.

"I was just explaining to Finn here what it means that he's having a baby with a Bailey," Hudson says to Finn.

Van chuckles. "It should come with a warning label."

My shoulders slump.

"I'm just kidding, man." Van squeezes my shoulder. "It can be a lot, no doubt. But honestly, it comes with such a big support system that it's worth the never-ending intrusions into your business. If you ever need anything, someone in that family is going to step up to help. Always."

Hudson nods.

"That doesn't sound so bad, I suppose." I sip my drink.

"Once you get used to it, you'll be happy for it." Hudson takes a pull from his beer.

I take his word for it. As if I have a choice.

twenty

HARPER

"You all right?"

Finn's deep voice draws my attention from the million thoughts swirling through my head. "Yeah, why?"

His large hand lands on my knee, preventing it from bouncing up and down as it has been doing since we checked in and sat down.

We're in the waiting room, waiting to see Aunt Stella for my first official doctor's appointment related to my pregnancy, and I'm nervous. What if she says there's something wrong with the baby?

"Sorry, nerves, I guess." I give him a tight smile.

He fixes me with his hazel eyes, rimmed with dark lashes. "I promise, everything will be fine. Whatever happens in there, we will figure it out, okay?"

The weird thing is, I believe him. "Yeah... okay, thanks."

A few minutes later, we're called into the office, and the nurse tells me to remove everything from the waist down.

Finn's eyes widen, and he looks away from me, thumbing over his shoulder. "I'll um... wait outside."

It would be almost comical if it didn't highlight the fact that we're having a baby together and barely know each other.

I undress and put the gown on before opening the door a crack and waving Finn inside. He looks at me warily when he steps in as if to make sure all my bits and pieces are covered. Finn sits in the chair, and I hop up onto the exam table, swinging my feet.

Before either of us can say anything, there's a knock on the door, and it opens, revealing my aunt Stella wearing her white doctor's coat, which contrasts with her dark umber skin and her red lipstick. She always looks so put together, even when she's working. Her dark hair is in braids and pulled back into a ponytail, and her deep brown eyes flick between Finn and me.

"How are you?" She steps over to give me a hug, which I return. "How's my girl? Staying out of trouble?"

I think my aunt would be happy if Maven continued living with her and Uncle Kingston for years, but she doesn't seem to hold it against me that I gave her a place to stay.

"She's good. Perfect roommate."

"Glad to hear it." She squeezes my upper arms then turns to address Finn. "And you must be Finn. Good to meet you." She extends her hand.

He takes it, telling her it's good to meet her as well.

"So." She claps her hands together. "Congratulations to you both. Should we try and find out when you might expect this bundle of joy?"

I smile. "Yes, please. Though I can tell you the exact date of conception, since it was a…" I trail off, not wanting to say it was a one-night hookup.

"That makes things easy. But I'll still do a physical exam

today if that's okay with you, Harper, just to make sure everything is progressing as expected."

I nod, thankful she's not making it a big deal. I knew my aunt would probably be cool about it, but I'm happy that initial awkwardness is over.

My aunt asks me a bunch of questions about how I'm feeling and what I've been able to eat. "Are you taking prenatal vitamins?"

"Yup." My gaze flickers to Finn's.

"Oh, of course." She laughs. "That's how you two were outed on Buzz Wheel." She shakes her head. "I haven't talked to your parents since I heard the news. How did they take it?"

"Surprisingly well."

She makes a few notes in the computer then looks at me. "Did you doubt them?"

I shrug. "I knew eventually they'd be okay with it, but I was surprised how fast it happened."

She heads to the sink and washes her hands. "Maven tells me you're staying with the girls until you can find a place, Finn?"

Finn glances my way, looking a little unsure. "Yes, that's right. Hopefully it won't be too long."

Aunt Stella cringes. "Small town means that sometimes it can be difficult to find a place, but I'm sure it will work out." She looks between us. "All right. Are you ready to get your first look at your baby?" She grabs some gloves from the box on the counter and pulls them on.

My stomach flutters with excitement and nerves as I nod enthusiastically.

"Lie down on the table and get comfortable, Harper. We're going to have to do a transvaginal ultrasound since it doesn't sound like you're that far along."

Once I'm lying down, she arranges one of the blue paper blankets over my lower half. Finn remains seated where he is, watching my aunt intently. When my aunt pulls out the wand for the ultrasound, Finn's eyes widen.

"You're going to put that *in* her?" He looks at me with something akin to horror. "Is that safe for her and the baby?"

His panic and protectiveness are kind of cute, and I can't help but notice the way he included my wellbeing in that sentence along with the baby's. My chest warms.

"I can assure you that it's perfectly safe. I won't insert the whole thing, and once Harper is further along in her pregnancy, we'll use a different wand, but this allows us to get a good look now." My aunt turns her attention to me. "You ready?"

I nod, and she wheels around the machine so I can see it better.

"Finn, if you want to see, you're going to have to come around here."

He gets out of the chair and comes to stand by my side near my shoulder. "Is it okay if I stand here?" he asks me.

"Of course." I turn my attention back to my aunt.

"All right, open your legs a bit."

I do as she says while she slips the wand under the paper and finds what she's looking for, then she presses some buttons on the screen. It goes from black to black and white with some grainy visuals. I can't make out what we're looking at, but my aunt takes pictures with the ultrasound on the screen while I keep on trying to piece together what I'm seeing.

Finn bends down so he's near my ear. "Do you have any idea what you're looking at?"

I meet his eyes. "No."

We both laugh, and when I notice the image on the screen flickers, I stop.

"Sorry," I say to my aunt.

She smiles. "No worries. Honestly, there's not much to see here unless you know what you're looking for, so don't feel bad about it." She points at the screen with her free hand. "This bigger end here is the baby's head, and this here is the body. And do you see that little flicker there?"

I nod, not removing my eyes from the screen.

"That's your baby's heartbeat."

I suck in a breath.

"Should we see if we can hear it?" my aunt asks.

I glance at Finn, but he's not looking at me. His attention is wholly fixed on the screen with a look of awe. "Yes, please."

She does something to the machine, then a whooshing sound rings through the room.

"It sounds really fast, is that okay?" I bite my bottom lip.

"It's perfectly normal. It's a strong heartbeat."

Finn's hand slips into mine, squeezing it. I glance up to find him looking at me, a serious expression on his face, then he gives me a small smile.

I squeeze his hand back. "That's our baby."

His nostrils flare, and he nods before looking back at the screen.

My aunt finishes up the ultrasound, and it's only then that Finn and I realize we're still holding hands. He drops my hand, seeming uncomfortable, and goes to sit back down in the chair.

"Do you know the due date?" he asks.

She nods. "Based on when you said your last period

started and when you're sure you conceived, I think we have a pretty accurate date."

She tells us the date, and I smile. An April baby.

"I'm going to send you to the lab to give a blood and urine sample to make sure everything looks okay there, though I don't see any reason to expect any issues. You can make your next appointment on your way out."

"Thanks so much, Aunt Stella."

She smiles and gives me a hug. "I'm excited that there will be a new member of the family." Then she turns to Finn. "It was wonderful to meet you. I'm sure I'll be seeing you often."

He thanks her, then she leaves us alone in the room.

Finn and I stare at each other for a beat, some kind of emotion swirling between us, but I can't quite put my finger on it.

He clears his throat and stands. "I'll let you get changed. Meet you in the waiting area."

Before I can say anything, he's out the door, closing it behind him.

I can't read him because I don't know him well enough yet, but I plan to change that.

FINN

I plunk down in a seat in the waiting area knowing that today will be marked in my memory as a defining moment in my life. There will be a before and after to hearing my child's heartbeat for the first time. For really comprehending that Harper and I are bringing another human being into the world.

Well, let's face it, she's doing all the work. I only participated in the fun part.

I couldn't have predicted how much hearing the heartbeat would affect me. How close it would make me feel to Harper.

She walks out of the office, and I watch her make her way down the hall to check out, picking up the paperwork she needs for the lab and making her next appointment. When she's done, she makes her way to me, smiling. God, that fucking smile. It's like a ray of sun cutting through the thickest winter clouds.

I stand and meet her halfway.

"The receptionist gave me this to give to you." She holds out a purple sticky note.

I take it and look down, seeing the name Kingston in feminine script and a phone number.

"It's my uncle who's the firefighter. Aunt Stella left it for you. Said he'll be expecting your call."

It's hard to get used to what a large family Harper has. It's as though she has a contact for literally anything. I wish I didn't have to call in a favor this early, but I can't afford to let my pride get in the way. There's a baby coming this spring.

"That's really nice of her. I'll be sure to call him tomorrow." I slide the paper into my back pocket.

"Okay, I just have to go to the lab on the main floor, then we can go home."

I hold out my hand. "Lead the way."

"I hope you're better than me with needles because your first job is right now. You have to hold my hand," she says as we make our way out of the waiting area. When I chuckle, she looks over her shoulder at me. "I'm not kidding."

***

She wasn't kidding about not liking needles. As soon as she sat down in the chair for the phlebotomist to draw blood, her head bobbed, and her eyes fixated on the tubes. Her breathing sped up, and she had tears in her eyes. When she reached for me to take her hand, a deep protective instinct in me took over. All I wanted to do was be there for her.

Then the nice lady smiled and revealed the needle she was about to poke into Harper's arm, and she almost crushed the bones in my fingers, causing me to question my thinking.

But as soon as we walked out of the doors of the clinic, the Harper I know returned—bright, energetic, and funny.

Since we met at the clinic, we drive back to the house separately, and the entire drive, all I did was replay the sound of the baby's heartbeat, the little flicker on the screen affirming life. It has become real. My baby. Not a baby, mine. Ours. Harper's and mine.

If I think too long and hard about how much my life has changed in such a short time, I'd probably panic as much as Harper did while getting her blood drawn, but in some weird way, none of it feels wrong.

It will take time for me to get used to the size of Harper's family, but if I'm honest, I like that she comes from a large family. I like knowing that our son or daughter will have so many people around, supporting him or her.

My family is small, just my parents and me. It sucks that they won't be closer to me and their grandchild, but we'll make the most of it when they come to visit. Maybe Harper will come with me to Vermont or allow me to take our child once they're old enough.

I stop on the way back to the house to grab some dinner from Wok4U, and since it's a small town, I'm able to ask the owner, Li—who already knew who I was—if he knows what Harper and Maven usually order. After the order is ready, I head back to the house and find Harper's car already in the driveway. I texted her while I was waiting to let her know that I'd pick up dinner.

She's coming down the stairs when I walk through the door. I almost drop the takeout bags. She's changed into her pajamas—a short-sleeve button-up shirt with white and red stripes and matching shorts. But those shorts are short as hell and show off her shapely legs.

My dick twitches in my pants.

Harper seems oblivious to my reaction as she walks over, arms outstretched to help with the bags.

"I've got them," I say and head toward the kitchen ahead of her, leaving her to follow me.

"Maven is out with Landry. She texted me back when I told her you were bringing home Chinese food."

"That her boyfriend?" I set the bags on the counter, purposely not turning around to look at her. I'd only be tempting myself.

"No, just a friend. I feel bad. You bought all this food."

I turn to take in her expression, and she's frowning.

"Don't worry about it. It just means more leftovers for tomorrow." I lightly hip check her.

It's an innocent enough action, but it sets off a series of chain reactions in my body. First my breath rushes out of my lungs, next my heart beats faster, then my dick perks up to pay attention. Our gazes lock and hold for a moment, and she licks her lips.

"I wanted to talk to you about something." Her voice is soft and a little breathier than normal.

"Oh?" I arch an eyebrow.

"When we were at the doctor's office today, I realized that we don't know each other that well. Here we are having a baby, yet we barely know anything about one another."

I know how beautiful you look when you come, I want to tell her. I think about her flush a lot. "Okay..."

"I thought that maybe we could get to know each other. You know, so that when the baby is born, we're not complete strangers."

I nod. It's a good idea. It would certainly make coparenting easier.

"What did you have in mind?" There's clear insinuation in my voice even though it's not something I did consciously. I turn to face her wholly.

She looks up at me with her big eyes hooded with desire. "I... I thought we could spend time together."

Somehow, we've moved even closer to each other. Her breasts brush my chest with every inhale.

"Like?" I don't know what possesses me, but I trail my finger from her shoulder, over her sleeve, and down her bare arm.

Harper's eyes drift closed as she basks in the sensation. "Whatever we want," she whispers.

I breathe her in as we stand in the kitchen, the tension as thick as an autumn fog between us. She tilts her head up slightly, and I dip my head down, our mouths a breath apart. When Harper places her palm on my chest, my control snaps, and I capture her mouth, my hand pushing into the long, luscious strands at the back of her head.

She opens immediately, matching my fervor with her own. When our tongues meet and I get my first taste of her again, I'm reminded of how addictive she is. How even after I left Lake Starlight that first time, she constantly floated back into my consciousness. Yearning for her thousands of miles away and wishing I could have her for just one more night.

The hand in her hair slides free and inches down her back until I reach her ass and squeeze. She groans, and I capture it with my mouth. My other hand slides up past her waist to cup her small breast, and she squeaks, a noise I'm pretty sure wasn't pleasurable.

"Sorry, my boobs are super tender right now," she mumbles against my lips before resuming our kiss.

It takes my brain a minute to catch up since all the blood in my body is presently rushing to my dick.

Pregnant.

Harper's pregnant.

With my baby.

I rip away from the kiss. "Fuck." I thread my hands through my hair. "I'm sorry, I shouldn't have done that." My chest heaves, and my dick is so hard, begging to be let free from my jeans.

A momentary flash of hurt crosses her face, but it's gone quickly. She nods, stepping away from me. "You're right. Anything physical between us is only going to further complicate things. We need to be clear on what this situation is." She motions between us with her finger. "We're never going to be together like that, right?"

I'm not sure why, but I feel as if this answer matters, maybe more than I even realize. I nod. "Right. We're just going to be friends and coparents. Anything else is too risky."

She gives me a sharp nod. "Agreed."

And I agree too. But seeing her swollen lips, looking equal parts cute and sexy in her pajamas, makes me wish things could be different. But they can't. I need to focus on building my life here, maintaining my sobriety, and getting ready to be the best father I can be. I can't allow myself to fall into a physical affair with the woman who will be the mother to my child. There's too much room for resentment to breed and poison what could be a healthy coparenting relationship.

"You're right though, we should know each other better before the baby is born."

"Maybe this weekend we can do something together then, hang out for a bit." She walks around to the other side of the counter and opens the takeout bags.

"Sounds like a plan."

Neither of us mentions making plans or the kiss as we dish our dinners onto separate plates. When I ask Harper whether she wants to eat at the table or in the living room in front of the TV, she tells me that she's going to get her laptop and bring it to the kitchen table because she has some things to catch up on for work.

I take her decision for what it is—a dismissal—and eat alone in front of the TV with the sports channel. I might not get to share my meal with Harper, but I can watch her brother on the baseball field instead. Even though the kiss made things awkward as fuck, I can't find it in myself to regret it, only the fact that there won't be another.

HARPER

The awkwardness that was left behind after our kiss has abated in the week that's followed. Finn and I didn't end up doing anything last weekend. I was so tired, and my stomach was bothering me again, so I just laid around the house taking it easy. Unfortunately, my stomach is still bothering me. I miss those blessed couple of weeks when I was able to eat normally and feel good.

But we have plans tonight to do something, though I don't know what. Finn insisted it be a surprise. All I know is that he told me to be ready to leave by five.

He walks through the door at 4:50 on the dot with a couple of grocery bags in his hands.

"Hey." He gives me one of his charming smiles and heads straight to the kitchen.

I follow him. "What do you have there?"

"I know you said your stomach has been bothering you lately, and you're finding it hard to eat, so I stopped and picked up a few things." He pulls items out of the bags.

There are saltine crackers, pickles, potato chips, chocolate, ice cream, and cheese.

"Interesting combo." My head tilts to the side.

Honestly, looking at the arrangement of foods on the counter makes my stomach turn. I swear I can smell the vinegary tang of the pickles, and the thought of eating ice cream makes bile race up my throat.

"I googled what pregnant women crave. Figured if you can't eat full meals, maybe you can have snacks throughout the day." He shrugs then holds up the ice cream with a smile.

All I can picture is it curdling in my stomach.

I slap a hand over my throat and race for the bathroom, managing to get down on my knees moments before I vomit. I'm not aware of anything except purging my stomach until a large set of hands gathers my hair and holds it at the nape of my neck.

Oh god, how embarrassing.

I continue vomiting until my stomach is empty, then I reach up blindly and flush the toilet, sitting back on my heels. Finn lets go of my hair.

"I'm sorry." I wipe under my eyes with a finger, sure that my mascara now looks like shit from my watering eyes.

"Why are you apologizing?" Finn slides to the floor beside me, somehow not looking repulsed.

"Isn't it obvious?" I chuckle and use the toilet for leverage to stand.

Finn stands up too, and I suddenly realize how small this bathroom actually is. His presence presses in on me from all sides.

"I should be the one apologizing. Obviously, I didn't buy the right stuff."

I shake my head. "No, it was very thoughtful of you. This is the first time I've thrown up. There's no way you could have known. I hope this isn't a sign of the next pregnancy stage."

He looks at me with concern. Something in his expression feels wholly intimate, so I turn away.

"Just let me go upstairs to brush my teeth, and then we can head out."

I wait for him to step out of the bathroom so that I can get past him, but he shakes his head. "We aren't going anywhere."

My forehead wrinkles. "What do you mean?"

"I'll rebook it. Let's just stay in tonight in case your stomach wants to go another round."

I do a mental check of how I'm feeling. Though my stomach definitely feels more settled now, I still have that queasy feeling at the back of my throat. Though I was looking forward to getting out of the house and doing something, Finn is probably right.

"Okay, maybe that's best. Thanks." I cringe.

"Why don't you go change into something comfortable, and then we can chill?" He turns and steps out of the small bathroom to let me pass.

I head upstairs and change into leggings and an over-sized thin sweater, pulling my hair up into a messy bun. When I get back downstairs, I find Finn with the TV on the home page of a streaming service. He's taken a blanket out of the blanket box and has it on one end of the couch, and he's lit the candle on the coffee table.

The vibe is chill and cozy and exactly what I need. If I didn't know better, I might even think it's romantic.

My mind drifts back to the kiss we shared, but I quickly push the thought away.

"What do you want to watch?" I sit near the blanket on the couch and pull it over my lap.

"You choose." He motions toward the TV.

"Do you like reality TV?" I ask.

He chuckles. "Never really watched it."

I pick up the controller from the cushion beside me. "Well, you're in for a treat then."

By the end of the second episode, my stomach seems to have come around, and I decide to try to eat something. I settle on crackers with peanut butter and head into the kitchen to make some. Finn follows to make himself something to eat since he hasn't had dinner yet.

Ten minutes later, I'm seated at the breakfast bar, slowly eating my snacks and watching Finn make an omelet on the stove.

"Have you heard back from the fire station?" I ask.

My uncle put in a good word for Finn, and though the Anchorage station doesn't need anyone at the moment, the local Lake Starlight one does. My uncle has worked out of Anchorage all his life, but around here, everyone knows everyone, so he was still able to put Finn's resume at the top of the pile.

"I did. Meant to tell you that I have an interview on Monday." He lifts the corner of his omelet to check it, then turns down the burner.

"That's great news." I reach for the glass of water Finn set in front of me a couple of minutes ago.

"Yeah, I'll have to call your uncle back to thank him."

"I'm sure he doesn't mind. It's one of the perks of having such a large family." I take a sip of my water then set down the drink.

Finn looks at me over his shoulder. "Is it ever overwhelming to have such a big family?"

I seesaw my head back and forth for a moment. "It can be at times. Mostly when there's a big event, and *everyone* is going to be there. Or if something big is going on and everyone is talking about it, and you find yourself somehow involved." I point at my stomach and chuckle.

"I'm sure the news about our baby must have made your phone ring."

Hearing the words "our baby" from Finn's mouth does something to me. Something it should not. I brush off the feeling.

"You have no idea how many calls and texts I had to field." I shake my head. "It took a few days to get through them all."

"But do you like it?" He turns off the burner and plates his omelet.

I nod. "I do. Wouldn't have it any other way. I mean, in a family this size, it's almost like there are little subsections of family units. I'm closest with my cousins who are around my own age. But I know that if anything ever happened, and I needed someone in my family to step up, they'd all do so in a heartbeat. There's something comforting about that." I shrug.

He grabs a fork and a knife from the cutlery drawer and stands opposite from where I sit, cutting into his dinner.

"Do you come from a big family?"

Finn shakes his head and frowns. "No, it's just me and my parents. Neither of them had any siblings and both sets of grandparents have passed so..."

My chest squeezes. Jeez, I'd hate that. I'd feel so alone. My family can be overbearing and intrusive at times, but I can't imagine not having them in my life.

"How do you feel about..." I was going to say being a part of a large family, but that's not exactly true, is it?

Despite being my child's father, we're not together, and he'll always have one foot on the outside. "...our child being part of such a big family?"

He finishes chewing and smiles at me. "I love it. For all the reasons you said. I like knowing that he or she will be surrounded by so many people who love them."

The tension in my chest eases.

"Have you told your parents about the baby?" I've been curious but haven't wanted to ask.

"Kind of had to since I relocated here." He brings his fork to his mouth.

"How did they take the news?" I brace myself.

"They were surprised... obviously. They thought I was getting married for love."

"Did you tell them the truth?"

He shakes his head. "Didn't see the point. I might in the future." He shrugs. "I don't know."

"They must hate me for taking their only son away." I frown.

His forehead wrinkles. "Not at all. Honestly, I think they were proud of me in a weird way. For taking responsibility."

"Most guys wouldn't have, you know." Our eyes lock and hold as I say, "Or at least to the extent that you are."

He breaks eye contact and looks at his plate, cutting into his omelet again. "I've always wanted kids. Granted, this isn't how I thought it would happen. I have a good relationship with my parents, and I want that with my own child. I can't build that from thousands of miles away."

"Well, I guess as far as baby daddies go, I picked a good one."

Finn's mouth drops open, then he tilts his head back and laughs. When he looks back at me, there's a sparkle of appreciation in his eyes. I recognize it from the night of the wedding when we ended up in bed together.

I clear my throat and push my plate away, sliding off the stool. "I think that's enough for me. Ready to watch another episode?" Leaving the kitchen, I don't wait for him to answer.

Whether it's pregnancy hormones, proximity, or just *him*, I can't afford to be attracted to him. I've always let my emotions run my life, but not anymore. Not when I have a little one who is depending on me.

twenty-three

FINN

Living with Harper gets more challenging every day. Which is why it's a good thing I'm now officially employed with the Lake Starlight Fire Department. Now I can keep looking for somewhere to live and be able to afford the rent without dipping into my savings.

I've been looking, but Harper wasn't kidding when she said it can be hard to find something in town. I've eyed a few places in Anchorage that are available. It's not as though it's five minutes away, but it's under an hour. But now that I have the job here, I definitely want to find a place in Lake Starlight. That way I'm close to work and Harper. I mean my child.

We've been getting to know each other for the past few weeks at her place. Her stomach has been bothering her, and she's been spending more time with her head in the toilet than anything, so it seemed the safest bet.

However, she's come around the last couple of days and insisted that we go do something tonight. I guess she's tired of being holed up in the house. So, I rebooked what we were originally meant to do the day that her sickness really took hold.

I was out on a run this morning when she left the house and in the shower when she returned from work, so I haven't seen her all day. When I walk in the kitchen, I find her wearing black leggings and a thin cropped sweater, but it's not how sexy she looks that catches my attention—though she looks incredible, and my dick notices too. I'm taken aback by the small swell of her belly.

She must notice where my gaze transfixes.

"I know, right? It just kind of popped. I noticed it this morning." She gently pats her stomach.

Some weird surge of male pride swells my chest. "It seems like it came out of nowhere."

"Tell me about it," she says with a smile, but she must notice my eyes haven't left her stomach. "Do you want..." She shakes her head.

"Yes," I answer, hoping we're talking about the same thing.

"Okay." She removes her hands from her stomach, and I slowly walk over to her.

My hand reaches, but I hesitate for a moment, my palm stretched over but still millimeters away.

"It's okay." She takes my hand and places it on her stomach. I cradle the small swell in my palm, and my fingers widen.

"Damn," I say softly. "They're growing." I push back the tears in my eyes.

"Let's not use plural. Twins do run in my family." She laughs, and I look up at her. She stops, and our eyes catch.

"Amazing, isn't it?" I ask.

"Yeah."

I remove my hand, and she straightens, both of us ignoring that pull once again.

She clears her throat. "So where are we headed?"

"Anchorage."

Her head rocks back. "Really?"

"Do you want me to tell you what we're doing?"

"Hell no. I love surprises." She walks past me toward the front door, and the scent of her flowery perfume trails behind her.

Fuck. There goes my dick again.

That scent throws me right back to the night we spent together. It was all over the sheets after she left the hotel room and had me reliving everything we'd done on said sheets until I checked out the following day.

"You coming?" she calls from the front door.

Not at the moment, but I have a feeling I will be later tonight to thoughts of you.

"Yup." I grab the truck keys off the counter. "Let's do this."

AN HOUR LATER, we pull into a parking space at the community college.

"Newsflash, I sucked at school the first time around, Finn. I'm not keen to do it again."

I turn the truck off and shift in my seat to look at her. "I thought you liked surprises?"

"I do, but not the kind that involve school." She's frowning, and there's something more behind her reaction, but I want to keep this light.

"We're not here for class. Well, not really."

Her head tilts. "Not helping."

"Come on. It will be fun, I promise."

With a sigh, she puts her hand on the door handle and exits the truck. I meet her at the front, and we head inside.

"I know I said I like surprises, and I do, but I'm feeling a little anxious now. Can you give me a really big hint?"

I stop her with a hand on her elbow. She turns and looks at me before we enter the building.

"We're just doing a cooking class. I noticed that neither one of us is even close to line cook status—no offense—and I thought we could brush up on our skills."

Her shoulders relax, and she smiles. "That I can handle. No promises I'll be able to do anything more than boil a pot of water by the end though."

I chuckle and hold the door for her, then tell her the classroom number we're supposed to find. It takes us a few minutes, but we do locate it.

The classroom is for the culinary arts students and is essentially a large kitchen with all the cooking equipment running in a large U shape along three of the walls and rows of stainless-steel tables in the middle of the room.

There are already some other people in the classroom when we enter. It appears that it's mostly couples, which I guess I should have expected, but I didn't really give it a lot of thought.

"Welcome, welcome." The instructor, an older woman in her fifties with curly dark hair to her shoulders and glasses on, waves us inside. "Just pick any station you want. We're going to get started in a few minutes."

When she starts the class five minutes later, it's us and five other couples.

She claps her hands together, and the quiet conversations going on around the room trail off. "I'd like to take a moment to welcome everyone to class. We're going to focus our efforts tonight on preparing a meal from start to finish, including an appetizer and a dessert. And the best part is that you get to take everything with you to enjoy."

A few yelps and woohoos ring out through the class.

"My name is Ellen, and I've been an instructor here for more than twenty years. Before we get started, I always like to get a quick introduction from everyone so we know who we're working with tonight. So when I point to your group, please let me know your names and what brought you here tonight."

She points at the couple farthest from us, who are here to celebrate their anniversary. Next up is an older couple who have been dating a while, then a couple who thought it would be something fun to do to have a night away from the kids.

It's not until she points in our direction that I realize we probably should have talked about what we were going to say. Harper looks at me wide-eyed, waiting for me to answer.

I raise my hand in greeting. "Hi, everyone. I'm Finn, and this is Harper." I clear my throat and decide that I'm just going to be honest about the reason I brought us here, minus some of the details. "We're expecting a baby in the spring, and neither of us is particularly adept in the kitchen, so I thought this would be a fun way to better our skills."

"Can you put chicken nuggets and fries on a baking sheet and turn on the oven? If so, you'll be all right," says the woman who said she was here with her husband for a night away from her kids.

Everyone else in the class laughs, including Harper.

"Congratulations," Ellen says, then moves on with the class, explaining what we'll be doing first.

I lean down to speak into Harper's ear, and her floral

scent hits me again, making my dick twitch. "I hope that's okay. Seemed easier than explaining to everyone what the situation is between us."

She turns her head to look at me when she responds, and our lips brush. She blinks and covers her mouth, stepping back. "Sorry. Yeah, that's fine. No biggie." Then she turns and gives her full attention to Ellen.

We do a pretty good job of putting together the appetizer and the main dish, and while the pork tenderloin cooks in the oven, we move on to making a chocolate mousse for dessert. We've got our chocolate, butter, cream, sugar, and eggs ready to go in front of us.

"Okay, it says to beat the sugar and egg whites together until they're foamy."

Harper looks at me. "Do you know how to separate the egg whites from the yolk?"

I cringe and shake my head. "No, but I can give it a try." Ellen demonstrated for us before she sent us off to work on our own.

Harper slides the glass bowl in front of me. I pick an egg from the carton, crack it on the side of the bowl, and try to do what Ellen did, moving the yolk from one half of the shell to the other, allowing the egg white to fall into the bowl. It's going okay until the third pass when it slips off the edge of the eggshell and falls into the bowl.

"Shit."

Harper giggles.

I arch an eyebrow. "You think it's easy? Why don't you give it a try?"

She doesn't back down from the challenge, shrugging. "All right."

She bumps me with her hip, and I slide to the side so she can stand in front of the bowl. That's one of the things I hope our child inherits from their mother—her backbone and the way she seems to go at everything straight on.

Harper cracks the egg, but she doesn't even get the chance to separate the yolk from the white because she cracks it too hard and the entire egg slides into the bowl.

"Shoot." She frowns at it.

"Hey, guys, how's it going?" Ellen looks at our bowl and cringes. Yeah, we're not killing it at this cooking thing.

"Neither of us can crack an egg and separate it," I say.

"Not to worry, that's why they invented these." She holds out something that looks like a large metal spoon with slim gaps along the outer edge. "It's a yolk separator. Toss those eggs in the trash, and I'll show you how it works."

Harper dumps the eggs in the bowl into the garbage, then slides it in front of Ellen. She shows us how to use the separator, and the egg whites slide nicely into the bottom of the bowl, leaving the yolk resting on the large spoon.

"Oh, that's so much easier," Harper says. "Making us do it the hard way, I see, Ellen."

Ellen hands a kitchen tool to me. "I just like to get everyone to try to do it themselves because not everyone has one of those." She winks, then walks over to next couple to check on them.

"This should be easy now," Harper says with a smile.

We work through the recipe, not having any more trouble now that we've handled the egg white situation.

We work well as a team, one of us naturally stepping in to handle a step in the recipe while the other one plays the role of assistant, then we switch without even discussing it. I'm hopeful it's a sign of things to come when we coparent together.

"Can I ask you something?" I ask as Harper folds together the cream and egg yolks.

She glances at me quickly before returning her attention to the bowl. "Sure, what's up?"

"You seemed to have a reaction to being at a school when you thought maybe I'd signed us up for a class or something. As if you thought I'd planned for us to prep for the ACT test."

The corners of her lips tighten. "It's a sore spot for me. I was never good at school. I got by, but it was always a struggle." She shrugs. "My dad was a teacher, and my mom was a principal, so I always felt like it should come easier to me, you know?"

The impression I've always gotten from Harper is that her parents are supportive, though I've yet to meet them. "Did they make you feel that way?"

She shakes her head. "Not especially. I mean, they'd be on me when I didn't study for a test—which was most of the time—or if I handed in an assignment late. But any parent does that. I just always felt like because they worked at our high school, I should have represented them better than I did. God knows my brother did."

"He did well at school?"

"Easton wasn't a scholar, but he did better than me. He had to be a good student so it would help him get a scholarship to play baseball in college." She sets the rubber spatula against the edge of the bowl. "I think we're ready for the chocolate."

"I'm sorry. That sucks." I hold the bowl of melted chocolate over the other bowl, and Harper uses the spatula to slowly fold it into the mixture.

"It's partly my own fault. I think when I realized that I could never live up to anyone's expectations, I just stopped trying and maybe went too far the other way to make sure they didn't have any expectations for me, period."

My chest pinches. I hate hearing her feel anything but the way she should—proud, confident, and successful.

"Were you good at school?" she asks. She's done folding in the chocolate, and she brings the spatula up to her mouth. Her tongue darts out, and she licks off the chocolate mixture.

My eyes widen, my heart rate picks up, and my dick twitches. I have to dart my glance away. "I was okay. Not a star student, but I got by."

"Well then, hopefully our baby will inherit your genes in that regard."

My gaze snaps back to hers, and I frown. "Hey, don't do that."

"Do what?" She appears genuinely perplexed.

"Sell yourself short." Harper has some chocolate beside her mouth, and I can't stop myself from bringing my hand up to cup her cheek and swiping it with my thumb. "You're an intelligent woman who runs her own successful business. A woman who was fully prepared to raise this child on her own if it came down to that. You're kind, almost always look at the bright side of things, and you care deeply for the people who matter in your life. Just because you didn't pull an A+ average in high school or college doesn't mean shit. None of that determines your worth."

Harper's eyes widen, and the space between us heats. My palm feels as if it's on fire where it rests against her cheek, and my lips tingle, wanting to feel hers again.

"All right, everyone." Ellen claps her hands at the front of the room. "We should be finishing up with the mousse right about now so that we can take the pork out of the oven in a few minutes."

I drop my hand from Harper's face, and she looks away from me, turning back toward the table to spoon the mousse into the smaller takeaway containers so we can leave with it.

I'm not sure what it is about this woman that makes her so irresistible, but I need to get a handle on my attraction to her before it ruins everything we're trying to build.

twenty-four

HARPER

The weekend after our cooking class, feeling emboldened by how well we did, Finn and I go to the grocery store together to grab some items for a recipe we're making tonight. It's a Mexican lasagna recipe with green chilis. Not super complicated, but it seems like something that will be good to make a few nights after the baby is born. Or we can make some ahead of time and freeze it.

Finn grabs a grocery cart, and we make our way through the store, working from the list we made. My appetite is back again, so we're grabbing some staples too.

"Oh shoot, I need to grab more prenatal vitamins while we're here. Don't let me forget."

"Why don't I just run and grab them now since they're not on the list?"

I smile. "Okay, that would be great."

"Here, you take over." He rolls the cart in front of me. "Be right back."

He walks down the aisle, and he has a really nice ass. It's perky and muscular. Must be from all his working out.

It's getting colder out at night now, but I'll still find him in the backyard going through his routine from time to time. He said he plans to join the gym in Sunrise Bay once it gets too cold outside.

I glance at the list and push the cart down the aisle but stop when I hear a familiar laugh from around the corner.

"Shit," I whisper, wondering if I should turn and head down the other way.

But it's too late when my mom and dad come around the corner together, my mom pushing a grocery cart as my dad looks to be chasing her. Gross, can't they at least keep their hands off each other while grocery shopping?

"Eww," I say, and my mom looks up. My dad's hand smacks my mom's ass.

Double eww.

"Harp," Dad says.

The next second, Finn says behind me, "Are these the ones you need?"

And this is the problem with small towns. Only one grocery store and my parents decide to go shopping the exact same time Finn and I do, meaning their first meeting is in the bread aisle. Great.

Giving my parents a smile, I motion to Finn beside me. "Mom. Dad. This is Finn. The baby daddy." I hold out my arm to him as if I'm a game show host showing the prize they won. Hello, this is Finn, and he's going to be a part of your life forever because he's the father of your first grand-child. I hope you like him.

Finn makes a choking sound and whips his head in my direction then looks back at my parents.

My mom rolls her eyes and shakes her head while my dad looks him up and down, appraising him as if he's the new RV he just won.

My mom is the first one to recover from the shock. She wheels her cart to meet mine and holds her hand out to Finn. "Forgive my daughter's bluntness. I'm Holly Bailey. It's good to finally meet you, Finn."

He shakes her hand, his face as red as the tomatoes we picked while asking how we know if they're ripe. "Likewise. Good to meet you too, sir." Finn moves his hand in front of my dad.

"Austin." The four of us stand in awkward silence before my dad breaks it. "Any luck finding a place?"

"No, sir. Nothing has come up in Lake Starlight. I'd considered moving to Anchorage for the time being, even if it wasn't ideal, but that feels too far from Harper and the baby. Plus, I'm working at the fire station here in town now, so—"

"Yes, congratulations," my mom interrupts, and I give her a look of gratefulness that she's stopped the conversation of us living together. "Stella told me you got your foot in the door there. That's wonderful. You were a firefighter back in Vermont, I take it?"

Finn goes on to explain how long he'd been in firefighting in Vermont and how he got into it in the first place. I listen with rapt attention as he details a fire at one of his friend's houses when he was there for a sleepover growing up and how as soon as he saw the firefighters fighting the blaze, he knew that's what he wanted to do.

He's still holding the prenatal vitamins, and I reach for them while he's talking. He passes them over while chatting with my parents, and I realize these aren't the ones I want.

"I'm just going to go grab the right ones," I say.

"Shit. Sorry, I thought those are the ones you have on the counter."

"It's not a big deal."

I turn to leave, but my mom calls, "I'll come with you." She steps up beside me.

"Holly," Dad says.

"You boys can find something to talk about until we get back." She hooks her arm through mine. When we're walking down the aisle that houses the vitamins and supplements, she leans in and says, "You two look... comfortable with each other."

We stop in front of the vitamins, and I jut out my hip and cross my arms. "What's that supposed to mean?"

She raises her hands in front of her. "Nothing at all. Just that living together must be going well."

I roll my eyes. "There's nothing going on between us."

She nods slowly. "Hmm."

"I'm serious."

She raises her hands. "It's not any of my business."

My head tilts. "True. But just so you know, there is nothing going on."

"All right, all right. I'll just say that, as your mother, if you *were* considering pursuing something, be very sure you think it has legs. Getting into something casual with the father of your child could make for problems down the road."

I huff out a sigh. "I know, Mom."

"I just worry about you, sweetie. And this little one." She pats the small bump on my stomach, eyes alite with joy. "You've popped."

"Yes."

My hands drop to my sides. As annoying as it is sometimes, I know my mom is coming from a good place. Oh god, that's going to be me some day offering unsolicited advice to this little one, isn't it? The thought makes me want to groan, but the realization tempers my mood.

"I know, Mom. Honestly, Finn and I have discussed it, and we both feel it's best to remain friends only."

To my surprise, she looks almost disappointed by this news. Isn't that what she just warned me about?

"All right, well, your dad and I would like to have you and Finn over for dinner so we can get to know him a little better. We were talking about it last night. We've laid off so that you guys could settle into... whatever you've settled into. Your brother will be back in town for a while once his season is done next week. How does that sound?"

I give her a tight smile. It doesn't sound ideal to me, but the fact is that Finn will be a part of their lives too, and it would make things easier if they at least knew him by more than his name and face.

"Just let me know a date, and I'll check with Finn and his work schedule."

She squeezes my shoulder. "Perfect. Well, I'm off. Your dad and I are headed over to Savannah and Liam's for game night, and you know how she gets when you're late."

We both laugh. My aunt can be a bit of a drill sergeant sometimes and is known to be super competitive on game nights.

"Have fun and tell them I said hi."

"Will do. I'll send Finn back your way." She waves over her shoulder and disappears around the corner.

I return the bottle in my hand to where it belongs and look for the bottle I want. A minute later, I'm hunched down, grabbing said bottle from the bottom shelf.

"Let me do that."

I turn my head to find Finn rushing down the aisle, pushing the cart in front of him.

"I'm fine." I grab the bottle and straighten. "There will be a time soon enough when I can't pull off that maneuver, and you can grab them. You don't need to baby me yet."

"I'm not trying to baby you." He takes the pill bottle from me and sets it in the cart. "I'm just trying to be helpful."

"You are. You have been." I glance behind him to make sure my parents are out of sight. "Sorry about the parental ambush."

He shrugs. "That's okay. I've been wanting to meet your parents anyway."

"You were?"

"Yeah." He heads down the aisle, and I walk beside him. "They're going to be the grandparents of our child. I feel like I should develop some kind of relationship with them, don't you think?"

"Yeah, for sure."

He smiles and holds out his hand. "Let's see what's left on the list so we can get out of here and start that lasagna. I'm starving."

I dig into my pocket and pull out the now crinkled piece of paper, passing it to him.

I know I just told my mom that nothing will happen between Finn and me, but he's making it really hard when he shows what a great guy he is. At least he'll be a great dad.

FINN

I'm back in Anchorage with Harper. There are only a handful of maternity clothing stores in Alaska, and we're at one of them.

Her stomach is only a little bigger, but she mentioned that the waists of her dress pants are getting snug and uncomfortable, so I suggested we go see if she could find something she'd be more comfortable in.

Shopping is far from my favorite thing to do, but that's beside the point. Harper needs something to wear throughout this pregnancy, and when I take a look at the first price tag on a sweater when we get into the store, I can see that this will cost a small fortune. She'll only be wearing these clothes for a few months.

"I want to pay for half of whatever we get here today."

She whips her head around from a dark green dress she's looking at on the rack. She wears green a lot—probably since it looks good on her. "I don't need you to buy my clothes, Finn."

"I know. But why should you have to pay for a whole new wardrobe? I can chip in. I want to."

She studies me, shrugs, then says, "Fine. If that's what you want."

Harper works her way through the store and picks out a few things. The saleswoman comes over and takes the clothes from her to start a changing room. Once Harper is satisfied that she's grabbed everything she's interested in, she turns to me.

"Come see what they look like on. I want your opinion."

"I'm not sure I'm the one to ask for fashion advice." I look down at my jeans, Henley, and light jacket.

She sets her hand on my chest and rolls her eyes. "You always look good, Finn." She shakes her head at me before walking to the back of the store.

I follow. The sales lady is waiting and directs Harper to the room with the clothes she picked out. Then she hands Harper a circular pillow.

"What's this?" Harper inspects it and looks at me as if I'd have any clue.

The sales lady says, "You strap that around your waist so that you can see what the clothing will look like when you're further along in your pregnancy."

"Oh, fun." Harper takes it into the dressing room with her, closing the door.

I sit in the chair outside the room, and a few minutes later, Harper comes out wearing a pair of dress pants and a black sweater. I do a double blink when I see the size of her belly. I know it's not our child that's made her stomach look swollen, but seeing her like this... my dick perks up and takes notice.

I think I have a pregnancy kink.

No. I have a Harper-pregnant-with-my-baby kink.

"You look great. I mean, the outfit looks great. How do you feel?"

"I think it will work." Harper rests her hands on her fake belly.

I swear to God, I already know I'm jerking off to thoughts of her rubbing her protruding belly later tonight.

Definitely a pregnancy kink.

I clear my throat. "Awesome."

Harper's head tilts, and she looks at me for a beat before going back into the changing room.

She continues in and out of the dressing room for three more outfits, and each one is hotter than the last. Every time she walks out of that doorway, I have to inhale deeply and try to think of something terrible—like some of the fire scenes I've been on—so that I don't sport wood.

She takes a while on the next outfit. When she doesn't come out after a few minutes, I ask if everything is okay.

Her head pokes out around the changing room door. "Can you zip this up for me?"

"Sure." I get up off the chair and join her inside the changing room, closing the door behind me.

Harper stands in front of the mirror, holding up her hair. The dress she has on gapes open, revealing her bare back.

I remember pressing my lips there the night we were together and running my tongue up her spine. When our gazes meet in the reflection of the mirror, I know she's remembering the same thing I am.

Our eyes remain on each other as I take the zipper in my fingers, slowly pulling it up. My knuckles drag against her heated skin as I work the zipper, and Harper's breath catches. A cascade of goose bumps races over her skin and a groan slips from my lips.

A sharp intake of breath sounds from her as our eyes meet in the mirror again.

I'm overwhelmed by her. Her beauty, her floral scent, her long, shiny deep red locks—the strands wound through her fingers where she holds it above her head—her energy, all of it.

Before I can think better of it, I lower my mouth to the curve of her neck. Rather than push me away, she exhales, eyes drifting closed, and leans back into me.

God, all I want right now is to worship this woman. Bring her pleasure. See her come.

My tongue traces a line up to her ear, and Harper whips around. I wait for her to push me away, tell me all the reasons why we can't do this. But she grabs my shirt and pulls me forward, her lips crashing to mine. I trace the seam of her lips with my tongue. She opens for me, and I get my first taste of her since the last time we kissed, which was way too long ago.

My dick is hard as stone between us, and when I jut my hips forward, I'm met with the softness of the fake belly. Wanting to feel her, I reach under her dress from behind until I feel the strap. The Velcro coming apart sounds like a needle scratch in the small space, but it doesn't deter us.

Harper's hands are in my hair, and when she yanks on it, I toss the belly to the floor and spin her around, backing her up so her back is against the wall, and she's facing the mirror behind me. I continue kissing her and slide my hand down and up under her dress until my fingers rest at the edge of her panties.

"Can you be quiet?" I whisper before sucking her earlobe.

She bites her bottom lip and nods.

"Watch yourself come in the mirror. I've been dying to see you come since you left my hotel room the morning after."

My lips meet hers again as I slide my hand past the elastic of her underwear. My fingers crest over her mound and delve between her legs. She's already wet for me, and I bite back a moan.

I tease her, gently running my fingers from her entrance to her clit over and over again. Harper bites my bottom lip to hold herself back from moaning. Her hands fist my shirt as I tease her entrance with my middle finger, never giving her what she wants.

She pulls away from the kiss and pleads with her eyes to put her out of her misery, and it's my undoing. I push my middle and ring finger into her, using the heel of my hand to provide pressure on her clit.

In seconds, she covers her mouth with her hand to keep herself from making a sound. Her attention goes from my face to the mirror behind me, and a small moan does sound in her throat.

I rock my hand back and forth, my fingers soaked with her arousal, and I step to the side and turn my head so I can watch in the mirror.

Fuck. We look good. Harper's back is arched while she grinds her hips, so, so needy. My large body beside her, my hand between her legs, both of us fully clothed.

When I increase the pressure and the pace, Harper's eyes squeeze shut, and she wraps her other hand over the one already on her mouth, her hips bucking against my hand. Her body stiffens, and she jerks her hips again. Once. Twice. Then her body is like Jell-O. She's soft and pliant, and I know the only thing keeping her upright is my hand between her legs.

She lets her hands drop from her face and the back of her head hits the wall with a thud, eyes still closed.

I pull my hand from between her legs. I'm about to suck

her juices off each and every one of my fingers, but a knock sounds at the door.

Harper's eyes whip open in alarm, and her body goes rigid—so opposite of the relaxed and sated woman from moments ago. "Yes?" she croaks.

"How's it going in there? Do you need help with anything?" the sales lady asks.

"No, I'm good, thanks. Just finishing up." Harper widens her eyes at me.

"All right, just wanted to check on you because you've been in there awhile, and I don't see your partner here anymore."

"All good! He was just unzipping the dress for me," Harper says, sounding anything but natural.

I have to work to keep my laugh inside while Harper gives me a stern look.

As soon as it seems the woman is gone, she turns her back to me and whispers, "Can you unzip me?"

I do so quickly, and she turns back around, silently shooing me out of the changing room.

I sit in the chair and think about what just went down. How much I enjoyed it. How much she enjoyed it. How it feels as though we've been dancing around the inevitable for weeks and weeks.

Maybe there could be something between us. If anything, living with Harper since I came to Lake Starlight has proven that we can get along and that we enjoy spending time together. We're definitely attracted to each other and not at a loss for sexual chemistry. What if we could be something, could be a couple, a real family? Wouldn't that be best for our baby?

Suddenly, images of the two of us play through my mind—us pushing our baby on a swing in the park,

Christmas Eve tucking in an excited toddler and reading them a bedtime story, Harper bringing our child to the fire station and me showing him or her around.

Before when I used to think of the two of us together, I was scared and unsure. Now, it just feels right. And I think it's about time I tell her I want more than the coparenting thing we agreed on.

When Harper comes out of the dressing room, I open my mouth to address what just happened and what it might mean, but she speaks before I can.

"Thanks for the great orgasm, but that can't happen again," she says under her breath.

I blink several times. Every part of me wants to argue with her and tell her she's wrong, but there's a look of steely determination in her eyes. Determination and… fear. So, I nod. "Okay."

Disappointment soaks in like lotion on my skin, coating me from head to toe.

She nods and walks out, clothes in hand, without giving me a backward glance.

The problem is that every time I blink, the expression on her face when she came is all I can see, and it will haunt me forever if I never see it again.

twenty-six

HARPER

Things have been strained between Finn and me since the dressing room incident. Telling him we couldn't do anything like that again went against everything I felt inside. But it was the right thing to do.

I'm the screwup. No, I don't mess up enough to land myself in jail or anything. But if there's a mistake to be made, I usually make it. Like the time I accidentally put unleaded in my cousin's truck because I wasn't paying attention. Or the time my dad asked for help with dinner, and I got distracted, causing the entire grill to go up in flames. Once I referred to my brother's girlfriend by his ex's name, which caused a whole thing. Well, Easton should thank me for that one. She wasn't near good enough for him.

The point is, I can't trust myself yet. If I want something, it probably means it's the wrong decision to make. Sure, we all laugh about it, and no one is mean to me or tries to make me feel bad. They just think that's how I am, that bad things happen to Harper, but what if I'm the cause of them?

So, I won't screw this up. This is my child we're talking about, and I can't afford to do anything that could possibly lead to me messing up my relationship with his or her dad. I don't want her or him to be living in a situation where their parents can't be in the room together. I want a mature relationship, one where we have a great friendship.

It's a shame though.

It really is.

Because what we did in that dressing room was one of the hottest things to ever happen in my life.

I'm sitting at the breakfast bar, moving my oatmeal around with my spoon, daydreaming about what went down, when the front door opens. A quick glance at the clock tells me it's a little after eight in the morning, so it must be Finn.

He's been at the firehouse since yesterday morning and is just coming off his shift. When he walks in wearing his black uniform, it does absolutely nothing to ease the desire I've been denying.

"Morning. I grabbed you a decaf coffee at Brewed Awakenings and scored the last green tea donut from Sweet Suga Things."

It's not just his looks and our chemistry that attracts me to him, but things like this. He's thoughtful and considerate, and he's been nothing but supportive.

"Thank you. How was your shift?"

He sets the drink and donut in front of me. "Pretty boring. Which is a good thing. Just makes for a long shift."

"Yeah, I suppose a busy day for you is a bad day for someone else."

He chuckles and sits on the stool next to me. "Hey, good news. I have a lead on a place in town. One of the guys at the station bought a house and is moving out of his rental at the end of the month. Said he'd talk to the owner for me."

"Oh... yeah, that is good." I force myself to smile.

I know this was the plan all along, but his words take me by surprise. The truth is, I don't want Finn to move out. He's been easy to live with, and we get along. But I suppose it's for the best. Maybe a little distance will help me remember what this is and is not between us.

Besides, I think Maven's been keeping her distance with Finn here. She's barely home these days. I don't think she's uncomfortable having him here, but I think she assumes we have things we need to work out between us.

"With any luck, I'll be out of your and Maven's hair in no time."

I give him a tight smile then take a bite of my donut to prevent myself from begging him to stay. My phone buzzes on the counter beside me, and I take the opportunity for the distraction, picking it up. I see that it's a text from Palmer, so I unlock my screen to read it.

> OMG were you and Finn getting it on at the maternity store?

My eyes widen. "Oh, shit."

"What's wrong?" Finn asks from beside me.

I set the donut down, lick my fingers clean, then clench my phone in both hands to pull up the Buzz Wheel app. Usually I check the app most nights, but I was tired and bored last night with Finn at work, so I went to bed early and haven't seen what they posted.

"What? The baby?" Finn's worried voice permeates my thoughts, but I can't look away from the screen.

BABY BUMPS AND BABY DADDY

I have it on good authority that Harper Bailey, along with her baby daddy in tow, visited Anchorage to do a little maternity clothes shopping. But from what I'm hearing, they walked away with more than just some new outfits. Things got pretty hot and heavy in the dressing room from what I'm told. Does this mean these two are an actual couple now? Has Finn gone from baby daddy to boyfriend? Time will tell. Either way, good for you, Harper! Pregnant women deserve to have some fun.

I groan and pass my phone to Finn, feeling the tension in his body ratcheting higher as he reads.

When he's done, he sets my phone on the counter. "There really is no such thing as privacy around here, is there?"

"We were in Anchorage. We should have been fine," I grumble.

"This is my fault. I should have never…"

"It's not like I was an unwilling participant, Finn. Maybe I wasn't as quiet as I thought." I glance at him to see his nostrils flare, his jaw set. He hasn't been quiet about his feelings for Buzz Wheel. "I'm sorry you have to deal with this. That this kind of thing goes with the territory around here."

He frowns. "You don't have to apologize."

"You're angry. I should know better."

Finn cocks his head. "I'm not angry."

"Then why do you look so intense right now?"

His shoulders relax a little, and he chuckles. "Because you brought up how loud you might have been, and that made me remember you coming in that mirror and how hot it was. I'm not angry, Harper, I'm horny and trying to tamp it down."

All the air rushes from my lungs. I don't know what to say. "Oh."

"Yeah, oh." He has an amused grin. "Anyway, how do you want to handle this? Like what do I say if someone brings it up?"

"Just deny, deny, deny. That's all you can do. No one will believe you but deny it anyway."

He gives me a sharp nod. "Okay."

I pick my phone back up to type out a message to Palmer.

> I'll fill you in later.

I set my phone down, and it buzzes again almost immediately, but I ignore it. She'll have to wait for the juicy details.

The two of us eat in silence for a few minutes, both in our heads.

"Are you going to the gym tonight?" I ask once the silence feels too awkward.

He shakes his head. "No, actually I have to work."

I frown. "Shouldn't you have a few days off?"

"Remember how I told you I was going to talk to the captain about flying down to Vermont to pack up the rest of my things and drive my truck back here?"

I nod and pop the last piece of my donut into my mouth.

"He said I could take the time to do so. I'll leave in a couple of days."

"Oh, that's good." I ignore the way my chest pinches at the thought that he'll be gone for a bit. "So, you have to pick up some extra shifts before you go?"

"Sort of? He said that if I go do the annual safety and

first aid presentation at the Northern Lights Retirement Home, then I can take the time I need to drive back."

I try and fail to keep a burst of laughter inside me.

Finn's forehead wrinkles. "What's so funny?"

"Well, I'm pretty sure I know why he agreed." I continue to try to stifle my laughter.

"What do you mean?"

"You've been there, Finn. You saw the residents."

He shrugs. "They were definitely interesting, but they're just a bunch of senior citizens. How bad could it be?"

Any filter I had to not laugh breaks. "They're going to eat you alive, Finn. I need some entertainment, so I'm going with you."

He rolls his eyes. "Harper, I'll be fine."

"Even so, I'm coming." I shake my head and slide off the stool to grab a paper towel to clean up all the crumbs on the counter.

"Be ready to leave at six."

"Will do."

I don't need reality television. This will be like watching a reunion of my favorite show.

twenty-seven

FINN

I pull the truck into the parking lot at Northern Lights Retirement Home. I can't help but reflect on how different things are since the last time I was here. Tonight, the woman sitting beside me is my pregnant one-night stand and not my fiancée.

It dawns on me that this is the first time I've thought about Tamra in weeks. If that doesn't tell me that it was a bad idea to be marrying her even under fake promises, I don't know what does. I still worry about my parents though. When I called my mom earlier to tell her I'd be home in a few days to pack everything up, she said everything was okay, but I could hear the underlying stress in her voice.

I couldn't help feeling guilty for not being able to help them any longer, even if they didn't know about my plan in the first place.

After I've turned the car off and am reaching for the door handle, Harper's hand lands on the wrist of my hand that's still on the console. "Before we go in there, I just want to say that the most important thing is to not show fear.

They can sniff it out like a bloodhound, and if they know you're afraid, it will only make it worse."

"Why are you talking like I'm headed to war? This is a bunch of senior citizens we're talking about. It will be fine."

She opens her mouth to say something more, but I push open the door and exit the truck, grabbing the large first aid bag we use on our calls from the back seat.

I get my first indication that maybe Harper isn't exaggerating when we're met by Leann, and she takes one look at me and chuckles to herself. "I see they sent fresh blood this year. Well, good to see you again." She gives me a nod and a smile, then looks at Harper. "Are you here for moral support?"

"Something like that," Harper says.

Leann leads us around to a large room that's been set up with rows of chairs. A bunch of seniors are sitting in them and a few are in wheelchairs on the outside of the rows. At the front of the room is an open space where I suppose I'll be giving my presentation.

I follow Leann and set down the first aid bag. Harper sits in an empty seat in the front row.

Until this moment, I forgot that she'd be watching my entire presentation. I'm not sure why that makes me nervous, but it does. It shouldn't matter to me, but I want to impress her. I want her to see me as capable person who will be able to handle the stress of raising a child.

"All right, everyone, listen up." The murmuring in the crowd quiets down. "Finn is here from the Lake Starlight Fire Department and has been sent to do the annual safety talk with you all. Please give him the courtesy of your attention."

"He's cute," a woman says, though I'm not sure who.

"Must be a bad boy. Look at all those tattoos," another says.

"I've got some tattoos I can show you, Lois. Come to my place after," a man says.

I clear my throat and shift my weight from one foot to the other.

"Enough talking. Everyone, please give Finn a warm welcome." Leann turns, so only I can hear, and says, "If they're a real problem, have Harper come find me."

Smiling, I nod then turn my attention back to the audience. "Okay, thanks for having me here tonight. My name is Finn and—"

"Speak up, I can't hear you," a plump man in the back calls.

I raise my voice and continue with what I was saying. "My name is Finn and—"

"Louder," he calls.

A quick glance at Harper, and her lips are pursed together as if she's trying not to find the humor.

"My name is Finn, and I've been a firefighter for—" I feel as though I'm yelling at a rock concert.

"Too loud," the man in the back says, then he and his buddy to his left laugh. "We're just messing with you. I could hear you just fine the first time."

The entire room dissolves into laughter at my expense.

After inhaling a cleansing breath, I start over. "My name is Finn, and I've been a firefighter for almost a decade. I'm here tonight to go over some basic safety and fire prevention tips that will help you at the retirement home, and also some basic first aid tips should you need to administer them until someone else arrives to help. Feel free to let me know if you have any questions as I go, or I'm happy to take them at the end."

When no one says anything, I nod and start my presentation. I go through why space heaters can be a problem and why those who smoke have to do it outside of the building in the designated areas, then I get into first aid. So far, everyone in the audience has been attentive and quiet and no problem at all.

Maybe Harper and Leann were just trying to spook me or something.

"Now we're going to move into the first aid portion of the presentation, but before we do, does anyone have any questions about what we just talked about?"

"Aren't you the same guy who was here with his fiancée a while back?" an elderly lady with dyed red hair says from the front row.

I remember meeting her the day Harper was showing Tamra and me around. I think I remember her name being Alice.

"I, um…" I glance at Harper, unsure what to do. "I'm no longer engaged."

"No doubt since you knocked this one up," an elderly gentleman seated beside Alice says. He gestures to Harper at the end of the row.

"If we could stay on track, that'd be great." I bend down to grab the first aid kit to pull out some things to use for demonstration purposes.

A man calls from the second row, "I have a question."

I straighten up and nod in his direction. We also met him the last time I was here. Melvin maybe? "Sure, what's your question?"

"If my little blue pill makes big Melvin stand at attention all day, what can I do about that?"

I clear my throat and glance at Harper, eyes wide. I thought she was here to help me. Based on the looks of things at the moment, she's just here to enjoy the show. She looks as though she's trying her best not to laugh.

"Well, I'd definitely speak to a doctor about that, if it's a problem for you." I clap my hands together in front of me. "Okay, let's move on to some basic first aid. Things that are good to know and can help someone until the paramedics arrive."

I go through the basics of applying pressure to a wound and, if it's bad enough, tying a tourniquet to stop the bleeding. Then I tell them about the signs of a heart attack or stroke and how they can differ between men and women.

"Is anyone familiar with CPR?"

A few hands go up in the room.

There's no denying that it would be hard for a lot of the individuals here to effectively deliver CPR, but even a small intervention can be the difference between someone living and dying.

I begin to explain the basics of how to deliver CPR effectively, but a woman with dark gray hair stops me. "I think you should demonstrate on someone. That would make it easier for us to understand."

"Great idea, Jean. She's right," Alice says.

I nod. "All right. Would you like to come up and help me?"

She scowls and shakes her head. "None of us can do it. We'd never get up off the floor. Harper, dear, go help the poor boy."

I blink at Jean, taken aback by her referring to me as a poor boy.

But Harper stands and walks toward me. "It's easier to just go with it," she says under her breath. "It will get this over with faster if you do."

"Let me grab a blanket from the kit before you get on the floor," I grumble.

I lay it out flat on the floor, then help her get down. She stretches out onto her back, staring up at me. Positioning myself beside her and facing the audience, I get onto my knees.

I start with why CPR is so important and what it's doing, then explain compressions, pointing to where on Harper's chest would be the correct spot to administer it.

"I think you should show us. Where do we place our hands?" Alice asks, leaning forward in her seat.

With a sigh, I show them how to arrange their hands, then look down at Harper. "Are you okay if I put my hands on you?"

"You've already had your hands on her from what I hear," the man beside Alice says and laughs.

"Maybe it was an immaculate conception," Melvin says, and everyone laughs harder.

My face heats with embarrassment. I feel like a comedian, but I'm not telling any jokes.

Harper turns her head and looks at the audience. "Knock it off. Finn is here to help you guys out."

That quiets everyone, and I give her a small smile in thanks.

"You'd place your hands here." I place my hands in the middle of Harper's chest, just below where I gauge her nipples probably are.

Do not think of Harper's nipples.

I don't press down on Harper's chest, but I shift, showing them how if they move their weight over their hands, it can help to increase the pressure.

"What about the mouth? When do we do that?" someone from the back calls.

"How can we do it at the same time as the pressing on the chest?"

"Lois, let's practice. Come over to my place tonight."

I try to block out the talking, but it's impossible. Harper's smile and laughter is the only thing that's getting me through this.

"Over top of the other person's mouth," I deadpan.

"Show us," Melvin says.

"I don't need to show you guys. You know where the mouth goes."

"But how does it fit over it? Is it like kissing?" Jean asks.

I roll my eyes and lean down over Harper. "You're going to be on the side of them, so it's not like kissing. You'll plug their nose and make sure your mouth is covering theirs so no air escapes."

Harper and I lock eyes. I feel her breath on my face. I'm so close, and her flowery scent drifts up to me. My heartrate picks up, and everything around us melts away for a moment.

Until all the senior citizens in the audience chant, "Kiss, kiss, kiss."

I blink and look away from Harper, breaking the spell. Does she look disappointed? I think she does, but she's the one who said we need to stay platonic.

"This is ridiculous." Standing, I bend to help her up off the floor. "All right, everyone, I think that's enough for tonight. If you have any last questions, you can come up and ask me."

I pick the blanket up off the floor and fold it as Melvin makes his way up to us slowly.

"Oh boy," Harper says under her breath. "What's up, Melvin?"

He looks between the two of us. "If you guys are looking

for a third for your throuple since his fiancée is gone, I wanted to put my name in the hat."

"What is with this place?" I shake my head, ignoring his comment as I pack up everything in my bag.

When I'm done, most of the people have left the room, and I find Harper talking to Alice near the door.

I make my way over. "You ready to go?"

Harper turns to me and nods. "Yup, let's get out of here."

She doesn't waste any time saying goodbye to Alice, and neither do I, then we're making our way to the exit, saying a quick goodbye to Leann, and getting the hell out.

"Well, that was interesting," Harper says, then she laughs uncontrollably before we're even two feet out the door.

I felt bad for Finn, but at the same time, it was so entertaining to see his reactions to the residents' questions. I'm used to how rowdy these senior citizens can get by now, but to a newcomer, it must be bizarre.

"I don't know if I'll ever recover, Harper. Melvin asked to be in a throuple with us." He shakes his head, then he laughs too.

It takes us a few minutes to recover before we make our way to his truck. He puts the large bag in the back and comes around to unlock my door and help me up into my seat. I don't need the help at this point, but I accept the offer, eager for the feel of his hands on me.

Once again, I scold myself because I shouldn't be thinking these things. Maybe it's a good thing he's found a place to move into. Perhaps a little distance is what we both need.

"At least that's over with. Hopefully there's someone with less seniority than me to do it next year."

"One can only hope." I chuckle. "You did a great job

though. I've never given much thought into what your job entails. I could never do it."

He starts the truck and rests his arm along the back of my seat while he looks over his shoulder to reverse the truck out of the space. I have to look away because there's something so innately sexy about that maneuver.

"Sure, you could." He puts the truck into drive. "You could do anything you set your mind to."

I shake my head. "Well first, there's the whole blood thing. I could never handle that. Second, I'd probably freeze and not know what to do. Or make the wrong decision. Or plan and then second-guess whether it's the right one. Either way, I'm not built for emergencies."

He frowns as he pulls out of the parking lot. "I think you need to have more confidence in yourself, Harp."

I'm adjusting my seat belt when he uses the shortened version of my name, and I still.

He must notice because he glances my way. "What?"

"You just called me Harp."

Finn shrugs one shoulder. "It just came out. Is that okay?" He takes another quick glance at me.

Only the closest people in my life ever use the moniker, but I love the way it sounds coming off his tongue. "Yeah, it's okay."

He doesn't glance in my direction, but he smiles as he looks at the road.

I realize something about what I've just said. "Wait. Oh my god. What if something happens and our child needs me, and I just freeze and I'm not able to help them?"

"That's not going to happen." Finn shakes his head.

"But what if it does?"

"If you're not confident about what to do after tonight, then I'll show you again and again until you are."

"I was paying attention. That's not the problem. I just think that when it comes time to use the knowledge, I won't be able to."

"You will, Harper."

I sigh. "I think you're wrong. It'd be just like me to make a bad situation even worse."

"Hey." Finn places his hand on my knee and squeezes as we're stopped at a light.

It's just my knee, but to my libido, you'd think he's squeezing my breast. I want to press my thighs together, but he'll know what's up if I do.

"Stop thinking of yourself like some screwup. I understand that you may not have been straight as an arrow when you were a teen, but you need to shed that image of yourself. That's not who you are now. Not even close." He shifts to make eye contact with me. "You're a capable, smart, successful woman with a helluva lot of heart. There's no part of you that should be apologizing for that."

His words sink in and hit their mark, dead center in my chest. I smile softly. "Thanks, Finn."

He nods then looks back at the road, pulling through the intersection.

Maybe I do need to let go of how I saw myself growing up and embrace who I am today. Shed it like a second skin. Some of Finn's confidence seeps in. I just hope it sticks around when the baby comes.

TWO DAYS LATER, I get a text from Finn while I'm preparing a vision board for a client I'm meeting later this week.

> Think you can get away for half an hour?
> I'm going to check out that place that's
> coming up for rent before I catch my flight.
> Would love your opinion.

There's that pinching sensation in my chest again. What the hell?

I already woke up grumpy because today is the day Finn flies home. Between packing everything at his place in Vermont, selling what he's not taking with him, saying goodbye to family and friends, and driving back to Alaska, he'll likely be gone for three weeks.

The reality of that is setting in, and I don't like the way it makes me feel—lonely, grumpy, and a little sad. As does the thought of him moving out. Now that Finn spends some nights at the fire station, I realize how much I miss his company when he's not around.

But I can't tell him that. We agreed that we'd maintain a friendship and nothing more. Anything else has the potential to be too complicated.

> Yeah. Text me the address and I'll
> leave now.

He does, and after locking up the office, I head down Main Street where I'm parked. It takes me less than five minutes to get there, and Finn's car is already parked in the driveway when I do. I park behind him, and he climbs out of the driver's side when he sees me.

"Hey, sorry to drag you away from work at the last minute," he says, shoving his hands into the pockets of his coat.

"It's no problem." I glance at the house. "So has your coworker already moved out?"

"Pretty much. He said he just has a few boxes to take with him. Want to take a look?"

I force myself to put on a smile as I walk toward him. "Sure."

We walk up to the house side-by-side, and Finn knocks on the door. A man who's probably a decade older than us answers. He has dark brown eyes that complement his russet skin.

"Hey, Shane, thanks for letting me come by and take a look. This is Harper."

Shane gives me a kind smile and extends his hand. "Good to meet you, Harper. Heard lots about you from this one." He nods at Finn, and if I didn't know better, I'd think that Finn's cheeks look a little red.

"All good, I assume." I give him a smile, and he laughs.

"Nothing but. Come on in, you guys." He steps back to let us inside. "I'm going to work on loading these last few boxes while you guys look around. Let me know if you have any questions."

Both Finn and I thank him, then Shane grabs a box from the pile in the living room in front of us and makes his way outside.

"Shall we?" Finn arches a brow and leads us inside.

The house is small—smaller than mine—but that's not a big deal. When we go upstairs, I realize there are two bedrooms up here and one small bathroom that's been remodeled with only a shower.

"What do you think?" Finn asks as I look around the space.

"There's no bathtub for the baby. It's not the end of the world." I shrug. "You could always use those plastic portable ones or something."

Finn frowns, obviously not having considered that. I'm surprised I did actually.

We walk over to the second bedroom to check it out. One wall has the door, one has the closet, another the window. I walk inside the room and over to the window. It's not a huge room, but then again, a baby doesn't need a lot of space.

Stepping over to the window, I look out it. "This window is a little drafty, so you'd have to put the crib on this wall." I gesture to the only other wall available.

Finn doesn't say anything, just watches me.

We continue the tour, taking a closer look downstairs. The living room is a living room, nothing special, and we head into the kitchen.

"There's no dishwasher. You're going to have to wash all the dishes yourself."

Again, Finn doesn't say anything, but a slight frown mars his lips.

"Well, that's it for my boxes. Do you guys have any questions?" Shane says from behind me.

Finn looks over my shoulder at him. "No questions."

"So do you want me to tell the landlord that you want the place?" Shane asks.

Finn opens his mouth to say something, and I open mine at the same time—to say what, I'm not sure.

"Do you mind giving us a few minutes, Shane?" Finn asks, keeping his gaze locked with mine. "We just want to have one more quick look around."

"Sure. I have to grab a couple things from the store around the corner anyway. I'll go do that and be back in, like, ten. Take your time."

I hear his footsteps get farther away, then the front door opens and closes, and it's just Finn and myself.

"Do you not like this place?" Finn asks, concern lacing his words.

I look away from him, down at my feet where I keep shifting my weight from one side to another. "It's not that…"

"Are you not comfortable with our child spending time here?" He steps closer until his feet are in my line of vision.

I look up, and it hits me like a sledgehammer to the heart. I don't want Finn to move out. Not at all.

"I'm sorry. It's fine. It works great." I shake my head and step back. God, I'm being a bitch, complaining about a drafty window and no dishwasher. What the hell?

"So I should take it?" he asks, his voice so quiet no one would hear him outside of this kitchen.

I glance up, and our eyes lock. Questions fill his hazel eyes. I inhale. "While we were walking around this place, I realized that you moving here means that we'll have to buy two cribs, two changing tables, two rockers… two of everything. And then he or she will have to split their time between your place and mine."

"That's coparenting, Harper." He takes another step closer, and the scent of his cologne and a scent that I've come to realize is just Finn wraps around me.

"I know." For some reason, tears prick the corners of my eyes. I feel at war with my body, wanting to tell him everything I want, but fearful I'll ruin my baby's future.

He cups my cheek with his palm. "Do you not want me to move out?"

I squeeze my eyes shut. What am I doing? What am I doing? This isn't what we agreed was best.

"Do you want to move out?" I ask.

"No."

My eyes snap open. He's looking at me with an intensity

I haven't seen since the dressing room incident, and I realize that he's been holding back the same way I have or because of me. It would just be like him to give me the space I needed.

"You don't?"

He shakes his head, still maintaining eye contact. "No."

We stand in silence for a beat.

"What does this mean?"

He presses his lips together. "I don't know. And unfortunately, we don't have time to find out right now because I have a flight to catch."

I nod, disappointment flooding my chest like the gushing rivers after the spring melt in the mountains.

"But we'll figure it out when I return, okay? I'll tell Shane I'm not interested in the place anymore, and when I get back, we'll decide together what it means for us, for our baby." He sets his hand on my small protruding belly.

My eyes drift closed. Something about the gesture calms and reassures me.

"Okay, we'll figure it out."

He nods then drops his hand from my stomach, stepping back as though it takes great effort to do so. "To be continued then..."

Something about the way he says it makes my toes curl. These next three weeks apart from him are going to feel like a year.

twenty-nine

FINN

I've spent the past couple weeks in Vermont packing up my apartment and either selling or donating my furniture. I thought maybe I'd feel melancholy about leaving here, but since my conversation with Harper about our living arrangements right before I left, all I feel is desperation to get back to Lake Starlight.

I'm just thankful that she had the guts to say something because I know I wouldn't have. But of course, she did. That's Harper. She takes life by the horns and doesn't let go. It's something I admire and something I hope our son or daughter inherits from her.

I don't know what it means exactly that I'm going to continue living with her, but I know it means that things have changed between us. We've acknowledged, without saying the words, that there's something more between us than friendship and coparenting.

I've known it but haven't acted on it. Something that became harder with each day that passed. Everything about Harper draws me to her, but watching her stomach slowly get bigger as a result of our growing baby has my desire for her at a fever pitch.

I'm starting to think that maybe I really do have a pregnancy kink. Jesus.

I push my hand through my hair and seal the last box with tape, then look around my near-empty apartment. My parents should be here any minute to say a final goodbye.

When I had dinner with them last night, I confessed to them the arrangement I had with Tamra. To say they were shocked and a little pissed was an understatement. I debated not telling them, but apparently Tamra has been telling everyone I dumped her out of the blue. I don't care that she's trying to make me look like the bad guy to save face, not really. I did agree to the plan and then backed out of it, but my parents were still struggling to understand why things had ended so abruptly and why I couldn't try to make it work, even though Harper is pregnant. I felt I owed it to them to tell the truth.

"Knock, knock." My mom does that thing she always does. She opens the door a bit, knocks on it, and says "knock, knock" at the same time.

"In here," I call from the kitchen.

My parents enter, my mom with tears in her eyes. She wasn't like this the first time I left. I think now that I'm back, packing up and giving away my belongings, it tells her I'm really leaving.

"You all set?" my dad asks, looking around.

"Yup, just have to load these boxes into the truck." I motion to the few boxes at my feet.

"I'll take these out for you." He nods to my mom, silently telling me we need to talk.

"Thanks, Dad."

He grips my shoulder, squeezing, then pulls me into a

hug, and pats my back before pulling away and bending to lift the boxes.

When he's out of the room, I turn my attention to my mom. There are no longer tears in her eyes—full blown tears are running down her face now.

"Mom…" I pull her into a hug, and she comes willingly.

After a minute, she draws away and wipes at her face. "Everything is changing, and that's not necessarily bad." She holds up a hand. "It's all just happening so quickly. And you're going to be so far away. As will our grandchild."

It's my only regret about any of this—the fact that I can't be closer to my parents. I know they'll make wonderful grandparents, but they're going to be the kind who fly in for holidays and know their grandkid more via video chats than in person.

"We want to get up there to meet Harper," my mom says.

"Okay, I'm sure she'd like that. Let me know when you think you can swing it."

I nod, knowing that it won't be until the baby is almost due since skiing season starts in a couple months, and there's so much to do to prepare. Then once the resort opens, there won't be a second to spare.

"We will. Oh, Finn, you're going to be a dad." She pats my cheek. "You're going to make a great father."

I take her hand on my cheek and grip it, pulling it down between us. "Only because I learned from the best."

That sets her off crying again until a couple of minutes later when she's laughing at herself. "Look at me. Such a mess. I promise I'll stop now."

I chuckle. "Okay, Mom." I shove my hands in my pockets. "Well, I'd better get going. Long drive ahead of me."

We both laugh. That's putting it mildly. According to my GPS, it's about seventy-five hours of driving, with most of it going through Canada.

I lock up and give the keys to Mom, who said she'll make sure my landlord gets them, then we walk over to the truck where my dad is waiting for us. After another hug and round of tears from my mom, I'm pulling away from the town I thought my life would play out in.

Whoever said life is full of surprises wasn't kidding.

thirty

FINN

Stopped in Quebec for the night.

Did you have poutine?

I did in fact. It was delish.

Did I wake you?

I wish. I've had trouble sleeping so I'm
still up.

Everything okay with the baby?

Yeah, it's not the pregnancy keeping me up.

A lot on your mind?

You mostly.

I know the feeling.

HARPER

How's the drive today?

Good. Just stopping for something to eat
by Lake Superior. Going to try and get a
few more hours of driving in today before I
call it quits.

Don't drive if you're too tired.

Aw, are you worried about me?

Just practicing for when this little one
arrives. ;)

How are you feeling?

Good. Just tired from sleeping so crappy.

Don't worry I'll be home to tuck you in at
night very soon.

FINN

Done driving for the day. Made it to
Winnipeg today.

You're getting closer!

When I look at the map it doesn't feel
that way.

I miss you.

Miss you too. It feels like you've been gone
forever.

Does Maven miss me too? :P

I think she just misses when you bring
donuts home after your shift.

Good to know. LOL As long as you miss me
that's all I care about.

Then you have nothing to worry about. xo

thirty-three

FINN

Made it to Sasktchewan today. You still up?

Yeah, still not sleeping well.

Tell me a bedtime story. Maybe it will help
me sleep.

All right. Once upon a time there was a boy
who was driving across the country to get
back to the girl he couldn't stop thinking
about. Every minute felt like an hour, every
mile like a hundred.

Oh, I like this story! What was the boy
thinking about the girl?

Mostly, he was thinking about how much he
missed her. How he didn't realize until he
was away from her how much she'd come
to mean to him. How much he liked having
her be a part of his life.

He sounds obsessed. Maybe he should be paying more attention to the road.

Probably, but she's pretty unforgettable.

thirty-four

HARPER

Saw my aunt today. Everything with the baby looks good.

I'm bummed that I couldn't be there with you. 🙁

Close to the border between Alberta and British Columbia.

You'll be there for the next one. That one is a big deal because they'll do the anatomy ultrasound to make sure everything is progressing as it should.

No chance I'm missing that. Send me the date, and I'll add it to the calendar.

Will do.

My brother got back yesterday so I had dinner at my parents' house tonight.

How'd it go?

It was fine. I thought E's eyes were going to pop out of his head when he saw me pregnant.

Well, you're the most beautiful pregnant woman ever so that tracks.

Gross, it's my brother.

LMAO

But thanks for the compliment.

Not a compliment. It's the truth.

thirty-five

HARPER

> How far did you get today?

Still in British Columbia but almost to the Yukon.

I was tired when I was driving and had to quit for the day early, but now that I'm in my motel I'm wired.

> Maybe I should tell you a bedtime story this time.

All right. Let's hear it.

Once upon a time there was a princess whose prince had to travel far away. Every day she would look out her window and wonder whether she'd see him approaching the castle. But every day she'd be disappointed that he wasn't there. With each day that passed she'd miss him more and more and would look forward to all the things they would do together when he returned.

I like where this is going...

LMAO

Keep going...

Hmm... I think I'll make you wait until tomorrow night. Something to look forward to. ;)

Tease.

You have no idea.

FINN

Stopped in Whitehorse for the night. I'm ready for you to finish that story.

I think you should pick up where I left off.

All right. I think you were talking about all the things the prince and princess might do when he returned. I have some ideas.

Like?

We could go take another cooking class.

Seriously!?

LOL Did you have something else in mind?

Tell me more about tucking me in at night.

Ah, yes. I'm looking forward to it.

Will you be tucking yourself in beside me?

Do you want me to?

I think you know the answer to that question.

Fuck woman, now I'm going to have blue balls for the next 900 miles.

FINN

I was hoping to plow through today and make it back but there was a detour that set me back.

Finn, what are we doing?

You getting nervous now that I'm almost home?

Maybe? I just don't know what we're doing.

Harp, if this is you asking me what I want, let me be clear. I want to be with you. I want to give this thing between us a go. I think we owe it to ourselves and our child. If it doesn't work, it doesn't work, and I think we're adult enough to still be able to coparent together afterward. But I think it can work. All I know is that when I'm not with you I'm thinking about you and wishing I was. And then when I'm around you all I want to do is to strip you down and hear you scream my name in pleasure again. One night wasn't enough for me. I want you all the damn time. But if you don't want that, I'll respect your wishes and never mention it again. So I suppose the question is… what do you want?

You.

See you tomorrow then. xo

thirty-eight

My phone rings, and I almost leap up off my office chair.

I'm wound so tight because today is the day that Finn returns to Lake Starlight. Our daily check-ins when he was done driving each day have felt like foreplay, as though we've been edging each other for days and days, and now that he's returning, my body feels as if it's a hair's breadth from combusting.

I knew when he left that I'd miss his company. What I didn't realize was how much. So much so that I was willing to admit to it over text apparently. It felt so much easier that way, not having to look him in the eye and tell him that my attraction to him is about more than our sexual chemistry. It was the chickenshit way out, which isn't usually my style.

But this feels big. As big as when I found out I was pregnant in some ways.

I pick my phone up off the desk and see Maven's name.

"Hey, Maven." I try to keep my voice relaxed so as to not give away where my head is at.

"Hey. How's it going?"

"It's going." I close my laptop. I can't concentrate on anything today.

She gives me a knowing chuckle. "You still expecting Finn home tonight?"

"At some point, yeah. I haven't heard any differently."

"Then I'm going to stay at my parents' place tonight. Give you guys some privacy."

"You don't have to do that. It's not a big deal." I spin the pen on my desk in circles. Anything to get rid of this pent-up sexual frustration that's coursing through my body.

"Come on, Harp, I've seen the way you've been acting since he's been gone. I think you guys have some things to figure out."

I frown, though she can't see me. "How have I been acting?"

"Like a puppy waiting for its owner to come home."

"Seriously?" I say with annoyance.

"It's not a bad thing. In fact, I think it's awesome. Finn is a great guy, and if you two can make a go of it, that's amazing for your child. I'll spend a few days at my parents' place, and then we can talk about where you're at, see what it means for me."

Guilt slides down my shoulder like bird poop. "I feel bad."

"Don't. We knew when I moved in that it wasn't a forever situation. I'll figure it out."

"Okay, well thanks. You're the best."

"Don't mention it. Have fun tonight." She singsongs the last part, and I laugh.

"Talk to you later."

After I hang up, I flop back into my chair. With every minute that ticks by, I get more turned on by the possibilities of what might happen when I see Finn again and also more nervous.

What if he pretends the things we said over text never happened? What if with every mile he drives closer to town, he second-guesses the way we were over text and decides it would be better not to take the risk?

My phone buzzes with a text on my desk, and I pick it up. It's from Finn. I straighten up in my chair and read his message.

I'm home. Where are you?

At the office. Leaving now.

I quickly pack up my things, lock my office, and walk to my car.

My fingers tap on the steering wheel with anxious energy the entire drive over. This is it. This is where things will either shift between Finn and me, or where he'll ignore our text messages, and we will forever remain friends and coparents but nothing more.

I hold my breath as I pull into the driveway and walk on numb legs toward the front door. With my hand on the doorknob, I take a deep breath and step inside. Disappointment floods me that he's not there waiting for me. I drop my purse at the front door and hang my coat on the hook, stepping farther into the house.

When I reach the bottom of the stairway, the bathroom door at the top of the stairs opens, and Finn walks out wearing only a towel. He stills when he sees me, and the way he looks at me with such hunger in his gaze leaves no room for doubt as to whether he's going to acknowledge all the things we implied with our texting.

"I wanted to be downstairs to greet you, but I wanted to

have a quick shower first. Get the grime from driving off of me."

He must not have been shaving on his cross-country trip, as he has a short beard now. I like it. It makes him look more mature, more manly, and like a protector, which I wouldn't have thought I was into, but apparently, I am.

I don't say anything as I make my way up the stairs. Finn's eyes devour me, and I do the same to him, taking in his dripping hair, the muscles and the tattoos across his chest and arms, the way he licks his lips as I get closer.

Once I'm at the top, he tugs me into him. My hands splay on the damp, warm skin of his pecs.

"Are we doing this?" he asks, his gaze intense, asking me one last time.

I don't hesitate. "Yes."

His lips are on mine the next second, and I moan into our kiss. Finn's hands thread through my hair, and my fingertips dig into the skin on his chest when our tongues meet. He directs the kiss, using the hands in my hair to tilt my head exactly where he wants it.

The fresh, outdoorsy scent of Finn's body wash surrounds me, and I press myself into him, desperate for friction on my heavy breasts.

One hand leaves my hair and travels down my back until he cups my ass. I swallow down his groan when he squeezes, then his hand travels around to the front, cradling my small bump.

He pulls away and looks down between us. "Your stomach really popped when I was gone."

It has. I don't look nine months pregnant or anything, but it's clear that I'm pregnant now, not bloated after a large meal.

I have a heartbeat of self-consciousness until he says,

"Fuck, that's hot. Just so you know, I'm pretty sure I have a pregnancy kink."

I laugh, but he doesn't.

"I'm serious. I see why your uncle Rome got your aunt Harley pregnant so many times."

"Can we not talk about my aunt and uncle right before we have sex?"

"Okay, scratch all that. Starting over… fuck, you're hot."

His words heat the blood in my veins, and I don't want to wait any longer to have this man again. I've waited long enough. So I dip one finger under the towel and pull forward, causing it to drop to the floor around his feet. Finn's proud erection is a steel rod, and the space between my thighs hums in anticipation.

"I like a woman who knows what she wants," Finn says, bringing his lips to my neck.

I sigh and arch my head back, pushing my hands into his hair. "Finn, don't make me wait any longer. Please."

He straightens. "Now how can I leave you waiting when you ask so nicely?" Finn takes my hand and leads me to my bedroom.

I don't feel guilty at all for checking out his muscular ass as I walk behind him.

Once we're inside, he flicks on the light, but I turn it back off. The sun is low in the sky and will begin its descent soon, so we can still see each other enough. And although he seemed to like what he saw of my tummy in the hallway, there's a difference between seeing it in clothes and seeing me naked.

Finn turns to face me. "Why'd you turn them off?"

I shrug a little shyly. "I don't know."

He tugs me into him. "Please, Harp? That night we were together, just the lamp on the far side of the room was on, and I didn't get a good look at you. I want to see you this time. Especially this." He settles his hand over my belly.

The way he's looking at me makes me feel beautiful, so I agree. He flicks the light back on.

"Can I undress you?" he asks.

I give him the once-over, standing naked and proud in front of me, seemingly without any self-consciousness at all. "Yes."

He slowly undoes the buttons of my silk blouse. With every button he loosens, the tension in my body increases. When they're all undone, he slides the soft material over my shoulders, and it flutters to the floor.

His breath catches as he takes in the black lace bra with green trim I wore especially for him today. Then he presses a kiss to my collarbone before dragging his tongue up the column of my neck until he reaches my ear. Goose bumps break out over my flesh.

"Did you wear this knowing what it would do to me when I saw it?" he practically growls in my ear.

"Maybe." My voice is breathy and barely there.

He tsks in my ear. "I'm going to make you pay for that."

"I look forward to it."

His hands slide around to the back of my skirt, and he undoes the button at the top and slides down the zipper before pushing the fabric down past my hips, allowing it to pool at my feet. Then he steps back to take me in.

"Matching panties." Finn grips the base of his cock and strokes. "You look like a fucking smoke show right now, Harp. Barely covered in this lace, your belly swelling with our child." He groans and squeezes the tip of his length.

"Do I look better out of it?" I reach behind and undo my bra, letting the straps fall over my shoulders and down my arms. Then I slide my panties down my legs and kick them away.

"Definitely better." Finn strokes himself, and the corded muscles in his forearm flex. "Now get on the bed so I can feast on you before I fuck you."

I squeeze my thighs together, remembering how much I liked when Finn took control the one night we were together. I do as he says, making my way over to the bed, and when I crawl up on my hands and knees, my backside facing him, he audibly groans. I turn around and lie down with my head on the pillow, and Finn stands at the end of the bed still stroking himself, his gaze roaming over me slowly as though he's cataloging each and every feature.

"I've been thinking about this every day since I left. Considering all the things I might do to you if I ever had you again, and now that I'm here in this moment, I can't decide what I want to do first."

"Guess we'll just have to do it over and over again." I give him my sultriest smile.

He crawls up the bed and comes to lie beside me, bending to kiss me then bringing his lips over my jawline and down my neck until his lips are wrapped around my nipple. The suction of his mouth causes both pleasure and pain because of how sensitive they are, and I moan, my hand diving into his hair. The scratch of his short beard on my breast only adds to the sensations culminating in a throbbing between my thighs.

Finn moves to my other breast and delivers the same treatment, flicking the nipple he just left with his thumb. I grow slicker between my legs and arch my breast into his mouth. After a few minutes, he travels down between my legs, pulling them apart for his attention. When I try to close them, he holds them open.

"You're beautiful everywhere."

Before I can respond, he dives in, his tongue stroking from my opening to my clit, where he sucks. The sensation almost sends me flying up off the bed, it's so intense. I'm not sure if Finn is just really good at this or if pregnancy has made me more sensitive than usual, but with a few strokes of his tongue, I'm already close to coming.

Maybe it's the fact that I've been thinking about this for three weeks, and now the time is finally here.

Finn continues to lap at me, driving me closer and closer to orgasm. My hand is in his hair, tugging, and my hips move in tandem with his strokes. Just when I feel the wave of my climax ready to crest over me, Finn pulls away.

I cry out in dismay, my gaze on him.

"Told you I'd get you back." He's grinning.

The son of a bitch is grinning.

Something like a mewl comes out of my mouth as I arch my back, silently begging for him to return to the spot between my legs, but he moves up my body and cups my face, kissing me. I taste myself on his tongue, and the way he kisses me leaves no question as to how much he wants me.

After a minute, he pulls away and looks down at me. "There's no going back if we do this."

I place my hand on his cheek too, maintaining eye contact. "I want this, Finn. I want *you*."

With one hand on his base, he pushes slowly inside me. Neither of us looks away from the other as he pulls out then pushes in a little further, again and again until he's fully seated inside me.

He gives me a minute to get used to the stretch of him, then he's moving over me. Something in my chest shifts into place, and I know for certain that he was right when he said there would be no going back.

FINN

Being seated inside Harper again feels like nothing I've ever known. It wasn't as if I forgot how amazing it was between us the night we were together, but now that I'm here again, I don't ever want to leave. I want to feel this always. The way her body hugs my cock at the same time that I have the taste of her on my tongue is utter perfection.

I slide out of her, and Harper wraps her legs around me as though she wants to prevent me from going any further.

God, she's beautiful. Always. But even more so with the swell of our child growing inside her.

Her breasts rock every time I push into her, her dusty pink nipples begging for my mouth, but I can't draw my gaze away from her face and the way she's looking at me. Almost as though she can't believe that we're here as much as I can't.

What was supposed to be a one-night stand led us both here, and though it's all unplanned, something about it feels so right.

Harper's hands travel up my arms and into my hair. I

want so badly to kiss her, but I don't want to crush her belly underneath me. I increase my pace, and we're both panting in minutes. I can tell she's getting close again, as am I. But I'm not ready for this to end, so I roll to my side.

"Finn!" The sheer desperation in her voice makes me smile.

"Want to see all of you." I pat my lap, and she grins, moving to straddle me.

Jesus, she's like a fucking dream as she grips my length and feeds it inside her, bringing all her weight down on top of me.

I cup the back of her head, bringing her lips to mine. "You're perfect, you know that?" The words are murmured against her lips, then I'm kissing her as she moves over me.

Sliding my hand between us, my thumb finds her swollen clit, and she gasps, breaking the kiss. Harper straightens, putting the slight swell to her stomach on display for me, and though I didn't think it was possible, my dick gets even harder.

With my other hand, I roll her nipple between my thumb and forefinger, and she arches her back, moving her hands behind her and onto my thighs for support. It gives me the perfect view of her body, and my balls tighten, ready to release inside her.

Increasing the pressure on her clit, Harper gasps and picks up the pace. I'm so close, the tingling starting at the base of my spine. There's no way I'm coming without her, so I increase my efforts and feel the first flutter around my cock as it drives inside her.

The contractions increase, then she bears down on me with a loud moan, and she's milking my cock with her orgasm. I spill inside her, my cock twitching as she wrings out every last drop.

Needing to be close to her, I sit up, still seated inside her, and wrap my arms around her body, drawing her in. Our sweat-soaked skin sticks together, and I keep us like that until both our breathing returns to normal.

When I pull away to see her, I use both hands to push her hair back from her face.

"That was…"

She doesn't need to finish the sentence. I know exactly what she means.

"Yeah, it was." I smile and place a chaste kiss on her lips. "Stay here. I'll get a washcloth to clean you up."

She rolls off me and lies down while I go to the bathroom, clean myself, and return with a warm washcloth. Kneeling on the bed, I wipe between her legs. I'd be lying if the vision of my cum leaking out of her didn't already have me half hard again, but I check myself. We have things to talk about.

After I've put the washcloth in the dirty clothes hamper, I join her in bed, pulling her into me. "You're okay? The baby is okay?"

I did a lot of googling in hotel rooms on my way across the country to make sure that having sex while a woman is pregnant in no way harms the baby or the pregnancy. Everything I found said that in a normal, healthy pregnancy, there's no reason why a woman can't be sexually active if she chooses. Thank God. Not that I wouldn't wait for her.

"All good." She places a kiss to my chest, and I kiss the top of her head.

"As much as I want to just fall asleep with you in my arms right now, I think we need to have a conversation to make sure that we're both on the same page as to what this is." She stills against my side, and I say, "I want to be very clear about my intentions. I want to be with you. In every way that a man can be with a woman. I want us to be in a committed relationship and try to figure out if we can make it work. Not just because we're having a child together, though it would be wonderful if things work out because of that, but because I like you, Harper. I like your zest for life, I like that you unapologetically go after what you want, I like that you let me see your softer, more vulnerable side. Everything I've seen, I like, and I just want more of it."

"I didn't know you were so mushy," she says, pressing her palm to my chest.

"Well, not all mushy. I really like fucking you too. Definitely want more of that."

She laughs and smacks my chest, then she's quiet for a beat, and I worry I divulged too much. I could scare her away. Does she not want the same things?

"Harp, talk to me." I use the arm wrapped around her to squeeze her side.

"I want all those things too, but I've never been in a relationship before. What if I mess it up?"

"You haven't?" I look down at her, and she shakes her head. A smile slowly tilts my lips.

"I've dated or had situationships for a period of time, but not a real meaningful relationship. Why are you smiling?"

"Are you kidding me? It's the best thing. Now I get to be your first and hopefully last boyfriend."

She smiles back, and I bend my neck to kiss her lips.

"There is one more thing I want to bring up so you know what you're getting into."

A frown mars her beautiful face. "What?"

"You know I'm an alcoholic. I've been good since I got sober. Most days I'd say I'm in full control of my impulses, but I can't promise you that every day in the future will be like that. There might be times when I struggle more than others. I need to know that you're okay dealing with that, supporting me through them." I hold my breath, waiting for her answer.

"What were you like when you were drinking?"

I consider my answer for a moment. "I wasn't an out-of-control drunk, probably more what you'd call a functioning alcoholic. But if I started drinking, I couldn't stop. Couldn't keep myself in check. At first, it was drinking when I had a weekend off and I was out with my friends. Then it was drinking on a weeknight if I had it off. Two nights a week turned into three turned into four. Once I realized it was a problem and tried to stop, that's when I figured out that I had an addiction and needed some support because stopping wasn't as easy as I thought it would be."

"I want to support you, Finn. I don't see it as a terrible thing. I think you're brave for admitting you had a problem and seeking out help. My uncle Jamison is an alcoholic—though he's been sober forever now. I'll be here to support you, but you could always talk to him too. He'll understand it in a different way than I can."

The tightness in my chest while I waited for her answer eases, loosens. "Maybe I'll do that."

We lie there in silence for a while, the cadence of our breath becoming a matching steady rhythm. I'm close to drifting off when Harper bolts up from my chest, props herself on her elbow, and looks down at me.

"There's something I wanted to ask you."

I can't help but smile at how animated she is. How she went from being almost asleep and pliant beside me to full of energy in half a second.

"What?" I prop my arm behind my head and take her in. The wild waves of her thick red hair, the freckles on her nose, the sparkle in her eyes.

"My aunt told me that at the next ultrasound, we can find out the sex of the baby. What do you think?"

I consider it for a moment. The idea of knowing—being able to choose a name, decorate the nursery, and prepare in a way that you can't when you don't know the baby's sex— appeals to me. But so does the idea of finding out when he or she is born. More than anything, I don't want to influ- ence Harper's decision. I can live with either.

"What do you want to do?" I ask.

She shakes her head. "Nope. You tell me first."

I chuckle. "I want whatever you want."

"Finn..." she says with a slight whine in her tone.

"How about this... I'll count us down, and we both say what we want at the same time. That way we know neither of us is just saying what the other person wants to hear. We can discuss from there."

She nods. "That works."

"All right. Three, two, one..."

"No!" we say at the same time.

The two of us dissolve into laughter, and she lies back down beside me, cheek on my chest.

"It's decided then. We'll wait until the baby is born. You get so few surprises in life. I think it will be fun to wait."

"You were a surprise. This was a surprise." I move my hand to rest on her stomach. "Sometimes life gives you amazing surprises."

HARPER

few weeks have passed since Finn's return, and we've fallen into a good rhythm. It's not that much different from how we were before we decided to be a couple. Only now, I don't sit on the opposite side of the couch as him. Now I hold his hand when we're walking around downtown or in the grocery store. And now he's beside me when I retire for the night.

Oh, and we have sex.

A lot of sex.

I'm not sure if it's pregnancy or just Finn, but my appetite is insatiable these days, and he definitely isn't complaining.

I've had good sex in my life, but sex with Finn is on another level. I'm not sure if it's because he's mastered his technique or if it's because there's something more between us. Something is building that I've never felt before, and it's equal parts exhilarating and terrifying. There's no way I'm going to acknowledge it first though.

Thankfully, my family has pretty much left us to our

own devices, letting us stay in this little bubble we've created for ourselves.

Today we're painting what used to be Finn's room and will soon be the baby's nursery. Finn has spent the past week moving the furniture that was in here into storage. We went to the paint store last week and picked a light beige since we're going with a neutral palette that will work for a boy or a girl. He wanted me out of the house while he painted, but we went with a low VOC paint so that I can help.

We're about a half hour in, and Finn is doing all the cutting before I can help with the rolling. He wouldn't let me get up on the ladder and didn't want me crawling around the floor to cut in on the baseboards.

For some reason, it's kind of hot watching him paint our baby's room. Maybe it's the way the muscles in his back and arms bunch with every stroke of the paint brush. Or maybe it's just that I get to admire his ass while his back is to me.

So while he does that, I sit with my legs crossed, looking through the website of the baby store in Anchorage that my mom suggested we register at.

"Babies sure come with a lot of stuff." It's not as though I didn't know that. Enough of my family have had kids over the years that I'm aware, but it feels different when it's for yourself. "So many things to decide on."

"We'll figure it out," Finn says to me over his shoulder.

I frown, staring at the screen. "Just for baby monitors alone, there's, like, a hundred different options. Ones with cameras and ones without. Ones where you place this mat under the baby and an alarm goes off if they stop breathing. And who knows which one to pick? Based on the reviews, some people say they love the mat because it gives them peace of mind, and others say it just gives them anxiety because they're waiting for the alarm to go off. And then some people say the alarm went off, and it was a false alarm, and now they're always afraid for their baby. Then others say it saved their baby's life. It's overwhelming." My chest feels tight when I look across the room at Finn.

He comes down off the ladder. "Harp, whatever we pick will be fine. Don't stress yourself out over it."

I shake my head. "But what if we pick the wrong thing? And we haven't even gotten into whether we're going to use cloth diapers or disposable ones. Of course there're a million options for those too. And will we give our baby a soother or just practice letting them cry it out? There are literally hundreds of decisions to be made."

Finn rests the paint brush on top of the open can and comes over to me, crouching so that we're almost eye level. "Hey, it's going to be fine. We'll make all these decisions together. You're not alone in this."

"But what if we make the wrong one?"

Some of this is my past insecurities coming out to mess with me. I've never been good at handling stressful decisions. For other people's weddings? Sure. For myself? I've made a lot of wrong decisions in my life, too many to feel secure making such big ones that affect a helpless baby's life.

"Then we'll learn from it and make a different choice." He shrugs. "Isn't that what life is about? Living and learning and then trying to do better?" Finn holds eye contact, and I relax a little.

God, this man centers me in a way no one ever has. I draw in a deep breath and feel my shoulders relax down from around my ears.

Better. That's better.

"You're right." I give him a reassuring nod.

"One decision at a time, okay? No reason to think about them all at once. You'll drive yourself crazy."

"Thank you. You always make me feel better when I start spiraling."

"That's what I'm here for." He braces one hand on the floor and places a chaste kiss on my lips, then he stands. "Now what do you think of the color?" He motions to the wall where the paint is almost dry.

"It's exactly how I pictured it. Looks great."

"See? One decision at a time." He winks, then turns around and goes back to the ladder.

I watch him for a while, rather than returning my attention to the computer. The way he concentrates so hard on what he's doing as if he wants it to be perfect. The way he gets up and down the ladder with ease. How I can see a patch of skin when his T-shirt rides up when he reaches up with the paintbrush in his hand.

By the time he's done cutting in the ceiling, the apex of my thighs throbs with need.

Finn comes down off the ladder for the last time, sets the paintbrush on top of the paint can, and steps back to admire his work. I crawl over to him with an idea in mind. Without a word, I crawl in front of him then raise up on my knees and undo the button on his cargo pants.

"What are you—" Finn looks down at me. "Oh."

He watches intently as I unzip his pants and tug them down, along with his boxer briefs, until they pool at his ankles. His half-hard dick hangs between us, and I lean forward to gently suck on the tip.

Finn groans then reaches behind himself and yanks his T-shirt up over his head. "I want to see this." His voice is gravelly, and I love that reaction.

His length hardens in my grip, and I stroke him up and down, meeting his gaze. His hands go into my hair, and I sink my mouth down on him as far as I can go, using my fist to make up the difference. A huff of air leaves his mouth, and his fingers tighten in my strands.

The look of pure pleasure on his face spurs me on until eventually, I pull my mouth off him, moving down to his balls. I continue to stroke him as I gently suck one.

"Fuck…" Finn groans, tipping his head back toward the ceiling.

A minute later, when I return my mouth to his length, he pulls me off him and hoists me up to my feet under my arms. "I'm gonna come if you keep doing that."

"Kinda the point." I arch an eyebrow.

"I want to come inside you. I want *you* to come."

He picks me up bridal style, using his feet to divest himself of the pants and underwear around his ankles, and carries me to our bedroom, where he makes me come not once but twice.

Life just gets sweeter by the day.

FINN

After a little break between the sheets, we finished painting the nursery yesterday, then went to bed early because we were both tired.

The color looks good. When we were done, I was picturing what the room might look like once it's complete, and it really started to feel real. Not that it doesn't already with the changes Harper's body is going through, but it felt real in the way that I could picture our baby in the space. See Harper in a chair in the corner breastfeeding, picture myself at the changing table, imagine both of us leaning over the crib just to watch our baby sleep.

Everything with Harper has been full speed ahead since we met, and my growing feelings for her are no different. But I don't want to scare her off. We've both gone through so many changes in our lives recently that it feels best to keep it to myself for now.

We're in the kitchen eating breakfast at the breakfast bar when Maven walks in, dressed as though maybe she's going to work out.

"Morning," I say to her. "There's coffee made if you

want some." I nod toward the coffee machine on the counter.

Her phone is in her hand, her eyes wide as she looks between us. "Have you guys seen last night's Buzz Wheel?"

I look at Harper and groan.

"No..." She picks her phone up off the counter and pulls up the app.

"I swear I didn't say anything to anyone." Maven looks panicked.

"Shit," Harper says.

"What is it?" I look between them.

Harper's expression is a mix of annoyance and upset when her eyes meet mine. "It details how you were engaged to someone else a short time ago and how I was acting as the wedding planner for you and Tamra before we got together."

My stomach sinks. It's not as though it was a secret per se, but I could go without everyone in town thinking I'm some slimy piece of shit who jumps from one woman to another.

"I'm not the leak," Maven says.

"I know that. I would never think that." Harper slides off the stool and walks over to embrace her cousin.

"As soon as I saw it, I was worried you would think it was me since I'd talked to you about the flowers for the wedding."

I shake my head. I obviously don't know Maven nearly as well as Harper, but she doesn't strike me as the sort to throw people under the bus. Especially not someone she cares about as much as Harper.

My phone buzzes from where it's plugged in on the counter beside the coffee machine. Harper walks over and unplugs it, passing it to me.

A text from Hudson.

Dude this is not good.

I roll my eyes and type out a response.

No shit.

Before he replies, a new text comes in from an unknown number.

Finn, this is Harper's dad, Austin. I'd appreciate it if you could come by the house at noon today.

I swallow. Hard. "Um... your dad just texted me and asked me to go over to his place at noon."

Both Harper and Maven's eyes widen to the size of the toonies I used to pay for things when I was driving through Canada.

"Damn it." Harper closes her eyes and massages her temples.

"What should I say?" I look between the two women.

"You have to go," Maven says.

"She's right. My dad will just show up here otherwise, which will make it look more like you have something to hide."

I nod and type out a response with shaky fingers.

I'll be there.

Jesus. First, I get this man's only daughter pregnant after a one-night stand, and now he probably thinks I was engaged when I did it.

AT FIVE MINUTES TO NOON, I knock on the door of Austin and Holly Bailey's house, Harper by my side. I said I was fine to come face the music on my own, but she insisted on joining me. Secretly, I'm thankful for her presence. I'm hopeful that with Harper here, I might be able to at least get an explanation out before Austin clocks me. Especially after I spotted all the cars in the driveway. Clearly this won't be a conversation between just Austin and me.

The door swings open and Harper's mom stands on the other side. She glances between us. "I figured you'd join him," she says to Harper. "Come on in. Just let me get my coat. You and I are going to do some baby shopping." She steps back from the door to let us enter.

I step inside, and my first thought is how it feels like a family home in here with the warm wood and family photos displayed on the entry table.

"I'm not going anywhere," Harper says, crossing her arms.

Holly looks over her shoulder at her from where she's getting her coat out of the closet. "Finn will be fine, Harp. He can hold his own, can't you?"

It clear from her steely gaze that I'm expected to agree, but I would've anyway. If this is an ambush, I'd rather Harper not be here for it. It might upset her or get her worked up and that can't be good for her or the baby.

I take Harper's hand. "I'll be fine. Go enjoy the afternoon with your mom. I'll fill you in later."

She bites her bottom lip. "Are you sure?"

"Positive." I give her the best smile I can manage, then bend down and kiss her, aware that Holly is watching my every move. But when I straighten and look at her, to my surprise, she's smiling.

"All right, we will see you later." She hooks her arm through Harper's. "Good luck, Finn." They make their way out the door, and I hear Holly say, "So the dressing room, huh? Like mother like daughter, I guess."

"Gross, Mom. It wasn't a Jeep," Harper says, then the door closes behind them.

With a big sigh, I continue deeper into the house toward where I hear voices. When I enter the spacious living room, every head turns in my direction.

It's a room full of men, but at least one person here will be on my side. I give Hudson a nod, which he returns.

"Finn, good of you to make it," Austin says, getting up out of his seat and walking over to me. He clamps me on the shoulder and squeezes. "Thought maybe it was time for us to have a little chat, and some of Harper's uncles wanted to be included."

"Great," I manage to say, voice strained.

"Let me introduce you to everyone you haven't met." He starts on his left, pointing at each person he introduces. "This is her uncle Colton, her uncle Jamison, her uncle Kingston you already know, this is her uncle Wyatt, and her uncles Rome and Denver—yes, they're twins—her uncle Liam, and then finally her brother Easton. Her uncle Griffin is in Los Angeles right now or he'd be here too. We were going to conference him in, but he said he trusted us."

Not one of them gives me any semblance of a smile, but I force myself to smile anyway and raise my hand in greeting. "Hello, everyone. I'll do my best to keep the names straight."

No one cracks a smile at my lame joke.

"Why don't you have a seat?" Austin motions to the

chair that's set up in front of everyone as if I'm being interviewed by the FBI.

I nod and take my seat. Everyone is silent until Rome speaks up.

"So, you're the guy having a baby with my niece." He crosses his arms and studies me.

"What's this about you being engaged?" Easton asks.

I shift in my seat, uncomfortable with all these men in Harper's family staring me down. "That I can explain."

I launch into the story of how Tamra and I had broken up when I was in Lake Starlight for Hudson's wedding and the reason for us being engaged and how it wasn't real.

"So you only agreed to the engagement so you could try to help out your parents?" Wyatt asks.

"Exactly. And I didn't know that Harper was going to be our wedding planner, and I had no idea she was pregnant." I raise my hands in front of me.

"What's the name of the ski resort your family owns?" Wyatt asks.

I answer.

"How long did you keep the engagement going once you knew Harper was pregnant?" Liam asks.

"Harper told me one weekend when I was here on my own, organizing wedding stuff. Tamra couldn't join me. I called off the wedding when I returned and made plans to move up here. I didn't want to be thousands of miles away from my child."

"And so, what, you and Harper are together now?" Denver asks.

I nod. "We are. I care a great deal about Harper, and I plan to do my best for her and the baby. We may not have planned to have a child together, but I think that maybe this baby was what was supposed to bring us together."

Easton scoffs.

"What, you don't think that's possible?" Kingston asks him.

Easton scowls. "Hell no. I think they screwed around and weren't responsible, and Harper got pregnant. It's not fate." He shakes his head and rolls his eyes before looking at me. "Sorry, man."

"She was on the pill, and we used a condom every time." I look at Austin. "Sorry." Then I look at Easton. "You can't convince me that the universe wasn't working in our favor."

"C'mon, man, where's your romantic side?" Denver squeezes Easton's shoulder.

"I don't have one, remember?" he grumbles.

Most of the room laughs, clearly knowing something I don't.

"All right, are we done interrogating this poor kid? I want to turn the football game on. I have money riding on it," Denver says.

Everyone turns to look at Austin. He gets up out of his chair. "Yeah, I guess we're done. You did good, Finn. Held your own."

I look at all the guys whose demeanors have now relaxed. Gone are the stoic, pissed off looks, and in their place are a bunch of easygoing guys smiling at me.

"Was this a test?" I ask no one in particular.

"Hell yeah," Rome says. "Hudson already filled us in on everything before you got here. We knew you're good people." He claps me on the back.

Whatever my expression is makes everyone in the room laugh.

"You want a beer?" Austin asks me, walking across the room.

I blow out a breath. Might as well get this over with now. "No thanks, I don't drink."

He studies me for a beat.

"I'm an alcoholic, so no booze for me." I wait for their judgment to rain down on me, but it doesn't come.

Austin merely nods at Jamison. "Well, you're in good company."

Jamison gives me a small smile. "If you ever need anything, you let me know, all right?"

I give him a grateful smile. "Will do."

The rest of the afternoon is spent watching the football game, and by the time Harper returns with her mom, I realize that I'm completely relaxed. I'm a part of the family, even if officially I'm not.

Well... not yet anyway.

HARPER

I barely slept last night because I felt anxious about the ultrasound today. While I'm excited to get another peek at our baby, I'm also nervous my aunt will find something wrong. But I'm trying to keep that possibility out of my head as much as possible.

Finn is scheduled to work today, so he said he would meet me. The chief said it was no problem if he ducked out for half an hour as long as he kept a radio on him in case something went down.

I'm just leaving the office to head to my parked car farther down Main Street when some kind of commotion ahead draws my attention. I realize that a few people are gathered around an older woman's body on the road between two parked cars.

I rush over and see that one of the bystanders is on the phone, presumably calling for an ambulance.

"What happened?" I ask the elderly man crouched by his wife.

He looks up at me with glossy eyes. "I don't know. She said she felt funny and then she clutched her chest before she fell. Hit her head on the curb. I don't know if she's breathing!"

This man is starting to lose it. I glance at her head and realize that her head is bleeding profusely. My legs get weak, and I feel myself list to the side, but I draw in a deep breath and reach out to the car beside me for support.

So much blood.

"Can you help her?" her husband says.

Something in me snaps to attention at his plea, and I spring into action without thinking about it. I toss my purse on the ground and quickly pull off my jacket, holding it out to him. "Here. Take this and apply pressure to her head to stop the bleeding while I check for a pulse."

I think back to that night at the retirement home and how Finn demonstrated checking for a pulse, and I place my index and middle finger on her neck. When I don't feel a pulse, I try to find one on the other side just in case and find nothing.

Panic threatens to override my thoughts, but I push it away.

"We're going to need to do CPR. I need someone to tilt her head back, pinch her nose, and breathe into her mouth when I say." I look up at the gathering crowd.

A man in his forties steps up. "I'll do it." He gets down on the ground beside her head. There's not a ton of room, but he makes it work as best he can.

The elderly man looks so scared, my heart breaks for him.

"She's going to be okay. Just keep applying pressure on the side of her head where the cut is."

I reposition myself so I'm straddling her and count out the chest compressions, telling the man when to breathe.

This is hard work. I can fully see now why Finn said as much in his presentation.

Within a couple minutes, the sound of sirens fills Main Street. Then there're some shouts, and the crowd around us parts. I don't stop what I'm doing. Not until a pair of hands wraps around my shoulders, and I hear Finn say my name.

"Harper, honey, we'll take over."

I turn and look over my shoulder, and the relief I feel when I see his face is staggering. I let him help me up, then some other firefighters take over until the ambulance arrives. As soon as Finn has pulled me away, off onto the sidewalk, I burst into tears. He pulls me into his chest, and his familiar scent helps to settle me.

Finn sets me back by the shoulders and looks me over. "Are you okay? The baby?"

I nod and wipe my face. "Yeah. I don't know what that was."

He smooths my hair back from my face. "An adrenaline crash most likely." Then he leans in and places a kiss on my forehead. "Let me go talk to the captain and tell him I'm taking you to see your aunt. I want to make sure everything is okay with you and the baby."

I nod. "Okay."

The ambulance arrives while I'm waiting for Finn to return, and they get the woman on the gurney.

"All right, let's go. Guess I didn't have to worry about being late for our appointment when the call came in, did I?" He wraps his arm around my shoulders as we make our way down the sidewalk toward my car.

I don't say anything, still too in my head, replaying everything that just happened.

When we reach my vehicle, Finn holds out his hand. "Let me drive." I nod, wordlessly digging for my keys in my purse and dropping them into his waiting palm. "You know you probably saved that woman's life."

My gaze flicks up to meet his. "Is she okay?"

"Her heart was beating again when they loaded her into the ambulance, thanks in part to you. One of the bystanders told me you jumped into action."

"I guess I did do that." A small smile tilts my lips.

"Remember when you doubted yourself?"

My smile grows a little more as I nod.

"So... this is the part where you tell me I was right."

I smack him on the arm. "Open the door so I can get in. I'm chilly." I wrap my arms around myself, laughing.

Finn seems to notice for the first time that I'm not wearing my coat. "Where's your coat?"

"I gave it to the husband to apply pressure to his wife's head wound."

Finn's smile is blinding as he opens the car door for me.

We make our way to see my aunt, who tells us that everything looks great with the baby. And after getting her to print out a million pictures for us to take with us, Finn takes me home before he returns to the station.

Maven keeps me company all night. I try not to make it obvious that I'm missing Finn, but when he comes in the next morning, and I'm still sleeping, he wakes me up in the best way possible.

TWO WEEKS LATER, my entire family cheers from the audience as I walk across the stage to accept Lake Starlight's Medal for Good as a result of my quick thinking and action. Turns out I did save that woman's life, who I now know is Shirley Jackson from neighboring Greywall.

Her husband nominated me after the doctor at the hospital told him that Shirley wouldn't be alive today if I hadn't started CPR right away.

At first the idea of accepting an award for it felt silly, but as I stand next to the mayor, smiling and getting my picture taken, I only feel pride.

Not in a smug way, but now I know that even though I'm nervous about becoming a mother, I'm confident I'll be able to handle whatever is thrown my way. No more second-guessing myself, no more waiting for me to screw it up. Mistakes will happen, but not because I'm not capable, just because that's life.

When the photographer tells me he's got what he needs, Finn is at the stairs, waiting to help me down the steps because he's overbearing in the best way.

"You looked good up there. I can't wait to get you alone later," he murmurs into my ear.

I don't have a chance to respond before the rest of my family is upon us, and I move from one set of arms to another until I end up with my brother standing in front of me.

"I'm proud of you, sis." He pulls me into a hug, squeezing tightly.

When we separate, I give him the once-over. "What's gotten into you, E?"

"What? I can't be proud of my sister?"

"Of course you can, but the hug was a little much." I squeeze his shoulder, so he knows I'm joking.

He pushes a hand through his hair. "I've been thinking about what you said about living in my shadow growing up ever since we talked about it. I never really thought about it. About what it might have been like for you."

"Oh god, are you going to make me have another heart-to-heart? Didn't we already reach our quota with one this year?"

He chuckles. "I just want to say I'm sorry if I ever did anything to make it more difficult for you."

I shake my head. "You didn't. It is what it is, E. You were a good student, and I wasn't. That's not your fault. You were an amazing ball player. I'm happy about that, happy for all your success. I've come to realize that all my hangups were my own. I just had to get out of my own way."

He shoves his hands in his pockets. "You sure?"

I nod. "I'm sure. Now give me one last hug before you go back to being my annoying older brother."

He does as I request, and I have to work to hold in my tears. Happy tears this time.

Lately, I feel as though there's just so damn much to be happy about.

FINN

I'm at the fire station on duty when my phone buzzes in my back pocket. I'm expecting it to be Harper—or more accurately, I'm hoping it's Harper—but when I look at the screen, I see that it's my dad.

Got a big surprise for you. We're in Lake Starlight.

They are? I can't believe they wouldn't tell me they were coming, but I'm glad they're here.

For real? Why didn't you tell me you were coming?

It was kind of a last-minute thing. We'll explain when we see you. Are you and Harper free for breakfast tomorrow morning?

I'll just be coming off shift, but yeah. Let me check with Harper and see if she's free.

I pull up her contact and dial her number.

She answers on the first ring. "Hey, you." I can hear her smile through the phone.

"Hey, you're not going to believe this, but I just got a text from my dad. He and my mom are in Lake Starlight. They want to know if we can meet them for breakfast tomorrow."

"Seriously?"

"Yeah, I had no idea they were coming. My dad said he'd explain when I saw him. Are you free?"

"Yes, of course. I can't wait to meet them. But oh god, what if they don't like me? What am I going to wear? I need a haircut and a manicure and—"

"Harp, they're going to love you, and wear whatever you feel like. You look beautiful in everything."

"Thanks, Finn."

"I'll tell them eight thirty at Lard Have Mercy. Sound good?"

"Works for me," she says.

"All right. I'll see you then."

I hang up with Harper and text my dad back.

> She'll be there. Meet us at 8:30 at Lard Have Mercy. It's a diner on Main Street. I'm at the fire station right now so I have to go.

> Sounds good. See you guys then.

I'm excited that my parents are finally going to get to meet Harper, but I can't help but feel as though there's something more going on than I realize. My parents are about the least spontaneous people in the world, and it's ski season.

THE BLARE of the alarm wakes me in the middle of the night. As it always does, it takes me a split second to realize where I am—on shift at the firehouse. As soon as I do, I get my ass in gear and get moving.

Within minutes, we've all donned our gear and are on the truck, pulling out of the station. Apparently, a call has come in about a building fire just outside of town. The guys tell me it's an old factory that's been abandoned for a decade and that sometimes teenagers go out there to party.

By the time we arrive, flames are visible on one side, and the captain doles out the orders. We all get to work, and within a few minutes, we have a hose on the fire.

"Finn. Shane," the captain barks over the noise. "Go check out the other side to make sure there're no flare-ups over there."

We do as we're told, navigating through the few inches of snow on the ground and the dead grass that's been left to grow through the cracks in the pavement. The two of us use our flashlights to navigate, and when we come around the corner, we're met with a group of teenagers all huddled together. The girls are crying while the guys look as though they might throw up.

I know those looks.

Shane must too because we rush over to them, no small task with all our gear on.

"You kids need to get out of here," Shane says.

"Did all of you get out?" I ask.

"No." One of the girls shakes her head frantically. "Kelly's still in there."

Fuck.

"Where did you last see her?" I ask.

"We were partying on the second level," one of them

says. "We thought she was following us, but when we got out here, she wasn't with us."

"All right, you kids go around to the front where the fire trucks are and stay there," Shane says while I take my radio and report what the kids just told us, letting the captain know that we're heading in to look for her.

The two of us don our oxygen masks and head inside. The smoke is thick, and smaller flare-up fires are starting on this side of the building. We need to be quick.

"Any idea how to get to the second floor?" I ask Shane, breathing heavily.

"Yeah, I've been here for a call before that turned out to be nothing. This way."

We look around as we make our way through in case Kelly made it down to the first floor and got disoriented or passed out because of the smoke, but we don't find her. When we reach a pair of rickety, old-looking stairs, I get a tight feeling in my chest. Only one of us can go up at a time. First because of the width of the stairs and then because I'm concerned the weight of both of us and our gear might send it crashing down.

"All right. Let's do this," I say.

Shane heads up first, and once he's at the top, I start up. The entire staircase feels as though it rocks side to side with every step I take. Once we're both on the second level, we don't waste any time doing a sweep of the place. The smoke gets thicker, and all I can hear is my heavy breathing.

Finally, I see something. "Shane! Over here."

I rush over to the patch of white that I see through the smoke. It turns out to be Kelly's T-shirt. By the looks of it, she tripped on a piece of metal splayed out on the floor and either hit her head and passed out or was overcome by smoke.

I lift her into my arms and straighten up while Shane reports in with the captain to let him know that we found her and to have the paramedics and oxygen waiting.

We find our way back to the staircase. There's no way I'll fit carrying her like this, so I slump her over my shoulder and start down the stairs while Shane waits at the top so that both our weight doesn't have to be supported by the already rickety stairs.

I'm about halfway down when a crack echoes out, the world drops out below my feet, and I'm free falling.

The last thing I think about before it all goes black is Harper and our unborn baby.

I arrive at the diner on time and do a quick glance around, but I don't spot Finn. I tried to make it so that I arrived right on time so that he'd be here before me, but no such luck.

There's one couple I don't recognize in the diner, which doesn't necessarily mean they're Finn's parents, but when the man laughs at something the woman says, I know right away that it's his dad. They look so much alike besides the few decades separating them.

Rather than stand awkwardly, I decide to go over and introduce myself. "Hi, are you Len and Kathy?"

They turn and look at me in unison. The woman's eyes fall to my stomach and her face lights up in delight.

"Harper?" She slides out of the booth and pulls me into a hug. "Oh, it's so great to meet you finally. How are you feeling?" She pulls away, but holds onto my shoulders, looking down between us at my swollen stomach. "How is the baby?"

"Give her a chance to answer at least one of your questions before you fire more her way, Kath." I turn toward the voice and see that Len is now out of his seat too. "It's great to meet you, Harper." He holds out his hand, and I shake it.

"Great to meet you as well." A genuine smile forms on my face. All of my trepidation about today and whether Finn's parents would like me melts away. Finn is clearly cut from the same cloth as they are, which means they're going to be warm, welcoming, and wonderful people.

We all sit in the booth, them side by side and me across from them.

"How are you liking Lake Starlight? Did you just get in yesterday?" I ask.

Kathy nods. "We did, so we haven't had too much time to explore, but it seems like a lovely town. Finn mentioned that you have a lot of family living here."

I can't help but chuckle. "My dad has eight siblings, and between them, there are twenty-six kids in total. And some of us are starting our own families now." I lay my hands on my stomach.

Kathy's mouth drops open. I think I've left her speechless, which, if I'm guessing right, seems like a hard thing to do.

"Wow. Finn wasn't exaggerating." Len shakes his head in disbelief.

"No, he wasn't. Most of them live around here, so yeah." I shrug and look around. "I'm actually surprised that no one from my family is here by chance."

They chuckle, then Maci is beside the table, offering me a decaf coffee. I slide my cup to the edge of the table so she can pour, then she pulls a couple of creamers from the pocket of her apron and sets them on the table.

"Are you guys ready to order?" she asks.

"We're actually expecting Finn, so we'll probably just wait to order until he gets here."

"Sounds good," she says with a smile and turns to leave.

Kathy frowns at the watch on her wrist. "It's not like him to be late."

"I was just thinking the same thing," I say, checking my phone.

He's almost ten minutes late now, and he hasn't texted. Unease settles in my stomach, but I push it away, instead deciding to use the time to get to know Finn's parents a little better.

We chat for another fifteen minutes, but I can tell that all three of us are preoccupied with where Finn might be.

"Maybe I should call him," I say when there's a natural break in the conversation.

"Please do," Kathy says, worriedly tapping her finger on the table.

I pull up his contact and call him, but the phone rings until it goes to voicemail.

I look at Kathy. "No answer. I'll try him again to be sure. Maybe he just got hung up at a call right before his shift ended."

But before I can dial him again, the bell over the door rings, and we all turn, expecting to see Finn. But it's not Finn. It's my uncle Kingston, and the way he's searching the restaurant tells me he's not here for breakfast.

I know immediately from the way he scans the place with a frown that something is wrong. When he spots me, he heads straight over. I'm standing beside the table before he arrives.

"What's wrong?" I barely rasp the words out through my rapidly closing throat.

My uncle glances at the booth behind me.

I gesture with my hand. "These are Finn's parents, Len and Kathy." Then I turn to look at them and explain. "This is my uncle Kingston. He works for the Anchorage Fire Department, but he knows everyone at the station here in town."

With that news, they're both out of the booth too.

"Is it Finn?" Len asks.

My uncle sets his hands on his hips. "There was a call at the abandoned factory just outside of town. Finn was rescuing a teenager inside and had to carry her out of the building. The stairs he had to use gave way."

Kathy and I gasp in stereo.

"Is he okay?" Tears fill my eyes.

"They've brought him to the hospital. I don't know much more than that."

Kathy cries out, and my knees wobble underneath my weight. My uncle must notice because he steadies me with a hand to my arm.

"I'm here to take you guys over there."

I nod numbly, barely registering the sound of Kathy's tears. It's not as though I didn't know Finn has a dangerous job. I guess I just didn't think about what that meant. I didn't think of all the what-ifs every time he walked out the door for a shift.

"C'mon, I'm parked just outside," my uncle says.

We make our way to the door, and within a few minutes, we're pulling up at the emergency entrance of the small hospital. Kathy and I are out of the truck practically before the wheels have stopped turning. We arrive at the check-in desk together, Len right behind us.

"My son was brought in here. He's a firefighter," Kathy says.

"Finn McDonald," I add.

The nurse's mouth tightens, and she stands. "Let me check with the doctor."

"Is he okay?" The words are nearly impossible to push from my mouth.

"Give me a moment." She disappears behind the doors that lead to where the patients who have been called back are.

"Oh god." My hand instantly goes to my belly.

If something has happened to Finn, I don't know what I'll do. Our time together has been too short. And I didn't get to tell him that I love him. I was too afraid to put myself out there in case he didn't feel the same. I didn't want him to feel pressured to feel that way because we're having a baby together.

Jesus, what if our baby has to grow up without their father? The thought brings hot tears to my eyes.

When I come out of my thoughts, I realize that some of the guys from the fire station are here too. I'm about to go and see if they have any more details when the nurse comes out from behind the doors, another nurse at her side. She looks vaguely familiar.

The nurse from behind the desk speaks before we can pummel her with questions. "Allie here will take you back to see him and explain what's going on."

All our attention moves to the nurse named Allie. "I can't take everyone back there," she says, looking around the waiting room.

"We're his parents," Len says, stepping up behind Kathy and me and placing a hand on each of our shoulders. "And this is his girlfriend."

The word sounds so foreign in relation to Finn and me, though it's accurate. It just sounds so juvenile.

"All right, you three come with me." She walks toward the doors and we quickly follow.

"Is Finn okay?" I ask as she leads us down a hallway.

"He'll be okay," she says, and a surge of relief washes over me. "He has some cracked ribs, and he's going to be sore from head to toe from the fall. He also has a mild concussion. We're going to keep him overnight for observation, make sure nothing else presents, but he should make a full recovery."

From where she walks beside me, Kathy takes my hand and squeezes.

I swear I'll never again take for granted Finn's and my time together.

Allie stops outside a door and motions for us to go in. "He needs to rest, so you can't stay long."

I nod and step inside, still clutching Kathy's hand. As soon as she sees her son lying in bed, she rushes ahead to embrace him, and he winces in pain.

"Oh, I'm so sorry." Kathy backs up, flustered when she realizes she's caused him pain.

Finn's gaze meets mine, and the look we share, the feeling that passes between us without words, lets me know that I was silly for not telling him sooner how I feel. Len walks in past me and greets his son, telling him he's relieved that he's okay.

Then it's my turn.

I don't even realize I'm crying until Finn says, "Aw, Harp, don't cry. C'mere." He raises his hand as much as it seems is comfortable with his ribs, and I rush forward.

Since I don't want to hurt him, I don't crawl into the bed and mold myself to him as I really want to. Instead, I lean over the bed and cup his face with my hands and bring my forehead to his. "I'm so glad you're okay. You scared me," I whisper.

"I scared me too. All I could think about when I felt the

stairs give way underneath me was you and the baby and how I had to make it home to both of you."

His words set my tears off heavier this time, and they drip on his face.

With a grimace, he raises his one hand and gently wipes the tears from my cheek. I move back a bit so that I can meet his eyes.

"I love you." The words burst out of me. "I should have told you before now, but I was scared you didn't feel the same way or might feel pressured to feel the same because of the baby, but after what happened today, I can't keep it to myself anymore."

Finn shakes his head. "I can't believe you stole my thunder."

I frown. "What do you mean?"

"I mean, I had fully planned to tell you that I love you. As soon as I woke up and realized I was still alive, that's all I wanted to do."

"You love me?" I whisper.

"You're so easy to love, Harper. I never stood a chance."

I want to crawl into his lap and make out with him, but given his ribs, I settle for placing a gentle kiss on his lips. "Don't you dare scare me like that again. I can't have the man I love putting his life in peril all the time."

His eyes gleam with humor. "No promises."

Movement out of the corner of my eye has me remembering that his parents are in the room with us. Guess it's a good thing I couldn't climb onto his lap and make out with him.

I force myself to back up from the bed, my cheeks hot with embarrassment. "Sorry."

But Kathy and Len are grinning at us.

"Are you kidding me? Nothing could make me happier

right now than what I just witnessed." Kathy's smile lights up her entire face.

"We're so glad you're all right, son. What happened out there?" Len asks.

Finn tells us about the call and how after he fell, the next thing he remembers is being transported to the ambulance. "The doctor told me that the girl is okay and that Shane, the other firefighter, made it out."

"That's good news," Kathy says, pulling up a chair beside the bed.

Len brings another one over and motions for me to sit, which I do. Finn immediately holds his hand out so that I can hold it.

"Since I didn't make it to breakfast, I never got to hear what you're doing in town," Finn says.

His parents share a look before Len clears his throat then shoves his hands in his pockets. "Your mother and I have decided. We're selling the resort."

My attention goes to Finn to see how he's going to take this news. His face is laced with concern.

"What? Why?" Finn asks.

"It's time. It's been a struggle for years now, and your mom and I don't want to struggle anymore." He shrugs.

"But you didn't want to ever sell it."

Len glances at me for a beat before returning his attention to his son. "We didn't want to sell it to a big conglomerate. But we were approached by Harper's Uncle Wyatt, who made us a good offer. It will allow us to retire, and that feels right since we're going to be grandparents."

"That's why Wyatt was asking me all kinds of questions that day when I was at your dad's," Finn says to me.

My uncle owns the Glacier Point` Resort here in town, as well as some other resorts around the country. It makes sense that he might be interested in acquiring Finn's family resort.

"Are you guys sure you want to do this?" Finn asks them, obviously not sold on the idea.

Kathy nods. "We are. That's why we're in town. To meet with Wyatt and sign the papers now that our lawyer has looked everything over. It will be nice not to have to be tied to the resort for so many months of the year and have no time for anything else. To not have to worry during the offseason about what the coming months might be like. The stress of it was getting to be too much. We're too old for that now."

Finn looks between his parents. "What are you guys going to do with your time then?"

His mom grins. "Well... we had this crazy idea that maybe we'd move here."

Finn's eyebrows rise up to his hairline. "Lake Starlight?"

"Only if it's okay with you two. We want to be close to our grandchild, not thousands of miles away."

He looks at me as if trying to gauge my reaction. Obviously, I don't know his parents well, but they seem like lovely people, and I have no doubt they're going to love our child.

"That sounds wonderful. But you might feel different once you meet my family," I say, laughing.

Finn squeezes my hand, and I can tell by his smile that he's excited about this development and just needed to know I'm onboard.

And I am. I'm onboard for whatever life throws our way, as long as we're in it together.

FINN

She'd never believe me, but Harper looks so fucking hot today.

That's easy for me to say when I'm not the one with swollen ankles and heartburn, or the one who can't sleep for more than an hour at a time, but to me, she's always been beautiful. Even more so with her belly stretched as she has provided a home for our child for the past nine and a half months.

So yeah, it's official. I have a bit of a pregnancy kink, but only when it comes to Harper.

She's not due for another two weeks, but I know if it were up to her, she'd be happy to give birth any minute now.

Tonight is what will be our last official date night before the baby arrives. I'm taking her to her uncle's restaurant, Terra & Mare, since it's where we had our first meal alone together. Even if it wasn't officially a date.

It's crazy when I think of how far things have come in less than a year. Crazy mostly because it feels as though it's always been like this. I can't imagine Harper not being in my life, and more than that, I barely remember my life before her.

When we're shown to our table, I pull out her chair, and she takes a seat. She's wearing a black knit dress that I love because it shows off her curves.

The hostess lets us know the waiter will be over soon to take our order. But before the waiter makes an appearance, Rome comes out of the kitchen wearing his chef's uniform. He must've been made aware of our presence.

"Hey, sweetheart." He bends to give Harper a kiss on the cheek. "How are you hanging in there?"

Harper sighs. "I'm ready to meet this little human." She rubs her hands over her swollen belly.

Rome chuckles. "You remind me of Harley. By the end of each pregnancy, she'd about had enough." He turns his attention to me. "What about you? You make sure to give lots of foot rubs to my niece. That always improved Harley's mood."

"Doing my best."

Harper and I share a grin.

In reality, what I've been giving Harper is a lot of sex. Not that I'm complaining. Her libido has been through the roof lately, and I'm happy to provide what she needs.

"Your parents were in here last night, Finn."

"They were?"

He nods. "With Austin and Holly. Practically had to kick the four of them out because the restaurant was closing."

"Sounds about right."

My parents moved to Lake Starlight a few months ago and have settled in just fine, both in the community and with Harper's family. In fact, our parents spend a lot of time together. I think it started as them wanting to get to know each other better because they'd be sharing grandparent duties, but it's morphed into a real friendship.

When my parents first mentioned that they'd be moving here, I worried that maybe Harper would be averse to the idea, but she took to it with open arms. I don't have a big family like hers, so I appreciate, more than I can express, how open she's been to involving them in our lives since they arrived.

We chat with Rome for another couple of minutes until he sighs and glances back at the kitchen. "Well, I need to get back to work, but I just wanted to pop by and say a quick hello."

The waiter comes over and takes our drink order before promising to return in a few minutes to take our food order.

"It's weird to think that this will be our last dinner out for a while. At least with just the two of us." Harper reaches for her water.

"I know. I keep imagining what our baby might look like. I keep picturing you holding her and wondering if she'll get your red hair or my dark hair."

She chuckles and sets her water back down on the table. "You're still so sure it's a girl?"

"Team girl all the way, baby."

Harper shakes her head and singsongs, "You're wrong."

"We'll see, won't we?"

The waiter returns with Harper's mocktail and my sparkling water, and we order our food.

Once he's left the table, Harper lets out a big sigh. "I have to go to the bathroom before I can drink this. I need to make room."

I can't help but feel bad for her. She must pee fifty times a day now.

"Let me help you up." I get out of my chair and come

around to her side, helping to slide the chair back and letting her use my arm for leverage to get up.

"Thanks." She gives me a quick kiss on the cheek and walks toward the bathroom.

I'm not even back in my seat before she gasps. I whip around, and she's standing a few feet away, staring at a pool of liquid between her feet.

"Oh my god, my water broke."

I rush over, my heart racing. This is it. Oh my god, is it too soon? She's not due for almost another two weeks.

Harper looks up at me with wide eyes full of trepidation.

I take her hand and help her step away from the amniotic fluid without slipping. "It's okay. We got this. Let's head to the hospital, okay?"

She nods, and I lead her to the front door then grab our coats from the coat check. I don't bother looking around the restaurant to see if I know anyone. There's no point. I can already predict what will be in Buzz Wheel tonight.

Let it. Let Lake Starlight know that the woman I love is about to give birth to our baby. I'd shout it from the rooftops if I could.

GOD, it's so fucking hard to watch the woman you love be in so much pain.

Twenty hours later, we're finally at the part where Harper is pushing. She opted for an unmedicated birth, even after my insistence early on that she didn't have to be a hero and should get the epidural. Maybe that was selfish of me, but watching her writhe in pain and not being able to do anything about it, was pure torture.

But she stuck it out and now our baby is almost here. Harper has been pushing for more than half an hour though, and I can tell she's losing steam. I share a look with Holly, who is on the other side of Harper.

"I can't do this," Harper says with tears in her eyes. She's sweaty and spent, red-faced and exhausted, but she's never been more beautiful.

"You can do this, Harp."

She squeezes her eyes shut and shakes her head. "I can't. I'm so tired."

"Hey, look at me." When she keeps her eyes closed, I add a little more force to my voice. "Look at me."

Her bloodshot eyes open, and she meets my gaze.

"You've got this, Harper. You're the strongest woman I know. Now stop doubting yourself, because I know you can do this. I know how much you already love our baby and how excited you are to see them. It's gut-check time, all right? When the doctor tells you to push in a minute, I want you to take all that strength and determination and stubbornness I know is inside of you and focus it on pushing, okay? I'll be right here with you."

Determination settles into Harper's features, and she blinks a few times and nods. "Okay, okay. I can do this. You're right."

Holly gives me an approving smile and a nod.

"We've got another contraction coming up," the nurse says.

"All right, Harper. Are you ready to meet your baby?" Dr. Stewart asks.

She nods and clenches her jaw, and I know somehow that this next push will be it.

When the time comes, Holly and I support Harper's

back. She grunts and screams and cries, but this time, the doctor tells her to stop.

"The head is out. Just one more, Harper," the doctor says, and Harper pushes again. "It's a boy!" Dr. Stewart calls.

Seconds later, we hear the shrill cry of our son.

I bend down and wrap my arms around Harper, who's crying now. "You did so good, baby. You did it. We have a son." I back up enough so I can see her eyes, my own filled with unshed tears, and slide some of the sweat-slicked hair off her face. "I'm so proud of you."

The nurse brings our son over to Harper now that he's been checked out and given a clean bill of health and sets him on her bare chest, then she eases the blanket over them up to his shoulders.

Harper's arms instinctively go to his bum and his back. "Hello, little man." She looks up at me. "He has your hair color."

We share a small laugh as it's been a big question in our minds.

"You did so well, Harp," Holly says, tears streaming down her face. "What's his name?"

Harper looks at me to tell her.

"Hollis Benjamin McDonald," I say with pride.

"We wanted to work your name into it somehow, and since it's a boy..."

Holly's hand flies to her heart. "Mine? Why?"

Harper reaches out with one hand to take her mother's. "If you hadn't tried so hard to have me, I wouldn't even be here. I know you weren't able to carry me, but you went through a lot to make it happen. This little guy wouldn't be here if it weren't for that."

Holly dissolves into tears and kisses Harper's forehead.

After a few minutes, Harper looks up at me. "Do you want to hold him?"

I have to press my lips together to keep from bursting into tears at the thought of holding my son for the first time. I strip off my shirt and ease myself into the bed beside Harper. As if she's an expert, she gently hands our son to me.

I place him against my chest and cover him with a blanket, making note of every squeak and small noise he makes. And when I look over at Harper looking at the two of us, I know that I was right. The universe did play a role in getting me here because I'm exactly where I was always meant to be.

***

"OKAY, no more visitors for a while. You need some rest."

No sooner have the words left my lips than there's another knock at the door.

I love Harper's family, I do. But there are a lot of them, and they all want to see the newest addition, which has left little time for Harper to rest.

When I turn toward the door though, I know it will be a while before she's resting now because Jack stands there with a wide smile. He must have flown in from Los Angeles as soon as someone told him Harper was in labor.

"Jack!" There's no missing the excitement in Harper's voice.

I've met Jack and his wife, Shelly, a couple times when they've been up here visiting over the past few months.

"Heard someone had a baby and had to fly up to see if it was true." He walks in holding a gift bag and sets it on the table in the corner with the rest before making his way to the bed and giving Harper a hug.

"I'm so surprised to see you," she says.

Jack reaches over the bed to shake my hand. "Congrats."

"Thanks."

He returns his attention to Harper. "I told you I'd be up to meet the baby as soon as I knew you were in labor. Did you doubt me? I'm a man of my word."

She chuckles. "It's so good to see you."

"So where is the little guy?" He looks around, spots Hollis in the glass bassinet, and makes his way over.

Harper has told me a little bit about his and Shelly's struggle with infertility, and when he looks at Hollis, I can see that while Jack is happy for us, this also causes him some pain.

Harper must see it too because she says, "Where's Shelly?" She looks behind him toward the doorway.

Jack turns to face us and swallows hard, then looks away from her, shoving his hands in his pockets.

"Jack, what's wrong? Is Shelly okay?"

"She's back in LA."

"She couldn't make the trip?" Harper's head angles to the side.

"I'll tell you, but please don't tell anyone else in the family. I'm not ready to deal with all their questions yet."

Harper takes my hand, clearly knowing her cousin better than I do.

"Shelly and I have separated."

Harper's other hand flies up to her mouth. "Oh, Jack, no."

The End

My Almost Ex

My Vegas Groom

A Greene Family Summer Bash (Novella)

My Sister's Flirty Friend

My Unexpected Surprise

My Famous Frenemy

A Greene Family Vacation (Novella)

My Scorned Best Friend

My Fake Fiancé

My Brother's Forbidden Friend

A Greene Family Christmas (Novella)

Plain Daisy Ranch

One Last Summer

The One I Left Behind

The One I Stood Beside

The One I Didn't See Coming

Chasing Forever

Chasing Love

Chasing Home

The Nest

Mr. Heartbreaker

Mr. Broody

Mr. Swoony

Mr. Charming

Hockey Hotties

Countdown to a Kiss

My Lucky #13

The Trouble with #9

Faking it with #41

Tropical Hat Trick (Novella)

Sneaking around with #34

Second Shot with #76

Offside with #55

Chicago Grizzlies

On the Defense

Something like Hate

Something like Lust

Something like Love

Kingsmen Football Stars

False Start

You Had Your Chance, Lee Burrows

You Can't Kiss the Nanny, Brady Banks

Over My Brother's Dead Body, Chase Andrews

Modern Love

Charmed by the Bartender

Hooked by the Boxer

Mad about the Banker

Single Dads Club

Real Deal

Dirty Talker

Sexy Beast

Hollywood Hearts

Mister Mom

Animal Attraction

Domestic Bliss

Bedroom Games

Cold as Ice

On Thin Ice

Break the Ice

Chicago Law

Smitten with the Best Man

Tempted by my Ex-Husband

Seduced by my Ex's Divorce Attorney

Blue Collar Brothers

Flirting with Fire

Crushing on the Cop

Engaged to the EMT

White Collar Brothers

Sexy Filthy Boss

Dirty Flirty Enemy

Wild Steamy Hook-up

The Rooftop Crew

My Bestie's Ex

A Royal Mistake

The Rival Roomies

Our Star-Crossed Kiss

The Do-Over

A Co-Workers Crush

Holiday Romances

Single and Ready to Jingle

Claus and Effect

Merry Kissmas

cockamamie unicorn ramblings

Thank you so much for reading! We hope you enjoyed returning to Lake Starlight!

After we released The Drawback of Single Dads (Palmer & Hudson's book), the book prior to this one, we realized that a lot of readers thought that the hero of her book was going to be Matt (Hudson's snowboarding friend). We wondered if we'd missed an opportunity even though Finn's name had already been used at the end of that book. Should we go back and change the name to Matt and make Harper's hero the professional snowboarder? But something told us no, Matt was not the man for her. Her kind of man was going to be a blue-collar hero, the type of man who always strives to do the right thing, the kind of man who doesn't need to travel the world and spike his adrenaline flying down the mountain terrain to be satisfied.

In our estimation, that was the right call. While Harper brought a little excitement and spontaneity to Finn's life, he settled her and helped her realize that she was enough just the way she was.

As writers, it's always fun to revisit the Bailey family. It has a real nostalgic feeling of returning home for us, and we hope you have the same feeling.

The family keeps growing with all the babies everyone keeps having. At some point it might not prove feasible that they all fit into one person's house for their gatherings. Not sure what we're going to do when that happens! We'll figure something out. LOL

As always, we have a lot of people to thank for getting this book into your hands...

Nina and the entire Valentine PR team.

Cassie from Joy Editing for line edits and attention to detail.

Ellie from My Brother's Editor for line edits and proofing.

Olivia Winston for the second proofread.

Hang Le for the cover and branding for the entire series.

Wander Aguiar for the wonderful photo of our Finn and Harper.

All the bloggers who graciously carve out time to read, review and/or promote us.

Piper Rayne Unicorns, both in our Facebook group and on IG who give us life!

Readers – There's so many options to choose from these days and we are beyond grateful that you invested your time and energy into this little world we created. We hope you found it worth it and that you'll consider visiting again sometime!

Up next is Jack's story and it will be a trope we haven't tackled yet—marriage in trouble! If you're a fan of our Baileys series, Jack is Phoenix and Griffin's youngest son.

This is going to be an emotional one and we can't wait to dive in! Until then...

xo,
Piper & Rayne